NINE LIVES TOO MANY

a novel by

John F. Rooney

Senneff House Publishers
Fort Lauderdale, Florida

Senneff House Publishers
P.O. Box 11601
Fort Lauderdale, FL 33339
www.senneffhouse.com

Cover design by Fusion Creative Services
www.fusioncreatives.com
Inside Book design by Dawn Von Strolley Grove

Manufactured in the United States of America

ISBN 0-9752756-8-2

Library of Congress Control Number: 2004102627

A cautionary tale

1

That morning, a Tuesday, June 11, Felix turned to his driver and stoically announced, "Today I'll be courting death more than on any other day of my life, but if the Fates will it, or Allah so desires, I'll bring annihilation to many and fear to all." Hundreds of men, women, and children were to dic or be maimed that day at the hands of a mediocre screenwriter who had been given the nickname Felix the Cat by his conjoined terrorists. The driver, Seleb, nodded his head solemnly several times in sync with the head of the felt dog sitting atop the dashboard. Seleb knew that Felix could at times sound pompous, but he also knew his leader to be ruthless and relentless.

At the corner of Lexington and East 87th Street in Manhattan, Felix climbed out of the grimy, well-dented, and battered van. Through the van's side door he wrestled the heavy black bag with the built-in rollers onto the sidewalk. Over his shoulder he hung the strap of the bulky black carryall. As the van pulled away and merged with traffic, Felix stood on the corner briefly.

In his mid-thirties, Felix was well-muscled, a man who obviously worked out. Balding with his black moustache and tinted glasses, he looked ordinary, rather nondescript, a man whose face didn't particularly stand out in a crowd. People would later say that his was the face of a thousand other men—not handsome, not striking, not noteworthy, just a dangerously ordinary face.

Felix stepped into the street by the curb and raised his hand to hail a yellow cab. Two occupied cabs drove by, and then a cab driven by a Pakistani driver screeched to a stop. The driver popped the trunk without getting out. Felix loaded the big bag into the deep trunk, closed the lid, and climbed into the back of the cab with the carryall.

"Grand Central Station."

The driver said nothing, glanced in the rear mirror momentarily to confirm his dislike of the type, and pulled away from the curb. Though a taped Whoopi Goldberg reminded Felix to fasten his seat belt, he ignored the message. After a few turns the driver was soon heading south on Park Avenue toward the station. As the traffic lights came up on them, the driver slowed so that he didn't have to come to a complete stop at each light.

They passed the Waldorf Astoria Hotel on their left, and where Park Avenue ran under the archway of the Helmsley Building, the driver veered west instead to Vanderbilt Avenue, past the looming Met Life Building, formerly the Pan Am Building. The cab entered the line of traffic on Vanderbilt adjacent to Grand Central Station. The sullen, sour-faced cabbie braked at the west side entrance of the terminal. Felix handed him the fare with a two-dollar tip. The driver took the money without even a grunt of acknowledgment. He had no use for his co-religionists from the Middle East. Again he popped the trunk lid without getting out. Felix hoisted the heavy bag from the trunk cavity. The cab sped away.

On the sidewalk Felix lifted the suitcase's pull handle so it perched above the big bag. He arranged the bulging carryall on top and strapped the two bags together with two canvas straps. He was about to start into the station when he happened to glance across Vanderbilt Avenue. What he saw made him stop: a man in a somewhat disheveled suit hurrying across the street. The man, in his early thirties, was heading in his general direction. Close to six feet tall, he was handsome, that black Irish look, with thick black hair, striking brown eyes—a man at whom both women and men would sneak a second look. Insistent and suggestive ebony eyebrows. Today his brown irises were set amidst somewhat bloodshot whites. Whereas Felix had a tendency to dissolve into a crowd, this man had the knack of defining a crowd. Felix did not know the man's name: Dennis Delaney.

Felix recognized him. A man involved in law enforcement. Perhaps FBI. Some kind of security. He angled off to the left to avoid contact. The approaching man had his eyes cast down as he hurried inside the station and did not see Felix. Good. This man might have screwed up everything. Felix knew that his mission would have gone on in any case, but he himself might have lost his future utility. And lost his future eight lives.

Felix rolled his burden down Vanderbilt to the corner of 42nd Street and entered the station's vestibule. He stood with his back to the people entering and leaving while he pretended to be adjusting his bags. No one paid him any attention. Felix stood there for several minutes; he wanted that security man well out of his way when he entered. Finally he started into the station, dragging his heavy burden behind him down the incline ramp. When he got to the Main Concourse, he plodded purposefully toward the center of the huge space.

As Felix reached the area around the circular information counter where many people were congregated, he selected two women standing together in animated conversation. He edged next to them, saw that they were oblivious to him, and positioned his bags a few feet away from them. Casually he abandoned his bags and walked toward the information booth, but as he neared it, sheered away and headed for the Lexington Avenue exit.

2

In a Grand Central Station men's room Denny Delaney was cupping cold water in his hands and dousing his face. He ladled one more handful and looked at himself in the mirror. His eyes were still bloodshot. His head was pounding from a hangover. When he looked in the mirror, he saw his own hell gaping back at him. He was late. Again.

Denny walked through the station's Main Concourse, which he and the others called the Cathedral. It was an enormous space, bigger than the nave of many cathedrals. Light was shooting down in shafts from the arched windows. Only a few years before, the station had been given a complete makeover. At one time it was headed for the wrecking ball, but it had been saved by the lobbying of prominent citizens like Jackie Kennedy. Now it was a Manhattan showpiece, one of the greatest and most celebrated indoor public spaces in the world.

The Main Concourse soars one hundred fifty feet above the floor of Tennessee marble. The vaulted ceiling with its zodiac design against a green-blue background has twenty-five hundred electrified twinkling stars.

At ground level in the center of the concourse is the circular information booth. Atop the booth is the signature station clock with its four clock faces, each watching the nave in a different direction. Two grand staircases on the east and west sides rise up to broad balconies that surround the vast space. Three sixty-foot arched windows on the east and west walls diffuse light into the grand space. A huge liquid crystal arrivals-and-departures board looks down, and egg-shaped chandeliers dangle above the floor in the concourse's adjoining anterooms.

Entering a major cathedral's central nave, even the most jaded person has a sense of awe and is struck by the loftiness, the size, and the grandeur, of the enclosed space. People entering the Main Concourse are awed by the same impulses. These soaring enclosed indoor spaces with sunlight filtering in make human beings proud, but they also make them humbled by the sight of such an overwhelming architectural achievement.

As he hurried through the crowd, Denny paid little attention to the concourse, which he loved, nor the swarm of travelers and commuters. He was distracted by his own problems and the pounding headache. Grand Central Station—this was Denny's turf. On a good day, when he wasn't nursing a Grade A hangover, he could stand on one of the balconies and admire this glorious space.

He neared the central information booth with its inquiry windows under the four-faced clock. He was hailed by the Ellises, the brother-and-sister team that helped service the counters. Even-tempered, patient to the core, each with a pitch-perfect sense of humor, they were ideal for the job. The sister shouted through her microphone, "Morning, Denny."

"Hi, Sandy. How ya doing?"

Timmy called out, "Top of the morning to you, Dennis. Looks like a grand morning, eh?"

"Morning, Timmy. How do you guys manage to stay so chipper?"

Timmy replied, “It’s the touch of the old sod that does it.”

Then both turned back to their questioners.

Denny passed a New York State National Guardsman, still on duty nine months after Nine-Eleven, still patrolling in his heavy boots and combat camouflage gear. Denny started up the marble stairs of the East Staircase toward his workplace, but he was not bounding up the stairs as in the old days. Each step brought more painful pounding to his head.

Above the main balcony was a short flight of stairs and a wheelchair ramp leading to a steel door that bore in small letters the legend Security. He pulled the door open and entered a big, windowless squad room with banks of stacked TV monitors set up on three long rows of desks. Four men were seated before monitors, but most of the monitoring positions were unoccupied.

At the first monitor was a cadaverous man in shirt-sleeves, his tie loosened: Tony—Antonio Tessitore. In a voice that was a little too eager and with a gotcha grimace, he said, “Better get in there. Mac wants to see you. Said as soon as you came in.”

Denny thought, *Once an asshole, always an asshole.* He looked at the big wall clock. Ten o’clock.

Seated two chairs away from Tony was Richie Walters, a twenty-eight-year-old who was Denny’s best friend on the squad. Richie had managed to stay upbeat and optimistic on a job that could be boring and full of numbing routine duties. He gave Denny a smile and a thumbs-up. Denny greeted him. “How’s she hanging, Richie boy?”

“Not bad, Den. You still on for that ballgame?”

“Yup. You bet, bro.”

Denny walked toward the back of the room.

In the far right corner was a room with one glassed wall looking out on the big squad room. On its door were the words *Tech Support.* Within the room Terry—Teresa Kerrigan—was in her wheelchair before a huge panel of instruments and small television monitors. An attractive young woman, brown hair, twenty-nine years old. In the corner of her area was a big screen, now blank. She saw Denny, waved, and grinned a greeting. He smiled and waved.

In the left-hand corner opposite Terry's area was another room with a glass wall and a door marked Supervisor.

The door was half open. Denny walked in. Mac—Jim Mackin—was a six-foot-three, overweight black man in his late forties, who looked older than his years and stressed out. He was obviously teed off. He sat up in his swivel chair and rolled closer to his desk.

"Shut the door."

Denny pushed the door closed and sat in one of the two chairs in front of Mac's desk.

"What the hell you think you're doing? I said I wanted everyone in here before nine from now on. You're pissing me off. Look at you. You look like shit."

Denny looked down at his lap. His trousers had stains and his suit had a tenuous press left, a slept-in look to it.

"In the old days it was easy to cover up for a fuck-up. Before Nine-Eleven our biggest worries were the winos, the homeless, the pickpockets. You know how everyone is on our ass now. I can't cover for you anymore."

He noticed that Mac was short of breath, was wheezing. His bronchitis was probably acting up, but this was no time to ask about his health. Denny's eyes met Mac's briefly, and then they dropped to a coffee stain on the lap of his own trousers. He looked up again as Mac continued his tirade.

"Shit, Denny, you're the sharpest guy I've got. You can outthink, outsmart any of those bozos on the squad out there. You think like a real detective, not like a cop on the beat. You've got brains. Why the hell don't you use them and straighten out? Why're you letting the booze take over your life? It's a wonder that Monny doesn't leave you."

Denny dropped his eyes again.

Mac's eyes widened. "Shit. I bet she's already left you, hasn't she? She's had to put up with a lot."

That dart hit Denny. He swept the walls with his eyes, looking like a man at the end of his wits. He sucked in his lips.

"Denny, are you going to let that dickhead Tony out there ease you out for the promotion? Shit, man, I'm trying to help you. You know there's a matter of obligation and trust here. After Nine-Eleven the FBI asked us to assign one of our best guys for temporary duty with them. I gave them you—TDY for six weeks, partly because of your previous stint with them—and you seemed to work out well with the Bureau, from all I heard."

"I did."

"But, Denny, you owe me one, goddammit. Remember that."

"I know, I know, Mac."

"Denny, this is my last warning to you. Our friendship is going to mean squat. You're out of here if I have to lay down the law again. As of now, you're suspended for a week with pay. Go home and sober up. Straighten up, or you'll be living in one of those train tunnels down below like the other bums. Get your life together before it's gone."

Denny had no excuses, no arguments, and he couldn't make any promises, either. He left Mac's office silently. As he left, he saw Mac using one of his puffers to aid his breathing. *Stress isn't helping him any,* Denny thought.

Denny shuffled across the squad room into Teresa's glass cage. All of the new sophisticated equipment was spread out in front of her on the control panels and monitors. It looked like the control room of a television or recording studio. Gate Nineteen was up on one screen. Commuters were hurrying toward the surveillance camera.

"Hi, Terry. How's it going, hon?"

"Hey, you look like you just got out of an all-night poker game."

"Yeah, yeah. Terr, how's your therapy coming?"

"The last week has been good. I think I'm making a lot more progress than I was. I've been walking a few more steps."

"Hey, great, hon."

Terry had been partially paralyzed by a bullet eleven months earlier in a station shoot-out.

Terry had a worried expression on her face as she said, "Denny, last night I had another one of those calls. I'm sure it was from one of Frankie Carrino's brothers or one of his other relatives. He said, 'You used excessive force. You killed an unarmed man.' Denny, Frankie Carrino had a gun. He shot first. I did what I had to do."

"I know, Terr. We all know. Of course you did what any of us would have done in your shoes."

"The guy on the phone. He was very careful. He made

no threats, just a not-so-subtle warning. Just letting me know that they're out there. They're probably watching me."

"Did you report it to Mac?"

"Yeah. He said that from time to time the city cops will be monitoring me. I just hope these guys phoning me don't decide to come after me. I keep my eyes peeled, but I haven't seen anyone following me."

Terry received a call. Denny used it as an excuse to back out of the room after signaling goodbye. By an unspoken agreement between them neither one ever mentioned their sexual encounter a few months before.

He had nothing to say to the bunch outside. Richie eyed him with a worried expression, while Tony couldn't hide his turd-eating grin. Denny just walked through to the outside balcony overlooking the Cathedral.

3

Outside on the balcony Denny stared at the mass of people below. Hundreds of people, some scanning the train arrival-and-departure boards; some lined up at the information or ticket windows; some hurrying, scurrying, dashing through the massive room. Denny's temples were still throbbing from his hangover. He'd have to take some Tylenol or something. He started down the stairs.

When he was halfway down, the explosion erupted with an ear-ripping sound, enormously amplified in that cavernous space—louder than any sound in the world. The blast caused an eruption of smoke, of hundreds of thousands of tiny objects hurtling through the air: blood, metal nails, ball bearings, bits of skin, body parts, powder, dust, shards of glass, timetable confetti, luggage bits, deadly shrapnel tearing into bodies. The awful sound echoed throughout the Cathedral. The smell of the explosive permeated the air.

Denny was rammed back against the stairs. His back hit the stair edge. He found himself—deafened, dazed, traumatized—lying on one of the steps. A small trail of blood was moving past his right eye. He reached into his back pocket for his handkerchief. He dabbed the cloth on his forehead. Then he blotted other parts of his face. He had small cuts on his cheeks and nose. The backs of both hands had lacerations.

Then, with eyes clouded by dust and smoke, he looked at the scene below him, the huge chamber of horrors. He was about twenty-five feet from ground level. He could see bodies writhing, parts of bodies, bloody smears and debris everywhere. Pathetic empty shoes strewn about. In the center of the hall a hole had been blown in the floor. Smoke, haze everywhere rising in plumes to the high ceiling above. Most of the glass panels had been blown out of the huge windows.

Denny was sickened by the horrible smells of the explosive, of blood, of bodily fluids from human beings who had been blown apart. Sounds came from everywhere: screams, calls for help, wailing, sobbing, sounds of agony, sounds of electronic beeping, whining sounds of devices activated, alarms going off.

The center of the blast was almost clear of any debris or remains. Moving out from the blast site were roughly concentric circles of devastation. In the circle closest to the blast were body parts and fragments of objects that had been blown apart. In the next circle were recognizable corpses and writhing bodies with severed limbs and fatal wounds. Some victims were trying desperately to crawl away from the center, away from that awful thing.

In the next circle were people who were still whole individuals but mortally wounded. At the perimeter of the blast people were sitting or lying, trying to assess the extent of their wounds and injuries. Numb, deafened victims wandered around, dazed, out of it. Some men and women were weeping uncontrollably. One woman clutched her arm that had been almost severed from her shoulder.

The squad members passed Denny as they ran down the stairs. Richie asked him if he was all right. He nodded and motioned him on. They had first-aid kits. As Mac passed, he took a quick look at Denny's face. He could see that he was one of the lucky ones. He patted him on the shoulder. Mac yelled, "If you're able, give us a hand." Then he headed down the stairs, breathing heavily. Mac's worst nightmare had come true. For him this was the end of everything he had worked to prevent; no matter what else happened in his life, this would be the worst.

Denny made his way down the stairs and started to help the injured. He held a man's coat sleeve over his bleeding knee until the man was able to hold it himself. He helped a woman with an infant to her feet. She was dazed. She wandered off toward an exit. He dried his own superficial wounds and leaned over to see about an old man with a very bad head injury. Denny checked. The man was dead.

As Denny ministered to the wounded and continued helping wherever he could, he heard sirens outside the terminal. Police, firemen, medics were starting to rush into the Cathedral.

Denny helped as many as he could. He kept whispering encouragement. He heard himself saying mantras, "Hold on. Hold on. The medics are coming. Help is coming. Hold on."

The cuts on his face, forehead, and hands had stopped bleeding. Mac saw him helping and gave him a thumbs-up sign. Mac was sweating heavily and his chest was heaving. Police, firefighters, and emergency medical people were pouring in. The streets outside the station were clogged with fire engines, police cars, and ambulances. Inside, it was barely controlled chaos.

People were sitting on the marble stairs leading up to the east and west balconies, some dazed, some weeping, some daubing their skin mottled with cuts, some staring robotically at the scene around them.

A woman was holding a bleeding young girl to her

chest. A medic eased the child from the woman's arms and started treating the numbed child. People stood dazed, disoriented. A boom box was blasting rap noise with obscene lyrics. A man furiously kicked it until it stopped. Then he fell down. Cell phones were going off. Pocketbooks lay open, their contents strewn all over. Tiny pieces of newspaper and the fragments of timetables kept circling around. The blown-out windows were bringing in air currents from outside. The smells were getting worse, noxious. The dry, coppery smell of blood was permeating thc air. Some people were vomiting from the smell, the dust, and the sight of so much carnage.

An old man, his face bloodied, his suit in tatters, grabbed Denny's arm and yelled, "What kind of animals would do something like this? Has the whole world gone mad?"

Denny couldn't answer the man. His only response was to tighten his lips and nod his head in affirmation, confirming the man's thoughts about the inhumanity of such creatures.

Rubber-gloved emergency medical workers were rushing into the station, quickly zeroing in on the more seriously injured. Doctors and nurses in scrubs and white coats hurried to victims. The area was swarming with first responders—the police, firefighters—grim-looking, motivated people. It had taken very little time for the FBI personnel in black windbreakers to arrive. They were fanning out around the station.

4

The concourse was now full of medics, firefighters, and police. With his limited medical training there was little Denny could do. His cop's instincts took over. He knew how to investigate. That was where he could do some good now. He rushed up the stairs to the Security headquarters.

Denny was halfway up the stairs to Security when his cell phone went off. It was Monny—Monica, his wife—calling him from her office at Morgan Stanley a few blocks away from the station.

"Denny, are you hurt? Are you okay?"

"Yeah, I'm okay. When the blast went off, I was coming down the stairs outside the office. I got grazed on the forehead with fragments and got some small cuts on my hands. I'm shaken up and my ears are still ringing, but I'm still here. I'm looking down at the concourse right now. It's awful. Worse than anything I've ever seen. A lot of people didn't make it."

"When I heard it on the radio, I almost fainted. I thought, 'He's there.' I'm so worried about you."

"Fifteen minutes before the blast I was walking through that crowd in the concourse on my way up here. And when the blast hit, I was on my back down there. I'm sure there are people I know who work in the station that didn't make it through. People who work in the information booth, the Ellises, other people."

"It's so horrible. What kind of people would do such a thing? Terrorists? Nutcases? Maniacs?"

"Any or all of the above."

"Denny, I'm sorry I haven't stayed in touch every day, but the way you were, the . . . drinking, I just couldn't take it. Are you sure you're all right, that you haven't been injured?"

"No, honestly, I'm okay. Just a few cuts, hon. Monny, I want us to be back together. Even more now."

"We'll see. I'm not shutting any doors. You see if you can get the drinking under control. You get straight. Then we'll see. I'm ready when you get straightened out, but, Denny, I can't go back to the bad old days."

"We need to be together, Monny."

"Now is not the time to be talking about this. What if there's another bomb in there somewhere? I do pray for your safety. Take care of yourself, hon. Please don't take unnecessary chances. I know how foolhardy you can be sometimes."

"Love ya."

"I love you too. Take care."

A few seconds after he deactivated the call from his wife, the phone rang again. It was his father, a retired New York police lieutenant, who now lived in Fort Lauderdale, Florida.

"Den, oh good. Are you okay? Your mother's here on the other line."

"Hello, Dennis, are you all right?"

"Yeah, fine. I was coming down the staircase when it hit. A few scratches, temporarily deafened, but still in one piece. The luck of the Irish."

"We've been watching TV. It's horrible. Were any of our guys right there when the bomb went off?"

"Not as far as I know. It's still too early to tell. Some friends of mine in the information booth were right in the center of the impact."

Denny looked at the scene below and saw a steady

stream of stretchers being carried out. It was the aftermath of a battle, a battlefield in a war zone. Denny described the scene to his parents.

Denny's mother said, "We're praying for you."

His parents were strong; they had faced a number of life-and-death crises over the years. He assured them that he was safe. After their admonishments to be careful, he wished them both well and broke off.

He put away his cell phone and rushed up to the Security office. He tore through the now deserted squad room. As he passed the monitors, he could see the carnage below on two of them. Rescuers were everywhere, trying to bring order out of the chaos in horror scenes out of Dante's *Inferno*. Two of the Main Concourse monitors were full of electronic snow and gray, blurry dots and a blizzard of nothingness—the cameras they were monitoring had been blown out by the blast.

Denny hurried to Terry's cubicle. When he came through the door, she spun her chair around, her face a portrait of pain. She had been staring at the two functioning concourse monitors and knew everything.

"Oh my God, Denny, it's so horrible. What do we do? I feel so helpless here in this fucking chair and with all this hardware. Hardware that didn't prevent a thing."

She pounded her fist on the desk.

"Terry, help me with the equipment. I need to look at what the cameras picked up right before the blast. I want to see those tapes."

"Monitors eight and sixteen in the Main Concourse were blown out in the blast."

"Yeah, but everything up to the moment of the impact will be on tape."

Denny sat at the master monitor with the big screen

in front of him, while Terry swung her wheelchair in front of her banks of monitors and mixers.

"Terry, run the tapes for me for cameras four, eight, twelve, and sixteen. Give me the last few minutes before the blast on each one."

Denny studied what each surveillance camera had recorded from its angle. He watched carefully as the tapes revealed what each camera eye had seen. After a few minutes Denny saw for an instant on camera twelve an unattended black bag with a bulky carryall sitting on top of it. The bags stood dangerously abandoned in the center of the Main Concourse. Two women were not too far away from the bags, but they were not on top of them either, didn't seem to be overseeing them.

"Terry, roll that tape again from two minutes back. Yes, that's it. Stop. Freeze that. Zoom in and give me two snaps."

The printer spat out two 8 by 11 prints, close-ups of the unattended bags. In the lower right corner of each print were the camera number, the date, and the time.

Denny went back to watching the tapes. On another tape he spotted something. "Stop. There, back up a little."

Terry was an expert at this technology. She backed up the tape.

Denny yelled, "Freeze it. Zoom in on the guy with the bags. There."

Denny pointed him out on the big screen with a laser pencil light. They saw a man standing with the bags. A clear, distinct picture of a well-built man, his face blank, expressionless.

"Print two of those."

The process continued. Denny would study the

tapes, then call out for Terry to freeze a shot, zoom in on the man, and print a copy of the frozen taped image.

In one printout he got a shot of the man approaching ground zero with his bags; in another he was some distance from the abandoned bags. He was hurrying away.

At one point Denny was studying a tape in slow motion.

"Hey, wait! Shit. Freeze that shot. Blow it up. Yeah."

Denny shouted, "I know the guy in the video. I know this guy. I swear it. Holy Christ!"

"From where?"

"Let me think. Jeez. I can't think who or where right now, but I'm sure I've seen him before. It'll come to me."

"You've got a good memory for faces."

"But I don't remember where I saw this guy. God, I wish I could remember. It's not somebody I know well or have seen a lot. Some casual sighting. Maybe in a bar."

Eventually Denny had two sets of five prints which he put into two manila envelopes. He handed one of the envelopes to Terry and tucked the other one under his arm.

"Here's a set of prints for the FBI or other investigators. I'm keeping one set for insurance, so please, Terry, don't mention that I've got it."

Terry was skeptical about Denny having a set, but she nodded out of loyalty to him.

"I'm going down to tell Mac. I'll catch you later."

"Watch yourself, Den. And have someone take care of those cuts you've got."

As he opened the Security headquarters door leading out to the balcony, carrying the envelope under his arm, Denny had to move aside to let in an officious Tony and a rush of six grim-looking men and women all in black windbreakers that blared FBI. Even in this crisis atmosphere, Tony had time to give Denny a look of contempt and hatred as he passed him. Tony led the agents to Terry's cubicle in the back of Security.

5

From the balcony Denny could see the battlefield cleanup going on below, the tumbleweeds of debris amid the awful carnage. EM personnel were carrying out stretchers. A group of firemen were engaged in the grisly task of gathering strewn body parts. They worked in two-person teams. One would put the body part in a clear plastic bag while the other would make out a label of where it had been found. Investigators were starting to set up grid markers so that Forensics would know the location of the retrieved remains.

Denny was still carrying the manila envelope containing the photographs of the mass murderer. He looked at the brown envelope. Since his school days, Denny had liked to get credit for his successes and his finds. It was a combination of ego and an instinct for survival. From his years in police work he had learned the essentials of "Cover your ass, baby."

Wearing his lanyard with the big laminated ID card with his photograph on it, he could go anywhere. He walked down the marble staircase laden with bomb aftermath. The air was heavy with that awful noxious, disquieting smell. He hurried through a maze of passageways and arrived at an office door marked Tasteful Travel by Design.

Inside, an elderly woman, Olive Patterson, was watching a portable television set, a handkerchief held to her mouth in a clenched fist. She turned and saw Denny. She rose and gave him a hug. Denny almost lost it for the first time since the blast. This was the first intimate contact he'd had with another human being in months.

"Oh, Denny, isn't it awful? Terrible. All those poor people. What's going to happen next?"

"It's very bad, Olive. But we'll catch the sons a bitches. Do me a favor and hold onto this envelope for me."

"Sure, put it in the top drawer of Lois's desk. She's on vacation. If I'm not here, you've got a key to the office. You can get it back any time you want. Take care of yourself."

Once back in the concourse Denny circled the devastated area searching for Mac. He found him near a marble railing, talking to two uniformed police inspectors who had brass and medals boasting of their rank.

Mac didn't look well. He was sweating heavily, and his chest was heaving from his breathing exertions. He spotted Denny.

"Thanks for helping out, Denny, I appreciate it."

"Mac, are you all right?"

"As well as can be expected under the circumstances."

"Mac, I've got to speak to you for a minute." Mac nodded to the two officers, and the two walked out of earshot.

"Denny, this suicide bomber really caught us napping. I feel like shit about it."

"It wasn't a suicide bomber, Mac."

"The FBI guys say that's what it was."

"I have the proof that it wasn't. I went to Terry's tech center. I looked at the tapes from the four concourse security cameras. The last few minutes on each one before the blast."

"What do they show?"

"This was no suicide bomber. This guy got away.

Just strolled away. I saw him on tape. He's there on tape for all the world to see, walking away from it all. Left two bags with the bombs sitting all by their lonesome in the middle of the concourse. Either the bombs were timed to detonate by themselves, or he detonated them by remote control from a distance. The tapes prove that he was well away from the blast."

Mac questioned him, "Did you get printout snaps of the guy?"

"Yeah. Terry's got the whole thing up there ready for the FBI. When they really study the tapes, they'll probably find other things too."

"Denny, why wouldn't someone report two bags just sitting there?"

"They weren't sitting there long, believe me. He planted them close to two women who were deep in conversation and didn't realize they were being used as decoys. The concourse was too crowded. People would assume that the bags belonged to the women, or that someone left them for a few seconds to ask questions at the info desk. Everyone is too interested in his own business. The bags weren't there long enough for any security people to get wise.

"We have four guys taking turns looking at twenty-six cameras. On the other twenty-two cameras people could be making atom bombs, and we wouldn't be the wiser."

"Denny, I'm going to alert the FBI to this right away. Thanks, kid. They've got something to work on. Go with these commanders. Show them the entrances where the bomber could have entered. I've got to see Captain Grayson."

Mac walked away. Denny didn't have a chance to ask him whether his suspension had been lifted in this crisis situation. It would be important to straighten that out with Tony around. Denny walked over to the two police top brass.

The taller of the police brass addressed Denny. "I'm Inspector Manginelli. This is Chief Inspector Montagna. We want to see where this suicide bomber might have come from."

"I can show you exactly where he entered. I've just seen some of the surveillance videos for this space. And this was no suicide bomber. He rolled a couple of bags in and just left them, walked away from them. He got away."

Manginelli said, "The FBI guys are saying this was a suicide bomber."

"I don't care what they're saying. They'll find the evidence up there in Security on the surveillance tapes. It's crystal clear, and there are perfect shots of him."

Denny pointed. "It's likely he came in from the western 42nd Street entrance and exited to Lexington Avenue. I would judge that by the time the thing went off he was hurrying north or south along Lexington."

Denny spent fifteen minutes showing the inspectors the probable entrance and exit. He left them conferring with other officers. As he headed toward the East Grand Staircase, he ran into June Levine, one of the workers in the information booth. She was disoriented, seemed out of it. She explained that she had just stepped away from the concourse when the bomb went off.

"If I'd been in the booth a minute later, I would have been killed, obliterated. Denny, Timmy and Sandy Ellis were at the counters when the bomb went off. Oh my God, they're gone."

She broke down; sobs heaved through her body.

Over and over again she repeated, “Oh my God, the poor Ellises.”

Denny hugged her to him, tried to ease her pain. She wanted to go home so he helped her to the street. So many emergency vehicles had blocked the surrounding streets that it was necessary for them to walk past the Grand Hyatt Hotel, the Chrysler Building, past Third Avenue to Second Avenue before they could find moving traffic and a cab.

6

It was two-thirty in the afternoon. Denny looked around the concourse; some semblance of order had been established, but the place still reeked like an abattoir. The central part of the great hall was now cordoned off with yellow police scene-of-a-crime tape. All of the injured had been taken away. The coroner's office had taken away those bodies that were intact or nearly so. The fire personnel and police were still collecting minute body parts. Groups of forensic people were trying to collect any shreds of evidence.

Denny used his cell phone. He called Terry on her cell phone so he could get through to her right away. She answered after three rings.

"Terry, what's happening?"

"Where are you? Tony told me you got suspended this morning. I didn't know that when you were in here. You shoulda told me. Has Mac reinstated you?"

Denny lied, "Yeah, hon, I'm back. What's been going on?"

"The FBI took all the surveillance tapes for the last twenty-four hours before the explosion. I had to reload all the machines with new tapes."

"Did you give them the envelope of printouts?"

"Yeah. I gave it to the senior agent. An Agent Wrightson. I didn't mention you at all or your extra set. They just took it along with the tapes and left. I wanted to make copies of all those tapes, but they said there was no time for that. Fucking Tony was a pain in the ass as usual, trying to pull rank on me and ordering me around. I insisted on giving them copies of the tapes, and Tony ordered me to turn over the originals. I tried to argue them out of it. I did get a receipt for everything. That's when Tony told me about your suspension."

"Tony is an asshole. Mac would never have let them have the originals. Never have let them get out of the building. If Mac were there they would only have gotten them over his dead body. He would have made them sit there and watch them in your room."

"Denny, we've got all the latest state-of-the-art equipment right here. I could have run the tapes for them. I could have given them copies of the tapes, all the printouts they wanted."

"Yeah, and Terr, the evidence wouldn't have been compromised. It would have been kept at its original site. They are the ones breaking the chain of custody. Seems like the Feds are trying to fuck up their own case or do a cover up. Who's up there now?"

"A few FBI agents are with Tony in the squad room. No one else. None of our guys. I haven't seen Mac since this whole thing happened."

"Okay, I'll be up there."

When Denny got to the door of the Security headquarters, two FBI agents blocked his way. They looked at his ID badge. The taller one said, "I'm sorry, Sergeant Delaney, but Sergeant Tessitore said you've been suspended and aren't allowed entrance."

Denny was pissed off. "Fuck Sergeant Tessitore. I have to get in there."

"No can do. Orders. Sorry."

Just then Tony came out of the Security office and pointed at Denny for the benefit of the two FBI agents. His face showed his hatred of his rival.

"This man is on suspension: he's not to be let in."

"Tony, I've been with Mac. He saw me working with the wounded down there. I'm sure he wants me off suspension."

"No one told me anything. I'm in charge."

"Who put you in charge?"

"Seniority put me in charge, wiseass. Mac and I have talked about how your drinking is affecting your work."

"Like the way your stupidity affects your job performance."

"You'll regret your digs at me, Delaney, when I'm in the saddle."

"At a time like this we shouldn't be at each other's throats."

"I ain't at your throat. Just get lost until your suspension is officially lifted. When I'm notified of that, I'll give you clearance. Otherwise, fuck off."

"Asshole." Denny stormed away from the door.

His mind was racing. *I gotta see Mac right now and get this straightened out. Gotta get this suspension lifted right away*. He rushed down the stairs looking for Mac. As he was circling the concourse, Richie raced up to him.

"Denny, Mac's down. He was suffering chest pains. The EMs think it was a heart attack. He looks like shit. Come on with me."

At the foot of the West Staircase, Mac lay on a gurney. His eyes were lolling back in his head. They had strapped an oxygen mask over his mouth and had an IV working. A doctor in green scrubs was looking after him.

Denny cried out, "Hang in there, Mac, don't quit on us."

He accompanied the gurney as the medics rolled it to

the 42nd Street. entrance. He helped them lift the gurney into an ambulance. “Hang in there, Mac.”

He questioned one medic, “Where are you taking him?”

“NYU Medical Center.”

After the ambulance pulled away, Denny stood staring after it. His universe was rapidly disintegrating. He had to be involved in the investigation. *I’ve got to get reinstated.* On his cell phone he dialed Captain Grayson’s number at headquarters. Grayson was Mac’s boss, his boss. He got through to Elayne, Grayson’s secretary. No, her boss was on the road. Denny told her about Mac, and she promised that Grayson would call him back.

“Elayne, would you please tell him to call me as soon as he can. It’s urgent.” He gave her his cell phone and home phone numbers.

7

Denny wanted to look at his surveillance shots. Events were getting out of hand, taking on a life of their own. Pretty soon he might be thrown out of the terminal altogether if that prick Tessitore had his way. He walked quickly to the travel bureau. Olive was standing, just packing up her briefcase. The television was still on, showing footage of the scene outside Grand Central. He saw brief playback shots of himself assisting Mac's gurney into the ambulance.

"Oh, Denny. I'm glad you're back. I've got to get out of here, get home. I went out in the hall. The dust, that awful smell, everything. I'm afraid."

"I'm going to use the office for a while. Okay?"

"As long as you like. Come and go whenever you want. You've got a key." Before she left she kissed him on the cheek and patted his arm.

"Denny, take care of those cuts or you'll get infected. Goodbye, dear. Stay safe. You want me to leave the TV on?"

"Yeah, leave it on. Thanks, Olive."

After Olive left, Denny pulled the envelope out of the drawer and brought it to the long table in the rear of the office. He pushed piles of travel brochures aside to make space.

Denny lined up the five photographs in front of him. He put them in chronological order and studied the pictures from left to right.

Picture number one showed a burly man in a blue suit and gray tie dragging a large black bag on rollers with a chunky black carryall bag strapped above it. He was coming from the direction of the 42nd Street entrance near Vanderbilt.

Picture number two showed the man stopped momentarily. He seemed to be adjusting something on the top bag. He was in the middle of the huge rotunda; crowds of people surged all around him. He seemed to have edged the bags close to two women who were standing together talking intently to one other.

Picture three showed the two bags sitting there on their own. People were obviously hurrying by the bags and swirling around them in the mob of people in the area. No one seemed to be paying any attention to them. The bomber had been careful about where he placed the bags. They seemed to belong to the two women who were very close to them. One woman was talking on a cell phone while her companion was staring up at the big display board.

Picture four showed the subject walking away from the upright pile of bags, walking toward the Lexington Avenue exit.

Picture five caught a view of the man far away from the bags and the big crowd swirling around the center of the Main Concourse. He was practically through the east passageway to Lexington Avenue.

In this last picture he was a considerable distance from ground zero. The time imprinted on the bottom of the photo said 9:31:38 A.M., a full thirty seconds before the blast. The explosion took place at 9:32:08 according to the time that camera eight went blank. Plenty of time for him to get away unscathed. He would have enough time to merge with the crowds on Lexington Avenue when the blast went off. He could even stand and act shocked by the explosion. If people started scurrying away, he could join them. Denny was sure that whatever he did, he would not have drawn suspicion to himself.

No, this guy had gotten clear away without a scratch. Denny was sure. His body did not end up in bits and pieces like those at the point of impact. He was somewhere well away, gloating and celebrating. *The fucking creep.*

Denny went to Olive's desk and picked up the big magnifying glass she kept there for close work. He sat down again in front of the line of pictures. He studied the man in the photo very carefully. Denny was good with faces. Back and forth over the pictures he searched.

I know this fucking guy. I'm sure of it. I've seen him. Heard his voice. Where do I know him from? Here at work? The bars? A waiter in a restaurant? It was something casual like that. Certainly not someone he had seen a number of times. He searched again, studying each picture very intently.

Then he sat with his eyes closed, leaned way back in the chair, thinking.

A news anchor's voice from the television set suddenly came into his frame of reference. He looked at the screen. The television reporter was standing outside the 42nd Street entrance near where Denny had helped load Mac into the ambulance.

He said, "Now, at three-fifteen here in New York, the FBI has confirmed that this horrible explosion was the work of one or more suicide bombers. Speculation has been rife all morning. I repeat, the Federal Bureau of Investigation is now convinced that this horrible blast was caused by one or more suicide bombers.

"It will be extremely difficult to track down the

bomber or bombers because the body or bodies are likely among those completely consumed by the explosion. The FBI has named Agent Bruce Wexler as the Special Agent in Charge; the SAC as he is called, is the key man in overall command of the federal investigation of this horrific terrorist attack. All of the tapes from the Grand Central Station's many surveillance cameras have been impounded by the FBI."

Denny was furious. Why was the FBI so quick to call this a suicide bombing? This wasn't like them at all. Often they had been criticized for their foot-dragging in labeling crimes. They seemed hellbent on labeling this particular crime a suicide bombing. Why didn't they wait to look at the tapes and the stills Terry had given them? He started to feel very uneasy about this whole thing. Very disquieted.

He went back to studying the prints in front of him. *Goddamn FBI jumping the gun, perhaps compromising the whole investigation. Where have I seen this guy? Fucking FBI making an early call that might destroy the case. That was it! The FBI headquarters on Vesey Street.*

It hit him. His preoccupation with the FBI announcement had triggered a distant, faint memory. Shit, even with all the booze my mind is still clicking. He couldn't believe his eyes. He took up the magnifying glass and studied the face again. *I know who this guy is.*

In September after the Twin Towers desecration, while he was working at the Manhattan FBI field office on TDY, he'd been sitting in the outer office talking with the partner assigned to him, Frank Millau. Then, at the door at the other end of the room, he had seen this man standing, talking to another agent. Somehow the man had not looked like an agent. He had stared at

Denny as if memorizing his features. Denny, always curious, had asked Millau, "Who's that guy?"

Millau had said, "Oh, he may be helping us on the investigation. Looks like Middle Eastern background to me."

Denny had asked, "An informant?"

"No, I think he's just helping us."

It seemed to Denny at the time that Frank Millau was being deliberately vague about the man, which was understandable. Good investigators compartmentalized.

Denny had heard the man's voice. A voice that projected, almost sounding like a trained announcer's or actor's voice. No real accent. Sounded like a general Middle American accent.

Denny felt that he had to tell Terry about his discovery, since he had told her that he knew the bomber from somewhere. He grabbed his cell phone and dialed Terry's number. When she answered, he said excitedly, "You're not going to believe this. The bomber, I said I recognized him? I saw him at the FBI field office when I was TDY there last fall. He could have been an agent, an informer, a consultant, whatever—but the FBI knows this guy."

"Den, what does this mean? What the hell was that bomber doing with the FBI? What the hell is going on here anyway?"

"Who knows? I've got to face them with what I know."

"Denny, if that guy is FBI or works for them, then this could be a much bigger thing than we think."

"Right. Oh, Terr, I've got some more bad news for you. Mac suffered some kind of an attack. Might be his heart. They've taken him to the hospital."

"Oh, no, what other terrible things are going to happen? What was his condition?"

"Looked comatose, out of it, but it's hard to say. Terr, can you call his wife Barb in case she hasn't been informed?"

"Yes, I'll do it. I've got numbers for her right here. I'll get on it. Watch yourself, Den. This thing is getting complicated. You're sure your suspension's been lifted?"

"Of course. See ya, Terr. I'll stay in close touch."

"I'll talk to you later."

Denny was excited and angry about his find. He thought briefly about Terry. She was his only link to working the case. He had no one close he could confide in or work with at this point. She had been great for him in the past. A great girl. He needed someone. Monny was slipping away.

Denny shuffled the pictures into a stack and put them back in the envelope. This time he decided to hide them a little more securely. He climbed on the table. He unscrewed a vent cover with his pocket knife and shoved the envelope well into a crevice. He redid the screws and climbed down.

He snapped the locking mechanism on the door and went outside into the hall. After he made sure the door was locked, he decided that now was the time to hook up with the FBI. He had no idea what was going down, but it worried him.

8

Denny circled the station looking for Bruce Wexler, the Special Agent in Charge. He had met him several times months before. At that time, hearing him use the expression *try to ferret out some* information and because of his lanky build, he had nicknamed him the Ferret. He had said to Monny that Wexler was probably the last one in the world able to ferret out anything. A bullheaded know-it-all. No sign of him. Finally he decided to ask one of the FBI agents. With so much going on, surely they all couldn't have been informed of his suspension. He approached an attractive blonde agent wearing a black FBI windbreaker.

"Ma'am, could you please tell me where I could find Agent Wexler?"

She glanced at his ID badge.

"He was here, but he went back to Vesey Street. They're setting up a command center there."

"Thank you."

Denny walked through to the station's sprawling food court. There was a haze everywhere in the station, and the awful smells persisted. Because of the attack, the famous Oyster Bar was closed. With the lights off, it was hard to see the gleaming tiles of the vaulted brick ceiling through the windows. Denny had spent many, many hours in there. The waiters and bartenders were his friends.

A lot of Denny's precious world was beginning to collapse. He thought that when politicians said that terrorists will never defeat us, they were wrong. When the victims were buried, and the surviving injured walked among us, and you looked at what you had before and what you had after, it was obvious to any one that everyone remaining had lost a precious part of his or her life. After all, the two great Twin Towers no longer soared above lower Manhattan. How could you possibly squeeze a victory out of that?

Now for at least a generation, thousands of people would no longer feel safe and comfortable in this station. People would rush through here apprehensively. No one would dare dawdle. Many would avoid it altogether. The bad memories would remain.

Some of the food concessions were operating and were busy with commuters, rescue workers, and investigators. Denny bought a cruller and a coffee and sat down at a table with some exhausted, dispirited firefighters. They nodded to him, but no one spoke. This was Denny's first food for the day. He glanced at the television screen mounted on one of the pillars.

The television host on CNN was saying, "This morning one or more suicide bombers set off an explosion in New York's Grand Central Station in the historic Main Concourse, which was crowded with hundreds of commuters, travelers, and ordinary New Yorkers. So far we know that over fifty persons were killed and at least one hundred eight were injured. Some of the injured are in extremely critical condition and are not expected to survive.

"The police, Federal Bureau of Investigation, the ATF, and many other law enforcement agencies are investigating this horrible attack. The FBI has labeled it the work of terrorists. The president has condemned the act. Here is what he said outside the White House this afternoon."

The president, shaken and clearly angered, was saying, "We and all civilized nations condemn this heinous and cowardly act. One or more suicide bombers set off bombs loaded with shrapnel which were strapped to their bodies. We do not know and may never know their identities. We may never know what group did this horrible thing unless some terrorist organization takes responsibility. This destructive act may be a continuation of the Nine-Eleven World Trade Center assault on our freedoms and liberties. This act will not go unpunished, nor will it deter us in our war to rid the nation and the world of such evildoers. Our prayers go out to all those who lost loved ones in this tragedy, to all those who lie gravely injured in hospitals."

From his wallet Denny removed a card with a number. It was Agent Frank Millau's cell phone number. After four rings, Frank answered. He asked Denny about the attack.

"Listen, Frank, I have some vital information about the bombing. I have to talk to SAC Wexler. It's urgent."

"Denny, you know the drill. You have to go through your superiors. They'll contact Wexler."

"I have to see him right away!"

"No can do, Denny. We're up to our necks in leads here."

"My boss, Jim Mackin, had a heart attack. He's in the hospital. I'm working through the only channels I know. Listen, Frank, this is urgent. I know who the bomber is. Set up a meeting with SAC Wexler. I have to see him. Now."

Millau knew Denny well. He was a good cop, but he was impulsive at times. He could explode if provoked. "Denny, what do you mean, you know who the bomber is?"

"Frank, get me in to see Wexler. If what I know gets out to the media, the FBI is going to look real bad, like there's a conspiracy going on. Do you think the Bureau can handle another scandal, another major fuck-up after the number they've had over recent years? I know who the bomber is, and that this was absolutely not a suicide bombing. I have the proof."

Denny didn't hear any sound for several long seconds. Frank's wheels were turning. What did he really have to lose by seeing him? Denny had sown doubts and fears in Frank's innate "cover your ass" FBI mentality.

"Okay, Okay. Come down to Vesey Street. I'll do what I can. I'll be waiting for you. But don't get here before seven-thirty tonight. Wexler can't meet with you before then. He's swamped."

"Thanks, Frank."

It took a threat to get through to him, Denny thought. *Typical of that bunch. Slow to act unless goosed by the threat of media disclosure.*

9

Denny had to get away from the station. He decided that he'd look in on his boss, Mac, at the hospital before going to the FBI office. Outside, Denny found that emergency vehicles had snarled traffic for blocks around. He had to walk three blocks from the station to find a thoroughfare where traffic was moving. He hailed a cab. He passed a clock tower that said five-fifteen. What a long, exhausting, horrifying day it had been.

As he headed downtown, he could see that the people in the streets appeared dispirited, defeated, demoralized. You could almost smell desperation in the air. They were grim; they seemed to walk hunched over and even faster than usual. Get to their families, their safe homes, anywhere but there. Traffic was moving at a slower pace; the drivers looked numb and somber. He called Monny on her cell phone and told her about Mac.

At NYU Medical Center he found a chaotic situation. Many of the victims of the explosion had been brought to the facility. Beds, stretchers, and gurneys were set up in hallways as doctors and nurses tried to cope with the injured. It was a hospital under siege in a city under attack.

Denny went to the reception desk to ask for Mac. It was staffed by two harried workers. A long line of worried relatives and friends was ahead of him. As he waited, Denny thought of Big Barb, Mac's wife, and he wondered if she had had time to make it to the hospital. His thoughts took him back over the years.

Mac had a deep, resonant singing voice. When he spoke of his wife in the Security office, he'd call her, in deep bass Tennessee Ernie tones, "Big Bad Barb." Mac's wife had been dubbed Big Bad Barb by her husband and subsequently by her relatives, friends, and neighbors. She was big—an impressive five ten in high heels, almost on an even par with her husband—but she wasn't at all bad, nor was she big implying fat. She was imposing, that's what she was. A force to be reckoned with. Together she and Mac had raised two boys and a girl, all of them winners because Mac and Barb willed it that way and planned it that way.

Mac had insisted on moving into a white neighborhood on Long Island, and the kids attended good schools. When white flight from the city was at its height, Mac went with the whites, bravely and with great determination. Mac had insisted that the family live in the lily-white enclave of Suffolk County on Long Island, where they had flourished with the sons and daughters of white policemen and firefighters who had fled the city.

At the beginning there had been threats and intimidation, an attempt to drive his family from the solidly white neighborhood, but one Sunday he had marshaled over fifty African-American and white police officers in uniform, many driving police cars, to his house while he held a barbecue on the front lawn. The neighbors had all been invited, and from that moment on Mac had started up the road from being barely tolerated, to be being accepted, to being the president of the local PTA. He and Barb were a formidable pair at PTA Back-to-School nights.

Mac had said to Denny's father, a close friend, "You can't hold a good fighting nigger down." He had earned a grudging respect from his neighbors. "The guy has a set of balls," they would say. Fear of cop had cowed the neighbors in a small desegregation battle. At his side during this was no little shrinking violet of a woman; no, it had been Big Bad Barb, as tough as nails, who had been at the schoolhouse when the least sign of a discipline problem had arisen regarding her children. No one messed with Big Mac and Big Bad Barb.

A receptionist told Denny that Mac was in Intensive Cardiac Care on the fifth floor. He could not go in, but he could take a chance that he might see Mac's wife in the unit's waiting room.

On five Denny saw Big Barb at the end of the hall. His eyes teared up as he approached her, and he couldn't keep himself from letting go a torrent of tears as they hugged each other. He desperately needed this human contact. If only Monny . . .

"Mac will make it through, Barb. We're all praying for him."

"Oh God, Denny, I hope you're right. Terry called me. She said you said to call me."

"I told Monny too. She's praying for both of you."

"You guys have been our greatest buddies over the years. Mac and I love you both."

Barb took Denny into the unit to see Mac. He was in a cubicle surrounded by curtains, hooked to monitors and IVs. His face looked very drawn. Barb whispered that he was under sedation at present. She held Mac's hand and gently caressed his forehead.

When Denny left the unit later, Barb was there—determined, strong, and holding onto hope for her beloved partner.

10

Outside the medical center Denny found a cab to take him to the Vesey Street FBI field office. At Vesey Street Denny sat in Frank Millau's cramped office. Frank was a neatly dressed, patrician type whom Denny had learned to trust while he had been on TDY with the Bureau. Frank was saying, "Denny, the White House has already confirmed that this is work of one or more suicide bombers."

"On whose say-so? The FBI. They're wrong. Dead wrong. Your guys went to our Security headquarters and confiscated all the tapes. You also took an envelope from Terry Kerrigan, our tech support officer. That envelope contains five stills of the bomber, which Terry and I made. It's all there in photos. Why won't you guys listen to the truth? What's going on here? A conspiracy again. More bullshit. More lies that the public is going to keep wondering about for generations to come? Like the JFK assassination?"

"Calm down. Stop being such a hothead for once. Denny, for Christ's sake, do you ever listen to yourself? You sound like a goddamn buzz saw. Come down to earth."

Denny spent a half hour working on Millau. He didn't tell him that he had his own set of photos, and he didn't tell him about seeing the bomber in this very office complex. Finally Millau became convinced of two things: that Denny wasn't going to give up, and that he wouldn't mind going to the media. And he knew that Denny was familiar with an awful lot of media types because of his neighborhood turf on Restaurant Row. One thing Denny had instant access to was a phalanx of media types. Millau left the office telling Denny that he was going to get him a meeting with SAC Wexler.

After ten minutes Millau came back in the room. "Denny, you're on. Let's go."

When they entered Wexler's office, the man stood up and shook Denny's hand. Wexler was tall, wiry, wearing his trademark bright red suspenders over his white shirt. Denny had told Monny when he worked with the FBI the previous fall that Wexler reminded him of a giant ferret in red suspenders. His wife had laughed as he strung out the cartoon imagery.

The three men sat around a conference table. Denny slowly and carefully told him his story, step by step. He arrived at a key point. "Your men have that envelope of the five blowup shots. You have the tapes. They prove that this guy got away. There was no suicide bomber. Homicide bomber, yes, but a guy who didn't waste his own life. He may have been dedicated, but he wasn't suicidal. He's out there ready to do it again—an even worse massacre, if that's possible."

Wexler replied, "I know nothing of a set of stills showing this bomber."

"Your guys were given them by our office technician. She gave them to Agent Wrightson. They confiscated all the tapes. A big mistake, in my opinion. Terry, our technician, has all the latest state-of-the-art equipment. She could have run each surveillance tape, given the exact location, made stills, mixed various sites. Your guys broke the chain of custody. She could have made copies of the tapes in minutes. Your guys fucked up."

Wexler was steaming. "Wait a goddamn minute here. Who made you judge and jury of our actions? You guys were responsible for the security of that terminal, and you didn't know your ass from your elbow. From what I hear you have a severe drinking problem that almost got you canned this morning. It sure as hell got you suspended. You're not even here in any official capacity. You're a loose cannon trying to fuck up the works!

"The scuttlebutt is that you are suspended and can't be working on this or any other case. Leave it alone. Let us do the work and the worrying. You're trying to open up a can of worms that doesn't exist. Go home and get drunk."

Denny was on his feet, his fists clenched. He reached over to grab Wexler and was restrained by Millau, who shouted, "Sit down, Denny. You're way off base."

Denny sat down, reluctantly, pissed. He thought that he had probably blown it. He'd soon be thrown out. Then he blurted out, "There are two things that are going to save my ass, Wexler. Number one, I have my own set of those five printout photos; and number two, I recognized the bomber. I saw him in this very FBI office when I was with Frank in reception one day last fall. How is it going to look when I announce at a major press conference that the perp was not a suicide bomber and may indeed be an FBI agent working at the Manhattan field office? Shit, I wouldn't want to be in your shoes when the director and the president get beeped on their crisis phones."

Millau looked at Denny in disbelief. "You didn't tell me that you had seen the bomber here in the building."

Wexler laughed. "Denny, that booze is making you paranoid and screwy."

Denny realized he had scored points. "When I was on TDY here last September and October, Frank and I were in the outer office one day. There was a guy at the other end of the office, looked Middle Eastern. I was curious if he was an agent. Frank said he thought the guy might be working with the Bureau. I heard the guy's voice. He saw me, sort of stared at me. I'm willing to swear on a stack of bibles that he's the bomber, the guy in the stills."

Wexler looked at Frank.

Frank looked confused, evasive. "Denny, I don't have any idea who you're talking about. I can't remember ever talking to you about such a person."

Denny stared at Frank, an incredulous look on his face. He was florid again. "What the hell is this? The JFK assassination all over again? Are you guys trying to snow me? What's going on here?"

Wexler pointed his finger at Denny. "I want that envelope of stills."

"Uh uh, no can do. You've got your own envelope. Find it. Get Wrightson."

"All right, Denny, let's do one thing at a time." He picked up a phone and spoke into it.

"Listen, I want to see Agent Wrightson. He was with the agents who picked up the surveillance tapes. I want an envelope of photos that was picked up at the same time."

Wexler hung up and turned back to Denny. "I want your printouts. They are evidence, and I want them delivered to me. Show me what you've got."

"You've already got it. Your agents took it." Denny was sarcastic as he said, "Special Agent in Charge Wexler, you'll get my set after you find the set that was taken from our Security office. When I see them spread out on your desk, you'll get mine."

Wexler was livid. "You're a hotheaded Irishman with a drinking problem."

"And you're a swellheaded Jew with an ego problem."

Denny was sorry the minute he said it. Why did he have to go and blow everything?

Wexler shot back, "I could have you taken into our Justice Department detention system, and you wouldn't be heard from for months. Lock you up pending the outcome of our investigation."

"I was expecting some bullshit like this. If I disappear, my attorney will go to the media with my story. I've already alerted him to everything. You guys are going to look like assholes once again, as you have any number of times in the past."

Denny was bluffing about the attorney, but now he was worried that they might sequester him, and the truth would never get out.

"Are you threatening us?"

"No, I want you to see the truth and to announce it to the world. It wasn't a suicide bomber. The other piece of news, that the guy was in your office after Nine-Eleven, is something I'll keep close to my vest until after we finish our investigation."

Wexler roared, "What's this *our* shit?"

"Yes, our, we. I expect to be assigned TDY to this office, tracking down the bastard who planted the bomb. I lost some good friends in that building. I owe it to them."

Wexler rose. "Get the fuck out of the building. Frank, escort this maniac outside to the street."

In the outer office Denny exhorted Frank. "Frank, I always thought you were a straight shooter. You gotta remember the guy we saw last fall. You told me he was working with the Bureau. Please, Frank, think."

"I promise you, Denny, when I see those prints, I'll study them and see if I can recall the guy. Go home.

Get some sleep. Have something to eat. Try to unwind. You're like a coiled spring ready to pop apart."

"Why can't you verify through the tapes that what I say is true? Why can't you admit that the Bureau made the wrong call?"

"Because once the wheels get turning, they can't always be reversed."

"Then I'll have to go the media. Hell, they'll make all of you look like assholes."

"Denny, wait until we've studied the tapes and looked at your stills."

"Tell Wexler I'll give him until midnight tonight before I break this whole story wide open. Frank, I'm going to be watching my back because I can only imagine what you guys are capable of doing to protect your own asses and the so-called reputation of the Bureau."

Frank explained, "Later, if we verify your information about the bomber, we'll tell the media we released misleading information to throw the terrorists off guard."

Denny scoffed. "It may only prove to the terrorists what saps you guys really are."

11

Many people were surprised when they learned where Denny lived. To some it would seem a glamorous place to live, while to others a seedy setting. His apartment—or more correctly, tenement—was on Manhattan's Restaurant Row on West 46th Street between Eighth and Ninth Avenues. Denny had grown up there, in what was known as Hell's Kitchen, or the more politically correct name, the Clinton neighborhood. A score of restaurants were located on the first floors and in the half basements of the brownstones along the street which had been upscaled with old gas street lamps. Many of the flats above the restaurants had never been modernized or rehabbed because for the most part they were still rent-controlled or rent-stabilized.

Denny had grown up in a tenement above a restaurant in a half basement that had over the years housed an Italian restaurant, a steakhouse, a Greek taverna, and for a number of recent years a traditional French restaurant called La Ferme.

It had never been a chic neighborhood to live in, but it was convenient to everything: the theater district, movies, hotels, and hundreds of bars and restaurants were in Denny's Times Square neighborhood.

Denny knew most of the restaurant owners on the street. He would drop into their small bars, where he was always welcome. He also frequented the theater bars on 45th Street like Charlie's and Barrymore's. In the theater district were hundreds of watering holes to choose from. He knew all of the saloons along Eighth Avenue. When he did one of his pub crawls, he would often drop into the small Rum House lounge in the Edison Hotel, kitty-corner from Monny's workplace.

In the bars Denny frequented he came to know many media people: reporters, columnists, news photographers, television anchors, and TV writers. If ever a person was well positioned to drop a story, Denny could be Mr. Source.

His mainstay neighborhood bar was Joe Allen's, a show business hangout where celebrities, star athletes, and politicos mingled with theatergoers and some neighborhood types. The actors, singers, and dancers in the Broadway plays would come into Joe Allen's below-street-level bar and eat and drink in the unglamorous restaurant that looked deliberately seedy, like a down-and-out Bowery bar. It had Paris, Miami, and London branches that mimicked the Manhattan saloon.

On the night of the Grand Central bombing, Kevin was working the bar in Joe Allen's as usual. Kevin, like most of the young people working in the Times Square theater bars, was a wannabe actor-cum-singer/dancer waiting for his big—or now even minimal—break. Of late he had been talking about walk-ons and industrial shows. Denny was seated at the end of the bar, staring up at the television set. The bar had few customers. The mood in the city that night was very somber.

Kevin knew where Denny worked. When Denny had entered, Kevin had said, "Bad break, man. This is horrible. It's getting real spooky and scary working in this town. How many of these things can New York take before it falls apart? Today I've heard a lot of people talk about moving out. What was it like in there?"

Denny sighed and looked down. "More awful than anyone can imagine. It was what hell must be like. Hell on earth. We're at war, and we're all combatants. It's bad, really bad."

"These suicide bombers . . . "

"It wasn't a suicide bomber. This guy got away. Clean away, the son of a bitch."

"But they say it was a suicide bomber . . . "

"They're full of shit!"

A half hour later Denny was working on his third vodka martini on the rocks. The glasses were small, but the drinks could still creep up on you. Sometimes leap up on you. He was finishing a hamburger and sweet potato fries, his first real meal of the day.

He was engrossed in the television news coverage of the attack. The story was the only thing on every television station. Kevin had given him the remote so he could surf the various cable and local channels. The channels were covering the basics of the bomb blast over and over again, with graphic footage of the wounded and of the inside of the station around ground zero. The floor had been cleared of bodies, body parts, debris—of all of the fragments scattered by the explosion. A hazy pall hung over the huge concourse. In the center of the floor was the gaping hole torn out by the explosion.

The news reader was saying, "Railroad execs, the mayor, and police have decided that to the extent possible, the station will return to normal operation. Only a small impact area at ground zero in the Main Concourse will be cordoned off. The mayor has said that if we are to function as a city, we must defeat the terrorists by resuming normal life as much as possible. He said that the area is not going to become a giant crime scene.

Trains will run as usual. The station will be up and running, but security will be at maximum alert. The governor has dispatched five hundred specially trained National Guardsmen, who will be at every station entrance to bolster security. Worldwide, there has been condemnation of this horrific suicide bombing."

Denny fumed every time they mentioned a suicide bomber.

"Fucking idiots. The FBI is lying through its teeth."

Kevin glanced down at Denny. Was he getting drunk again? He was a quiet drunk for the most part, not often belligerent or assertive. Kevin hoped he didn't go the other way that night. So many drunks were troublemakers.

Denny switched channels. A woman anchor on Fox was about to say something when she switched gears and said, "Stand by, please, we have just been given word that the FBI is going to be having an unscheduled press conference at their headquarters. Please stand by."

The screen showed a scene at FBI headquarters, a large room with some hastily summoned and assembled newsmen and camera crews. The reporter on the scene said, "The FBI Special Agent in Charge of the Grand Central bombing case has requested air time. Here he is now."

Kevin and a white-shirted waiter joined Denny at the end of the bar. When Denny saw Wexler—still in his shirt sleeves highlighted by the bright red suspenders—approach the podium, he grunted under his breath. "The fucking ferret."

A large screen had been set up behind the SAC. "My name is Bruce Wexler. That's W-E-X-L-E-R. As you know this has been a long, grueling day. We have had hundreds of agents working this case. We have gathered a great deal of forensic evidence and interviewed hundreds of eyewitnesses. Our video and photo experts have just completed an analysis of the tapes from the surveillance cameras located in all the critical areas of Grand Central Station.

"Security officers who are permanent personnel in Grand Central alerted us to some crucial information on these tapes. We had been withholding certain information while we did some intensive investigating. I am now in a position to announce that this terrible bombing was not the work of a suicide bomber. We have surveillance tapes that clearly show the perpetrator positioning two suitcase bombs and then walking away from the scene. Get the lights, please."

The room was darkened. On the screen came a still photograph of the bomber. Denny saw a very clear shot that the FBI had enhanced. *Maybe now they'd get on the ball.*

Wexler continued, "This is a photograph of the bomber. I am circulating this to all news media. Early this evening this photo was sent to all law enforcement agencies, all airports, all points of exit from the United States."

Denny whispered, "Yeah, and they lost valuable time. They might have caught this guy if they'd done it right away."

Kevin and the waiter stared at Denny. Was he right, or was this a drunk spouting off?

Wexler requested, "Please watch this screen, and we will show you how this man carried out this homicide bombing."

On the screen were the tapes showing the man rolling his deadly load into the station, placing it next to the two women, abandoning it, and walking out of the station. As he walked out, the camera caught the man in a close-up that was better than Denny's. Denny knew that the videotape had been enhanced by a process that redefined and expanded the pixel base. The tape was frozen at that point as they zoomed in, and the man was caught in a magnification that filled the screen. Wexler let that face remain on the screen.

Then they repeated the video. They had taken video from four cameras and spliced it so that it showed a continuous progression from the time the bomber entered the station, to the time he planted his bombs, to the moments of his exit.

"This is the man. We are asking anyone who recognizes this man to come forward and notify us. We have no ID for him as yet. We are attempting to get fingerprints and DNA for this individual from overseas sources.

"Lights, please. Now I would like to introduce you to a brave young lady who is assisting us in this investigation and who was partly responsible for the discovery of this individual's role in the explosion."

Denny was astounded as Terry rolled herself into the room. She had put on extra makeup and looked very photogenic and attractive.

"This young lady operates the television monitoring center in the Security center in Grand Central. She and others helped us to spot this individual as he was caught on the various surveillance tapes. She'll be available later to answer your questions. A big thank you to Terry and . . . and her coworkers who did fine police work."

Denny shook his head. No mention of Dennis Delaney.

After his statement, Wexler answered questions.

A television reporter asked, "Why initially were you so convinced it was a suicide bomber, and wasn't the announcement that it was the work of a suicide bomber premature?"

Wexler coolly answered, "We deliberately gave out misleading information to throw the bomber off track while we were analyzing our surveillance camera data."

"Follow-up, please. Explain to me how the bomber could be thrown off track. He knew what he did and how he did it. It really threw the public off track, didn't it?"

"We needed to buy time while we were conducting our investigation. Every indication led us initially to believe that this was a suicide bombing."

Denny loved this. Backtracking, stonewalling, spinning—all par for the course.

A print reporter asked, "I still don't get why the FBI was so quick to announce that this was the work of a suicide bomber. It's not like the Bureau at all. It usually errs on the side of caution. This was contrary to its usual practice."

"I've already answered that. Yes, you in the corner."

"What did this early announcement accomplish? It would seem that valuable time was lost in the search for the bomber."

"Hey, guys, you're beating a dead horse here."

Denny recognized the next questioner. It was Lenny Harrington from the New York Daily *News*, a friend of Denny's from his 46th Street drinking holes.

"Would you please give us the names of other Grand Central security people who helped with supplying the surveillance tapes?"

"Yes, we'll have that for you later."

At the end of Wexler's news conference Denny said

half aloud, "Better late than never. Now only one other thing to clear up. What was that guy doing working at FBI office?"

Kevin leaned over the bar. "What did you say, Den?"

"Only talking to myself."

Wexler was back on the screen, announcing, "We are making the stills and tapes available to all TV stations and other media outlets. Two of the surveillance cameras were destroyed by the explosion. The actual blast was shown on two cameras in the concourse that were not put out of commission. This footage will not be made available. There was a flash of light, then dust and debris. In the initial moments it is almost impossible to see anything, but when the smoke clears, they are horribly graphic, far too brutal to be released. We are not going to release those tapes."

Then he turned the stage over to Terry, who seemed in her element answering questions. She had apparently been warned not to identify Denny. Thank God. Otherwise the media would be all over him, haunting him. Denny thought, *This is not a wise move for her, to be out front there answering questions. It makes her a target. I have to warn her.*

12

In Joe Allen's, Denny was working on his fourth vodka martini. As he surfed the channels, he saw Terry being interviewed on every one, as well as the repetitive showing of the stills of the bomber interspersed with the aftermath scenes outside Grand Central earlier in the day.

Denny decided to call Monny. He pulled out his cell phone.

"I'm sorry I'm calling you so late, but I know you don't go to bed too early. How ya doing?"

"Fine, Den. Where are you calling from?"

"Joe Allen's. It's the first time I've had to unwind and relax."

Monica said, "Your girlfriend's all over the TV. She performed miracles from that wheelchair."

Denny ignored the girlfriend dig. "I don't think it's a good idea for Terry to be so public. It could be dangerous for her."

"Something tells me that you had something to do with those tapes too. Especially after being TDY with the FBI for six weeks."

"Yeah, I was the first one to ID the guy, but I'm afraid I burned some bridges when I was with Wexler in the field office tonight."

"It wouldn't be the first time you've burned bridges, Den."

"Monny, it's been a long day, a helluva day."

"Denny, I feel for you, I really do. I can only imagine

what you've had to go through. Please don't think I'm not praying for you."

"Pray for Mac too. I saw Big Barb in the hospital. She's bearing up well. He's in a coma. The stress brought on the heart attack, they think."

"Poor Mac. I'll call Barb tomorrow. Uh, it sounds like you've had a few. I should think on a night like this you'd swear off the booze. You've been through so much and you have so much ahead of you."

"I'm okay. Monny. Honestly. I'm not going overboard with the drinking." As he said it, he took a sip. "I'm not going to lie to you. I needed something. It's been a terrible day for me."

"I know, I know. It's been awful just following all the news. Hey, Den, why don't you go home and get a good night's sleep?"

"Monny. I'm all alone. I have no reason to go home to an empty apartment. I go home to that flat and see ghosts. You, Mom, Dad. Plus I'll see the ghosts I've already seen today."

"Denny, please . . . at a time like this I don't mean to seem bitchy, but for you the bars are your salvation. I don't want to share a life with someone who is more interested in drinking and schmoozing with barflies and bartenders."

"Monny, that's not me. That's all going to change. I'm getting a wake-up call, I can feel it."

"I hope so. When it happens, I'll be the first one to shout hurrah. Den, try to get some sleep tonight. Take an Ambien and go to bed. Go back now. You're going to have some awful days ahead of you. Denny, take care of yourself. Be careful. Get some sleep. Go home. Love ya."

"I love you too. G'night."

"I love you, Denny, I truly do."

When Kevin came back to Denny's end of the bar he said, "Den, are you and Monny getting along all right? I haven't seen her in here in a long time. You guys used to come in together after a Broadway show. She'd always have her one chardonnay."

Denny was about to snap at Kevin, tell him he was breaking the bartender's code by bringing up delicate matters, but he knew that Kev was a good friend and was well-meaning.

He answered, "There's been a bit of marital slippage, but I'm dealing with it. Kevin, you don't have to keep dipsticking me. I'm going with the flow, doing the best I can."

"Den, would you like a good cup of coffee before you go?'

"Uh uh, then I'd just be a wide-awake drunk. No one needs that."

Denny sat at the bar, pondering. He knew that it had been the most stressful day of his life. The day represented a failure for him and the unit. He was part of security in the most famous railroad station in the world, but he and the others had failed to prevent a catastrophe.

After Nine-Eleven there had been a lot of talk about setting up a perimeter around the station that would require people and their luggage to be screened through metal detectors. There had also been talk of some type of profiling to be put in place. But then what about all of the trains that came into the station? It was a big commuter hub with subway connections. The place was a sieve unless and until it was radically changed. The challenges were enormous.

Even though plainclothesmen like himself and

uniformed officers patrolled the station twenty-four hours a day, the place was a disaster waiting to happen. Everyone had known that for years, and no one knew exactly how to fix the situation.

There he was in his local, trying to fix the unfixable. Why had he come into the bar? The answer was easy. To unwind, to get the booze that had become his lifeblood. Lately he couldn't get through a day without his pick-me-ups, his nightcaps, his cocktails. Actually, because of all the action, his drinking had been delayed. Maybe he should just go home, take an Ambien, and get a good night's sleep.

When Kevin came over, Denny hesitated for a few seconds. Then he said, "Oh, what the hell—give me one last one. A light one."

13

The television finally drove Denny from the bar with its ceaseless repetition of the same scenes: horror, chaos, Wexler, Terry, the bomber, and then the same scenes and people all over, again and again, until the viewer was numbed into submission.

Denny left the bar and headed west on 46th Street, a few buildings down to his apartment. Restaurant Row was very quiet that night. Many restaurants had shuttered early or not opened at all. La Ferme, the restaurant in the half-basement of his brownstone, was dark. He walked under the restaurant's canopy and up the long, steep sixteen-step stairway to his building's front door, unlocked it, and slowly climbed the stairs in the dimly lit hallway to his second-floor apartment. When he got inside his flat, the telephone answering machine was beeping.

There was nothing glamorous about the five-room tenement where he lived. It had been his mother and father's apartment until they had moved to Fort Lauderdale. Denny's father had been a New York City cop for thirty years. Denny had spent his whole life in the second-floor walk-up. As a child he had accustomed himself to the street with its series of canopies for the various eateries. He grew used to the crowds of people walking up and down the street, going in and out of the restaurants for lunches and dinners.

The rent was very cheap by New York standards because the apartment was rent-controlled. His father and mother had rented it originally, and when they'd moved to Florida, he had inherited the flat and also the rent control prize. The landlord seldom repaired anything, but Denny had done a few upgrades on his own as time went by. It was a great location for Denny and Monica. Both of them had walked to work. She was a currency trader at Morgan Stanley on the corner of West 47th and Broadway, a block and a half away.

He collapsed onto the sofa and started to go through the messages from his answering machine on the end table. The first one was good news. It was from Captain Grayson saying that the suspension had been lifted. The next one was from Wexler.

"Call me whenever you get in. No matter the time."

Denny called him back.

When he came on the line, Wexler was apologetic and disarming. "I want to apologize. We went through the tapes. You were right. I hope you saw my news conference."

Denny, noncommittal, grunted, "Yes, I did."

"Thanks to your keen eyes and detective work, pictures of the bomber are going out everywhere. We've talked to your supervisor. You've been reinstated. Denny, I would like you to be temporarily assigned with us. Your chief has okayed it. Whattaya say? I'm imploring you. We need a sharp mind like yours working on this."

Denny didn't need time to consider it. This would give him access to the investigation. He'd be closer to getting the bomber if he was with the Bureau. "Fine with me. Sure. But aren't we forgetting something here? Seeing the guy in your field office?"

"Den, you were right about that. I'll have a complete rundown for you when you get here tomorrow afternoon. Tomorrow morning wait at home. Frank Millau will be calling you. You'll be working with him. I think he wants to go with you to Grand Central, so wait around for his call. We'll expect to see you here tomorrow. Frank will bring you in. Thanks again for all you've done. We appreciate it."

When he got off the line with Wexler, Denny dialed Terry's number. Her answering machine picked up, so Denny decided to leave a message.

"Terry, hon, I just saw you on TV. You looked great. You did a great job. But, hon, I don't think you should be out front talking to the media. You could become a target. The bomber and the members of his cell, if he has any, might think you know more than you do. You probably think I'm envious of you, but really, I'm not. I'm worried about your safety. Try to get some security. I'll talk to you in the morning."

Denny dragged a bottle of vodka out of his cupboard. He sat in the living room in his father's favorite recliner and turned on the television with the remote. The channel he pulled up was still running footage of the medics carrying the wounded and dead out of Grand Central.

Over and over again, showing the same shots. Searing the visions into the minds of the viewers like the Twin Towers falling again and again, or Oswald being shot over and over, or like the Secret Service agent repetitively diving on top of a wounded President Reagan. Images and icons being burned into the brain as one would burn CDs. He muted the sound and sat there with his glass and bottle of vodka, staring at the screen. He took slugs of the drink until he could feel the numbness setting in. Alcoholic numbness to twin with the visual numbing. His mind was drifting off. Dreaming . . .

He was a small kid playing on the front stoop of this same building. He had his die-cast metal fire engine and a police car. He sent them racing along the third step. The toy cars were both answering some kind of emergency. A bomb had gone off in a big railroad station. The boy imitated the sounds of sirens. From the street outside on Eighth Avenue, all-too-real sirens were sounding as police and fire raced somewhere . . .

14

It was 8:30 A.M. on Wednesday, the morning after the massacre at Grand Central Station. Denny was in a fog, a hazy half sleep, an alcoholic stupor.

Ring . . . ring . . . ring . . . ring.

The telephone slowly brought Denny back to a semi-wakeful state. He was on the sofa in his clothes from the day before.

Ring . . .

"Hullo."

"Denny, this is Frank Millau. Did you get Wexler's message last night?"

"Yup."

"You've been taken off suspension, and you're assigned to us on temporary duty for the foreseeable future. I've got a few things to do this morning, and then I'll meet you at your Security office in Grand Central at ten-thirty. Okay"

"Yuh."

"You all right?"

"Yeah, yeah. Fine. TDY again. Grand Central Security at ten-thirty."

"See you later."

Denny hung up the phone and raised his hands to his head. A headache, a sharp one, but not like yesterday's. He could deal with this. In the bathroom he glommed down three Tylenol tablets. He stripped off all of his stale, bloodstained, disreputable clothing except his briefs, and left it in a heap in the bedroom.

After struggling his way to the kitchen, he made a

pot of coffee, took his daily vitamins with a big glass of OJ, and emptied two thirds of a cup of water and an envelope of dry Irish oatmeal into a bowl and heated it in the microwave. The oatmeal, one of his comfort foods, began to ease his lightheadedness, and after he had drunk two mugs of coffee, the headache had begun to lessen and become manageable.

A long shower with a burst of cold water at the end finished the sobering-up process. Now at last he was almost a person again. He dressed in the only clean working suit he had left. Only the blue funeral suit hung in the closet, clean and pressed. In the days ahead he knew he would be donning it too often. With three wrinkled, dirty suits tucked under his arm he headed out the apartment door.

The day outside the apartment was deceiving. It was too nice a day. A beautiful day, clear, sunny, invigorating; but what had happened yesterday would darken everyone's thoughts. Denny dropped his suits off at the cleaners and headed on foot crosstown toward Grand Central. At the kiosks the newspapers had huge black headlines. He could see certain words blaring at the passers-by: BOMBING, CARNAGE, BLOODY, PANIC, TERRORISM, ATTACK, WAR, MASSACRE.

Two papers had chosen a signature portrait for this disaster and had featured it on their front pages. A little girl, abrasions on her face, stood dazed and bewildered on the street outside of Grand Central, her arm hanging down, the hand trailing a bloodied teddy bear with one of its legs torn away. The media had its defining portrait of the tragedy, which Denny thought somewhat cynically, might end up as a commemorative statue in the station.

Denny thought Americans of late had honed the

mourning process to a science; they had made a cult of grieving, embalmed the word "closure." They were better at post-tragedy grieving than they were at solving the complicated and difficult jobs of prevention and seriously trying to assuage grievances. Denny grieved too, felt tragedy deeply, but realized that grieving didn't have to be institutionalized and ritualized.

When he reached Grand Central, Denny stood on the West Balcony overlooking the Main Concourse. A hole had been blown in the marble at the center of the concourse floor. The information booth was a jumbled mass of wreckage, the huge clock a crumpled batch of metal lying beside it. Yellow police tape circled the area where the most damage had occurred. Much of the other debris had been taken away. The blood and gore had been washed and scrubbed away. Nothing remained of the human toll from the horrible blast.

A few forensic people huddled within the cordoned-off area. Outside of the plastic crime scene tapes thousands of onlookers shuffled past the site, most on their way to and from trains and subways. Some were crying. Almost all were aware that there at that spot, but for the luck of the draw or the will of God, their lives could have been snuffed out or their bodies maimed.

Denny asked himself if this would become another hallowed site for grieving Americans to memorialize. *America must not become a country living in the past, full of cemeteries, memorials, and mausoleums,* he thought. A country and its people had to look ahead, and life had to go on.

As Denny stood on the balcony looking down on the blast site he thought *I've got to put myself in the mind of the bomber.* Somehow, having been the first one to see images of him on tape, he felt he knew him, could get inside him.

You cased this bombing site, sometime before yesterday. Probably at the same time of day, probably the same day of the week, I think you walked into the station without any luggage. You looked around. Stood where I'm standing overlooking the whole Main Concourse. You studied people's behavior in here.

You saw which areas were most crowded. You figured out that you could choose some decoys, people distracted in a conversation, and plant the luggage close to them. I think you worked out in advance where you'd enter and where you'd exit. You left very little to chance. You did all of this ahead of time. You're a planner. You wouldn't want to die just yet, would you?

Yesterday when you were safely away from the bags, probably out of sight of them, you dialed a number on your cell phone. This activated the bomb. After the explosion you stood dead in your tracks, probably put your hands to your face and looked horrified. When people started to panic and hurry away, you joined the crowd and went with them. You were only a nondescript face in the crowd.

Would you come back here later to check your work? What for? Television would do that for you. No, you'd be planning the next one. You'd created a demoralized, fearful mob. You'd accomplished what you'd set out to do. You bastard.

Denny was startled back from his trance-like state by a pat on the shoulder.

It was Frank Millau with another agent—an eager, freshly scrubbed rookie, the perfect poster child for FBI recruitment. Mid-twenties. Strong. Dedicated.

"Hi, Denny, this is Chris Simpson. He's in his first

year with the Bureau, and the three of us are going to be working this case together."

"Good morning, Sergeant Delaney."

"Call me Denny. Hi, Chris."

"Denny, Agent Millau has been telling me all about you."

"Yeah, I'm the lush who is lucky enough to be assigned TDY with the Bureau once in a while."

"Chris, when Denny got out of college, Fordham . . . wasn't it?"

Denny nodded.

"Yeah, after college he trained at Quantico to become an agent. Before he was given an assignment, he changed his mind and decided to follow his father into police work here in Manhattan. He's a New Yorker to the core."

Denny said, "Can't help loving New York. I got into this transportation detail after I found out that advancement was faster."

Frank butted in. "Denny, in a few hours we're going to meet with Wexler on Vesey Street. He's going to explain about the guy you saw at headquarters last fall. Honestly, for the life of me, I can't remember anything about him. You're the one with the eagle eye and the memory. Meanwhile, here in the station, Chris and I want to see how the Security office works and the possible entrance and exit points of the bomber."

"Any make on him?" Denny asked.

"Lots of tips coming in. Supposed sightings. What we're looking for is an official ID from some official source here in the States or from overseas. The Bureau, the CIA, and Interpol are canvassing Middle Eastern countries intensely. Nothing so far."

Denny showed Frank and Chris the Vanderbilt

Avenue entrance behind them, where taxis disgorged passengers. FBI agents were greeting every cab that came in, questioning the drivers, showing the picture. They walked around to the corner of 42nd Street.

"This is where he entered."

They walked down the ramp into the Main Concourse.

The three stood looking at the now cleared blast site. Denny pointed out the point of impact, the exit that the bomber had taken. Each of them was engrossed in his own thoughts on what carnage and destruction had been wrought just the day before.

Denny then led the way across the Main Concourse, following the bomber's known path across the huge cathedral-like space. They ducked under the crime scene tape, and Denny simulated the bomb placement. Then he led them to the door on Lexington where the bomber had exited.

Denny said, "The whole thing only took a few minutes. He didn't linger, didn't draw attention to himself. Out on Lex he may have taken a cab, caught a subway or bus, or hopped in a waiting vehicle."

Frank said, "Whatever he did, we have no credible witness who can remember seeing him at the station—not yet anyway. He came from nowhere and left unseen except by the cameras."

Denny answered, "Inside, the cameras saw him, recorded him. He had to know he was being taped. Didn't care. Did what he had to do."

After Denny gave them the close-up of the Lexington Avenue exit, they ascended the East Staircase together. As they did so, Denny had a brief moment when he seemed to relive the explosion. That ear-wrenching blast, the smoke, the rain of tiny, blistering objects. He shuddered to think how close he had come to being annihilated. The smell lingered in the air, and a haze still hung over the space. The huge arched windows had almost all been shattered by the explosion, and unfiltered sunlight poured down on them.

15

Back upstairs, Denny led them into the Security rooms. Near the door was Tony Tessitore, seated at his monitoring station. He made a face and turned away as Denny entered. Denny could tell that he had been notified of the suspension lifting.

In the glass cubicle on the left he could see Mac's stand-in, Lieutenant Pressman, from headquarters. Pressman waved at Denny. He was busy talking to a police commander. In the right cubicle Terry was looking at some tapes.

Denny explained the working of the monitoring stations in the main room to Frank and Chris. He introduced them to Richie. The rookie agent and Richie were about the same age, both unspoiled eager beavers.

In the tech support room, Terry's domain, Denny introduced the agents to her. She explained to them how her high-tech stuff operated and demonstrated the equipment's capabilities as she switched from camera to camera, zoomed in, and printed stills of the cameras' constant surveillance. She showed them scenes of themselves, taped moments before as the three of them were walking around the ground floor.

Terry said, "The two cameras that were knocked out in the blast are already back up and running. No one is wasting any time on this."

She and Chris hit it off right away. He was impressed by her competency and her good looks. She was captivated by his boyish eagerness and his clean-cut handsomeness. After a series of questions, Frank said he'd like to talk to some of the men in the squad room.

Denny said, "Sure, be right with you. I have to do some checking with Terr." Frank and Chris went outside the cubicle.

Denny turned to Terry. "Hon, I don't think it's a good idea for you to be so public. Did you get my message on your answering machine? I think you could become a target for any crazies out there or any of the bomber's crew."

"Yeah, I know you're right. Wexler talked me into going public. I just didn't think. From now on I'm going to lie low. Afterwards I thought maybe he wanted to take the credit away from you. But, Denny, did the FBI acknowledge anything? Did they admit that this guy had been in the field office?"

"Not yet. I'm getting suspicious again. I never know what these guys are really up to. Frank out there is okay, but he's low down on the need-to-know chain."

"How do you know with them when they're telling you the truth?"

"With them, you don't."

"Couldn't it be they were snowing you, and that the bomber had been working for them and turned against them?"

"Yeah, the thought has crossed my mind. Why should I believe them? I don't trust them. They are either rushing to cover their asses or rushing to take credit for someone else's work."

"Denny, watch out for those cute buns of yours."

He leaned over and gave Terry a kiss on the cheek. "You smell terrific, hon. I love that perfume."

"How you and Monica doing?"

"We're still working on it."

When Denny was back in the main office explaining about the TV monitoring system, Frank gestured toward Terry behind the glass and asked, "What's the story on Terry? Has she always been in a wheelchair? She's a very beautiful young woman. I feel so sorry about a knockout like her in a wheelchair."

"No, the wheelchair is a recent thing. Eleven months ago Terry was a woman in top physical shape. She jogged, went rollerblading, rode her bike through Central Park and lower Manhattan where she lives. She was living a very out-of-doors, physical life. Then, in the railroad car of a commuter train one afternoon here in the station, she had her run-in with a spaced-out druggie, Frankie Carrino. He had an automatic weapon and was acting like a total nutcase, threatening passengers. He fired a shot at her. Wounded her. The shot went through to her spine. She reacted swiftly and got off three rounds to Carrino's chest. He died instantly.

"Her wound caused nerve damage in her spine, an injury that made her unable to walk. Doctors said that with aggressive therapy she could regain her ability to walk again. Terry's a real fighter. She went at therapy the way she does everything in life. All out. The doctors have become more optimistic as they see her dedication to the tough therapy program. Her legs are getting stronger."

"And she came back to work here?" Chris asked.

"Yes," Denny answered. "A woman in a wheelchair obviously can't be out on patrol, so they assigned her to the tech support position. She went through an intensive training program, and now she operates the equipment like an expert. It's an ideal job for her while she's recuperating.

"One other dark cloud in this whole thing. Carrino was from a big clan of no-goodniks on Long Island, hoods who think they're wise guys. Mob wannabes. Every once in a while Terry gets a call from some guy—sort of threatening but not quite. They call up and remind her of the shoot-out. The police have investigated but can't pin anything down. She's under a light watch by the cops. I'd judge a pretty light watch."

Denny added, "Terry lives on Water Street in downtown Manhattan, not far from the World Trade Center site. In the financial district. I wouldn't want to live down there. It's a spooky place at night. Creepy. Few people around. It's basically a daytime office area, but she has a big loft apartment she couldn't get in another part of town for the same money."

Frank reacted, "Denny, not everyone wants to live in the heart of Times Square where you live. They'd find your home turf a little too hectic."

"I love it," answered Denny.

"Chris, this guy lives no more than a few blocks from every major Broadway theater. If it's a play or musical on Broadway, this guy has seen it. Hey, it's time for us to hit the road for Vesey Street. SAC Wexler is going to be giving his big update at one p.m."

Denny, Frank, and Chris were headed out the squad room door when Tony rose from his chair and confronted Denny. He had been stewing as he watched Denny leading the two agents around.

"Look what the cat dragged in. Mr. Glory Boy himself. The boozer is back with his buddies at the FBI, reinstated on the squad, the conquering hero as always. Does the Bureau supply you with the sauce as one of your perks?"

Denny was furious. "Tony, you're a big mouth with a

major attitude problem. It doesn't go with that pea brain you carry around in that ugly hairless skull of yours."

"Fuck you. You've kissed ass so long with Mac that you're beginning to act like that nigger. You won't have Mac to back you up anymore because he's cramming for his finals right now and won't be around much longer."

Denny made a lunge for Tony. He had his fists up. This triggered quick reactions from Frank and Chris. They grabbed Denny and held him back. When Tony saw that Denny was being held back and couldn't retaliate against him, he shoved Denny in the chest. Then Richie grabbed Tony from behind and held him back.

Tony shook himself free and headed out the door shouting, "Fuck all of you. You're all lower than whale shit—the bunch of you."

Later, when the three were out on the balcony, Frank said, "Boy, Denny, you sure know how to push the right buttons to get someone all riled up. You had Wexler so pissed off last night I thought he was going to have a stroke. It's a knack you have. You're on a hair trigger. Your wife must be a saint if you try that on her. Especially when you've been drinking."

"No, Frank, I've never been that way with Monica."

Outside Grand Central, Frank, Chris, and Denny got into a black unmarked sedan that was parked in a "No Parking" zone. Frank got into the driver's seat. Denny sat in front. From the back seat Chris asked, "Denny, is your car parked around here?"

Frank laughingly said, "Son, you're talking to Denny, the carless wonder. Imagine that. He's part of a segment of Manhattan society that believes a car is a nuisance."

Denny explained, "Chris, I live on Restaurant Row, West 46th Street between Eighth and Ninth Avenues. Parking there isn't just a hassle; it's a nightmare. I'd have to spend every waking hour changing parking spaces, waiting for someone to pull out. Waiting for certain days when parking is legal on certain streets. Changing hours, changing days, changing spaces—the whole thing is insane for me.

"I'm not about to spend hard-earned money on an expensive lot or parking garage. Some people in my neighborhood pay three hundred bucks a month or more for parking."

Frank chimed in, "To most red-blooded American men Denny would be a freak, Chris. Carless in America. Might as well say you don't have any balls. Not wanting a car? What kind of American male would put up with such a state? A car is an extension of a man's penis, for God's sake."

Denny replied, "No, to me a car in Manhattan is a useless luxury, a nuisance. I don't mind taking the subway or hailing a cab. I have a bike I ride along the Hudson or through Central Park on Sunday mornings. I like to jog."

"No, Chris, Denny here is that breed of city kid who just doesn't care about cars. It's not a status symbol to him."

"I know how to drive, but don't choose to own a car. Never had a car, might never get one. Whenever my wife Monny and I want to get away from the city for a weekend or a week's car vacation, we rent one.

"One night while I was drinking in a bar in Manhattan I met four Brits. None of them owned cars;

none of them had any great desire to own one. Where they lived cars were an inconvenience and a nuisance. Just like my case."

Denny had noticed that Frank was deliberately steering the conversation away from the horrors of yesterday to other subjects. The blast and deaths were on everyone's mind, but what good did it do to dwell on them?

Chris laughed and said, "I grew up on a farm in Wisconsin. Cars, trucks, and tractors were our life. Without them we'd be lost."

Denny said, "Did you ever think that America's love affair with cars has a heavy price? All that oil Americans consume is probably the source of some of our problem with terrorists. Some of the money we spend on oil seems to be providing a cash cow for the terrorists. Saudi money for one."

16

At the Vesey Street field office Frank stopped outside the door to Wexler's office. "Denny, before he briefs all the agents, SAC Wexler wants to talk to us for a few minutes. Chris, you wait out here."

Denny thought *Oh oh, here it comes. Leave Chris outside. Keep the need-to-know circle to a minimum. Compartmentalize.*

Frank and Denny entered the office. Wexler stood up and greeted Denny with a handshake. "Denny, yesterday was a bad day for everyone. I want to apologize for being off base and also congratulate you on the great job you did for us. Your printouts were invaluable. We're glad to have you aboard for this TDY stint."

"Thank you, Agent Wexler. Sorry I shot from the hip yesterday. Not one of my best days."

Behind Wexler was a huge blowup of the bomber. Wexler made a brief call after the three were seated.

The door opened and an agent walked in. Wexler introduced him. "Denny, this is Agent Brian Hoffman. He'll tell you what he knows about the man you saw in the office last fall."

Hoffman recited his information like an automaton. He had rehearsed carefully.

"On October 20, 2001, this individual"—he pointed to the man in the printout on the wall—" came into the outer office. He explained to the receptionist that he wanted to volunteer as a translator and interpreter. I was called out to talk to him. He said he spoke Arabic, Hebrew, and most of the Middle Eastern languages and dialects: Lebanese, Egyptian, Syrian, and Saudi.

"He said he'd like to volunteer his services. He spoke in perfect, unaccented, general American English. He told me he had interpreted all over the Middle East. I told him that we were in need of interpreters, but that we'd have to vet him and do a background check; he'd have to fill out forms, basically go through a security check, a screening clearance. He said he could bring in as many documents as I needed."

Hoffman leaned over to Denny, "That's when you saw him in the office. I noticed you and Frank Millau on the other side of the room that day. I talked to him for about twenty minutes. I don't remember the name he gave, yet I do seem to remember him saying that one of his names was like Phoenix, something like that. I wouldn't bet the farm on it."

Wexler interrupted, "We've added that to his wanted identification list—that one name may be Phoenix or similar."

Hoffman continued, "Then I got called away. When I came back into the room, he had disappeared."

Denny said, "He was still here when Frank and I left the room. This Phoenix guy and I stared at each other, made a lot of eye contact for some reason. I'm sure he would recognize me again just as I recognized him. We might have even crossed paths yesterday morning as he was planting his bomb."

Hoffman said, "When I returned and found him gone, I didn't think much of it. We get a lot of crackpots and volunteers in here. He definitely was not a crackpot. I was impressed by him, but later I figured he didn't want to go through a lot of paperwork just to be a volunteer. I figured that maybe he had a shaky green card. He spoke all these languages, but he didn't volunteer a nationality. I didn't give him much thought until SAC Wexler asked if anyone here had seen the suspect in the office.

"When I saw the picture, it took me a long time to remember the exact occasion. After all, that was about eight months ago. An awful lot has happened in those months. There's really nothing more I can tell you about him. I do remember his eyes; he could stare you down. Very intense, very probing eyes, cold eyes . . . a tough-minded guy in my opinion, not swayed by emotion."

Wexler said, "That's it, Denny. We'd rather not have this information released to the media at this time. Well, guys, it's time for my briefing. Let's go."

Denny realized that he wasn't going to get much more out of anybody. If he wanted to work with the Bureau, he'd have to go along, at least for now. Wexler looked relieved that Denny wasn't following up on this. As they all exited the room, Denny felt uneasy. Everything seemed so pat, so scripted. It could be that this bomber, this Phoenix, had been more of an operative than they were willing to admit.

They filed into a large room, the room where last night's press conference had been held. Over one hundred agents were crammed into the room, with a large number standing along the back and side walls. They were grim-looking men and women. Denny squeezed himself in at the back, next to Chris and Frank.

Wexler began, "Fellow agents, welcome to what may be one of the most crucial investigations you'll ever be involved in. New York is in a crisis situation. Right, let's get started.

"That bomb was what they call a DRAB, meaning drop, run, activate, blast. It was planted and then activated from a distance, probably by a cell phone. The cell phone can be at a great distance from the bombs themselves. All the bomber does is dial the cell phone number present in the bomb trigger mechanism. It could also have had a timer set to go off a minute or two after the bombs were abandoned, planted by the perpetrator.

"In this case we know how the bombs were planted. And we have video and stills of the bomber."

The screen behind him showed a very clear still photograph of the bomber.

"Remember this face. Memorize the features. We've circulated our best pictures of the perpetrator to every media outlet and all foreign intelligence and security agencies.

"Now, which method did he use to get to Grand Central? Here are some suppositions.

"One, perhaps he stayed overnight in a nearby hotel. Check his photo with every hotel in the area. Would he risk a stop at a hotel ahead of time? Seems risky, but who knows?

"Two, he was dropped off by an accomplice from a private vehicle. Check all officers on duty outside the station. See if any of them recognize this guy. Somehow I doubt if he was dropped off in this way. Too obvious, makes him stand out. For months New York police have been posted outside the station in case a suicide bomber in a vehicle loaded with explosives tried to park at the station entrances. We were expecting a Timothy McVeigh kind of operation, but we got a much less elaborate scheme. If he were dropped off by a private vehicle, some officer might remember.

"Three, he took a subway, a bus. Check bus drivers.

"Four, my best bet is that he got a cab from somewhere

not too far away. Check all cab drop-offs at Grand Central.

"One problem is that there are a number of drivers who are having immigration problems and won't talk. Osama bin Laden could get into fifty percent of the New York cabs, and the drivers would never report it. A way-out possibility is that the cab driver may be sympathetic to this guy's cause or at least to his actions. It's possible that the cab driver dropping him off might have been part of the cell.

"Go to every cab company. Get the time and trip sheets for every cab that had a Grand Central drop-off that morning. Interview every one of the cabbies, show them the pictures. Sweat 'em. If anyone denies they've seen him but seems suspicious, pull him in and press him hard. This wasn't a one-man operation. This man was part of a cell or network. You don't get these explosives without help."

"Right now I don't think forensics is going to be much help. They will be able to pinpoint the type of explosives. It's probably a waste of time trying to track down the manufacturers of his bags. There are millions of these bags in existence.

"This guy had to know that surveillance cameras were taping him. He had to know that we would get shots of him, so in a sense this was a suicide mission. This guy was putting his life on the line. If he had been challenged by someone in the terminal, he probably had an alternate way of detonating the bombs. I would be willing to bet that that moustache is down the drain by now.

"What are the lessons for the future from all this? Some defensive measures are already being implemented. We need metal and weapon and explosive detectors at every entrance into this station, every gate to every track. But it's a railroad terminal. It was built for easy access. It is designed to move people in and out as efficiently and easily as possible.

"All those tracks down below bringing people and baggage into the station. Subway connections. It's going to be a tremendous job. The public won't like it, but at the same time they are demanding security and safety. Not only at this station but at all the railroad stations in the leading cities of the country. We are going to have to become an armed camp."

A woman walked up to Wexler. She whispered to him for about thirty seconds. He asked questions. She handed him a piece of paper.

"Listen up, folks. We've got a credible lead. A woman in an apartment house on 45th Street off Roosevelt Avenue in Queens. She claims our perpetrator was a frequent visitor to an apartment in her building, visiting three Middle Eastern men there. She hasn't seen him in a couple of weeks, but she's sure the other three guys he was visiting are still living there. She saw one of them last night.

"I'm sending in A and B SWAT teams. Also Response Team Zebra. Frank Millau, go with your team. Tommy, send in helicopters as well. This is a full-court press, the works. No media notification. Suit up gentlemen. Good luck and good hunting."

There was a rush for the door. Frank, Chris, and Denny went to the armaments room where they grabbed flak jackets and two shotguns. Shouts filled the room: "Suit up"; "We're going in"; "Let's roll." Adrenaline was flowing. Action. Payback time.

17

It was a Queens neighborhood of tightly packed tenements. Fifty nationalities could be living on a single street. It might quickly become a tinderbox if the people became inflamed, but the illegal aliens would try to lie low if authorities were in the area.

At a rendezvous at the corner of 45th Street and Roosevelt Avenue the agents gathered. New York City police had been ordered in as backup. The agents were pumped up. They could be proactive now.

Agents were donning flak vests. The SWAT teams were in full combat gear. The sense of an approaching battle was in the air. Scores of agents were swarming, converging on the subject tenement.

The back yards and rear entrance had been sealed off. The silhouettes of men with rifles stood out on the rooftops. The FBI SWAT teams started moving out, down the cordoned-off street. Ambulances had moved into position behind the lines. Medics were standing by. The crackling of two-way radios could be heard. So far the media hadn't caught onto this one, but soon they would. The sky would be full of the droning bugs, the whirlybirds. A dozen television news copters would be circling, moving in for the sight and smell of blood.

Denny had a bad feeling about this raid. He had no lack of courage, only doubts and unease about this assault. He, Frank, and Chris had been chosen to be in the advance party. He wondered if Wexler had deliberately put him in the line of fire, yet he wanted to be in the first wave. His station had been seriously violated, and friends had died wantonly. These guys might be part of the bomber's cell, and with luck they might nail the bomber himself. He was hoping it wouldn't turn out to be a false lead.

The tenement stairway was dark and narrow. Two advance SWAT agents, Charlie Snelling and Neil Fitzgerald, heavily armored and outfitted, were followed by Frank Millau and Chris Simpson, who had a shotgun and a battering pole on a sling over his shoulder. Denny had been ordered to bring up the rear of the first group. Another squad of five agents was right behind him. He had his Walther drawn. He was a good marksman; all he wanted was a clear shot.

The five men took up positions around the door. Frank and Chris thrust the heavy batterer into the door, near the locks. The door swung open in one blow. Snelling and Fitzgerald, automatic weapons poised, charged in. They took up positions in the living room and stationed themselves at either side of one of the room's three closed doors.

They were shouting, "FBI. FBI. Throw down your weapons." Frank and Chris cleared the kitchen area. No one there. Frank shouted to agents outside the kitchen window on the fire escape, "Two rooms cleared."

Denny crouched in the living room at an angle to the first closed door. Chris and Frank had now taken up positions at the side of the living room, one beside Snelling, one beside Fitzgerald.

Snelling and Fitzgerald kicked in the door to a bedroom. Immediately Uzi machine gun fire erupted from inside the room. Deadly fire. At least two machine guns. Deafening sounds in the tiny apartment. Snelling was down, badly wounded. Chris, his shotgun poised, ratcheted around the door frame and fired both barrels. One of the Uzi firers was thrown back by the blast, his chest riddled with shot.

Another deadly burst of Uzi fire. Fitzgerald was hit in the leg and was down. Then Chris was hit. Bad. In the head. He collapsed into a heap. Denny now had a clear shot at the assailant. He fired off four quick rounds. The man was tossed back from the impact. All was silent for a few moments.

Fitzgerald, on the floor with his body partly in the bedroom, shouted, "There's another one in the bathroom." He got off two shots. The man in the bathroom sent a hail of machine gun fire into the living room. When the chatter stopped for a few moments, Frank Millau ducked around the door frame just in time to nail the man with three clean shots to the chest. Denny climbed past the fallen agents and quickly checked out the room, the closets. He checked each of the fallen suspects. All three were dead. He felt like kicking their dead bodies. He examined each of them carefully. None was yesterday's bomber.

Frank was on the communicator. "Three agents down. Two very critical. Another agent with serious leg wound. Now clearing rest of the apartment."

Three new second-wave SWAT team members were positioned around the two remaining doors leading into the living room. Denny and Frank kicked open the next door. The three SWAT men entered and cleared the room. No one there. They carefully checked under the bed, the closet. The third door was kicked in; it was a shallow closet, empty.

When the apartment had been cleared, Frank announced it on the radio. Other agents and medics entered the battle zone. Frank leaned over Chris. He was gone. His head wound had been fatal, instantaneous. Snelling was badly injured and was taken away in critical condition. He didn't look like he would make it. Fitzgerald had a leg wound that they treated on the scene. Then he was taken away on a stretcher.

Frank had tears in his eyes as he knelt in the hall talking to Denny. "Goddamn it. Poor Chris. His first real operation. He didn't do anything that wasn't by the book, and he got hit so badly."

Denny whispered, "He did nail one of them."

Later Frank and Denny donned rubber gloves and led the search of the apartment. On the dresser in the bloodied bedroom they found the front page of the *Post* with a full-page shot of the bomber. Across the picture someone had written with a red marking pen, *Felix the Cat.*

Denny exclaimed, "We've got a name for the son of a bitch."

Frank asked, "Why, I wonder, a name like Felix the Cat?"

Denny said, "Felix, Phoenix. Hoffman could have heard Felix and later thought it was Phoenix. Close."

Searchers found copies of the Koran, cell phones, a laptop computer, hand weapons, and a stash of cash—over thirteen thousand in twenties. In the living rooms were stacks of videos: mainly action flicks, some pornographic. In the kitchen was a large stock of nonperishable food, enough to sustain them over a long period if they couldn't leave the house. Thrift shop furniture. Four single beds.

Agent Robinson had been questioning a neighbor downstairs, the one who had called in the tip. "She reports that once in a while one would go out and come back with bags of supplies. Always went out one at a time. She said no loud noise. The woman reports that up until a month ago the Grand Central bomber would enter the building, stay a short time, and leave. She's pretty sure he never stayed overnight, but can't be certain."

Frank said, "I guess from now on we call the bastard Felix the Cat."

Denny added, "They say a cat has nine lives. That's nine lives too many for this piece of crap."

18

After the bloody attack on the Queens tenement, two FBI agents lay dead, and three members of the cell were dead. Agent Snelling had been DOA at the hospital. That night when Denny and Frank were back at the FBI field office, they could see that Wexler was visibly shaken by the deaths of the two agents. He realized that this could be an investigation with a heavy price to be paid by the investigators. He talked about their enemy: "These guys will never give up. They are going to make every potential apprehension a firefight. For them it'll be a suicide defense."

It was nine-thirty that night before Denny was cut loose from FBI headquarters. He sat at the end of the bar in Joe Allen's. Kevin had greeted him with, "Denny, your name is showing up in the papers and a few mentions on TV. You're going to have to join our celebrity circle."

Denny grumbled, "Yeah, yeah." Thank God, the media hadn't started haunting him yet.

He ordered a bowl of potato leek soup and a steak with a baked potato. In front of him was his usual vodka martini, this time with a beer backup for thirst.

He stared at the television set, which was now recapping the raid in Queens. Videos of bodies being carried out on gurneys were the theme of the night's broadcasts. The morning before, in what seemed like another lifetime, the bomb had been detonated in Grand Central. The television announced that another two victims of the Grand Central blast had died from their wounds. It was getting to be litany of tragedy in New York. Looking at the all-but-empty restaurant, Denny could see the effect it was having on the public.

He had checked on Mac's condition with a quick telephone call to the hospital—not good, barely holding his own. A call to Terry. She was still talking of the possibility of an FBI plot. He told her about Chris, and she gasped. He was soon on the phone with Monny.

"It's been a wicked day. Two agents dead. One a rookie—Chris. I just met him this morning. I liked him right away. So eager, a really nice guy, selfless. Nice guys are hard to find in this business. The niceness gets wrung out of them."

Monny listened, reacted quietly as Denny talked his way through it. "His whole life ahead of him, now wasted by nutcases, fanatics. Snelling, another agent, is dead too. Sure we got three of them, but there are thousands of them all over the world ready to kill Americans."

Monny reacted. "It's all over television—they've got a name for the bomber now, Felix the Cat. Where did he get that name? What does it mean?"

"I have no idea."

Denny and Monny talked on about the day. Their call ended with the usual "Love you's."

As he drank Denny continued watching the television set.

The talk everywhere was full of Felix the Cat. They had a memorable tag. Felix the Mass Murderer. The enemy had a name now, a pedigree.

Kevin gave Denny the remote, and he surfed the news channels. One station reported, "A leak from an FBI source is saying that the U.S. is gathering evidence that the Grand Central bombing was the work of an

Iraqi national. The rumor has surfaced several times during the day both here in Manhattan and in Washington. There has been no rush by the Bureau to silence the rumor. They had a noncommittal 'no comment,' which has only served to fuel the rumor mill."

Kevin brought him a big bowl of soup and a basket of bread. Denny tore into the food. He was on his second rocks martini. The steak and baked potato tasted so great to him. Lately he had forgotten to eat during the day. He was drinking a cup of decaf when Jake Sigman walked in the door. Denny smiled. Hey, the world was still humming along. Sigman, a character actor and frequent fixture in Neil Simon plays, had a smooth, waxed-looking, heavily made-up face that gave him a Kewpie doll look. He waved at Denny. "Hiya, kiddo." As usual, he was accompanied by a blonde. *Where does he get them all?* Denny wondered.

Denny smiled as he thought back to the winter night when Sigman had come into the bar wearing a mink jacket. His blonde female companion had been wearing a cloth coat. A woman had approached him and said how much she liked the mink jacket, and boldly asked if he'd consider selling it. Denny wasn't sure whether it was a put-on or not. Jake had told the woman, "Oh I couldn't possibly consider selling this jacket, madam. This morning I had my hair dyed to match the coat. It would interfere with my fashion statement."

Denny was sipping his drink and watching the raid being played out again when Jake edged up to him at the bar.

Denny inquired, "Where's tonight's blonde?"

"Oh, she's one of those bimbos that lives in the ladies' room."

"I hear you're a hit in that new Neil Simon play."

"Yeah, in one scene I'm avuncular, in the next I'm addled—about par for the course. Typecasting. How's it going, bro? I seen your name in the tabs. You've been having a rough time of it. How's Monny?"

"Oh, we're taking kind of a breather. She's staying out in Mineola with her sister."

"Don't let her get away, Den. She's a classic." He pointed to Denny's drink. "And take some advice from a guy who's been there. Cut down on the sauce. It'll do you in if you let it."

"I know. I hear that a lot."

"Well, listen, you dumb shit, and put your eggs back together in the basket before it's too late. Becoming a souse is no achievement around these parts. When you see your dad, tell him how much us older guys miss him. We love the bastard. And you watch that cute little mick tush of yours."

Jake patted Denny on the lower back and went back to his table in the restaurant section.

Exhausted, and slightly looped after his third martini, Denny dragged himself back to the apartment. That night his home supply of vodka remained untouched because he was too beat to stay awake. He didn't have the strength or the will to check his answering machine. He shambled into the bedroom, threw his clothes on a chair, and fell into bed. In minutes he was in a deep sleep.

19

His telephone was insistent, loud, determined. Denny was completely out of it, in his morning post-alcoholic stupor. His eyes opened to slits; the thick black eyebrows scowled as he looked at the ghostly floating green numbers in the darkened room. It was 6:12 A.M. *God, what now?* He could barely get his mouth to imitate a voice, to make sounds. On a hangover headache scale of one to ten, Denny had a seven or eight.

A voice, obviously being disguised, inquired, "Dennis Delaney?" An educated voice, a general Middle American accent. "*The* Dennis Delaney, who is a security officer at Grand Central Station?"

"Yes, who is this?"

"I just glanced at a map and at your address, and I realized we had something in common. Grand Central Station, no?"

"Who is this?"

"Felix, le chat, mon ami. The feline Felix."

Could it possibly be? Denny decided he would have to lead this guy on just in case he was the real thing.

"How do you know me?"

"Well, my dear boy, you're something of a celebrity. I understand that you work security at the famous terminal, now known round the world. I saw your visage on television outside the station on that fateful day. I saw your face on camera at that infamous raid where three of my compatriots were slaughtered."

"How did you get this number? How did you get my name?"

"Don't be shy. Your name has been all over the media. I see your name in the tabs. And you are still listed in the directory. In addition, the gossip columnists did say you lived on Restaurant Row. *Frequenter of a number of taverns* is the way they put it."

"What do you want? How do I know you are the real Felix and not someone pretending to be him?"

"You want proof, my friend? The slug line would read: INTERIOR. FBI FIELD OFFICE—AFTERNOON. I think we saw each other on Vesey Street, the FBI field office some months ago, yes?"

Only the FBI and Denny would know that piece of information. Oh, and Terry. Had Terry told anyone? No, she wouldn't. This guy was the real thing. He had to be.

"Yeah, I believe you. Why the call? Why call me?"

"Because you are at the center of the maelstrom we are creating. And you've tweaked my sense of the dramatic, or should I say the melodramatic."

"Me?"

"We do not provide our enemies with attribution, claim responsibility for our actions generally speaking. We have a message to impart. Your people still don't get it. Our message is the bomb itself. No need for an oral communication to take credit. The bomb itself is the calling card. Get it, Dennis? Now in the movie there'd be a close-up of Dennis doing a double take."

"I think I get it, but what motivates you to do something so horrible? The killing of innocents."

"Not some vague, amorphous motive. Your country supports genocide by Israel against the Palestinian people. Until you stop your support of the Israelis, you can expect to be hit hard and often in your sacred homeland. Plain and simple motivation. Turn your spigot off, stop all aid to Israel, give the Palestinians back all their stolen land, get out of the Middle East, and then we'll see if you can get back your peace and quiet."

Denny didn't want to argue politics with him.

"Be watching television in the weeks ahead, and I'll supply the fireworks display. Ze pyrotechnics. Fade in, Cut to Next Attack. Have a nice day, Dennis. Split screen of Felix and Denny talking on phones."

"Felix, I want to . . . "

Click. Felix had hung up. Denny called Wexler's cell phone to report the call. Wexler was ahead of him. "We know all about it. We heard it."

Doesn't the son of a bitch ever sleep?

"You heard it? How?"

"We've been expecting something like this. We put a tap on your line and a simple caller ID, but no sophisticated tracer—yet."

"A tap on my phone? What the hell? Who's the enemy here? A tap without my permission? You fucks. Do you go through my garbage? Count the vodka bottles?"

"Easy, Denny, watch yourself. I'm sorry. Your name has been out there. He's reading what we're reading. We know you two saw each other in our field office. This is a war we're in."

"Yeah, so I keep hearing. Did you trace the call?"

"Don't know yet. I'm not in Vesey Street. We're trying to trace it. We didn't have time to set up a sophisticated tracking system on your phone as yet. Wait a few minutes. I'm checking with our office."

It was more than two minutes before Wexler came back on the line. "Felix's call was from a cell phone. A prepaid. It came from somewhere on the West Side of

Manhattan. He'll ditch the phone and never use it again. A prepaid phone purchased with cash. Untraceable. NYPD has dispatched every available car and man. They'll be on the lookout for him."

"So there's a tap on my phone. Am I being tailed?"

"I'm not aware of any tail on you, although it might not be a bad idea. What's interesting are the technical movie references Felix made. What do you make of the movie stuff, Denny? Felix was speaking like a director or a screenwriter. He used movie-making terminology. He wanted you to notice that stuff."

"Yeah, I caught that too. I'm sure that was deliberate on his part. This guy wants us to unearth his past. Why don't we have a make on this guy from overseas?"

"Because key Middle Eastern countries are holding out on us. They know, but they won't tell us. The CIA is sure that Egypt, Lebanon, Syria, Saudi Arabia, and maybe Jordan have dossiers on him, but they aren't going to share—not now, not yet anyway. Denny, get down to the office as soon as you can. I want to plan something with you."

Denny took little time getting down to Vesey Street. Soon he was sitting with Wexler and Frank in Wexler's office. The first few moments were tense. Denny was teed off.

"A tap without telling me. I would have said go ahead, but I'd like to be asked."

"Point made and point taken, Dennis. Now let's move on. We have a major investigation underway. We have the call on tape. What's interesting are the movie jargon references.

"He may be someone in the movie business. Perhaps either here in the States or overseas. Maybe the Middle East. If he's holed up somewhere, he could still do screenwriting. He could be writing a screenplay of what has happened so far. We'll have teams of agents circulate his picture among production companies, agencies, screenwriting outlets, the indies. Frank, what else are we planning?"

Again it sounded scripted to Denny. Frank said, "We're going to follow up on the movie references. It was all technical film script stuff that a screenwriter, a director, or someone engaged in making films would be aware of. We're including that in our alerts to law enforcement and intelligence forces all over the world. Here in the States we'll send men out to film schools to see if anyone picks up on this guy."

Denny added, "He's probably the type that goes to a lot of movies, rents videos."

Wexler emphasized, "Good thinking, Denny. We'll get on that."

Denny had some ideas. "I'll tell you why I think he's called. My wife and I see all the latest movies. This guy has a movie buff's or movie director or screenwriter's sense of the cinematic. He knows what plays on the screen. In the movies the investigator and the perp have to establish a relationship, a bond that ties them together. It makes for a dramatic film setup. It personalizes the bigger conflict. The audience gets off on it. It's been used thousands of times.

"In a way the protagonist and antagonist are above the fray, on another level from the bigger conflict. They are combatants on a different plane. While the perp is doing his dirty work, the audience's interest is grabbed by the man-to-man aspect. Good versus evil is personified in the good guy–bad guy conflict. It's a way of personalizing the struggle for the audience."

Wexler said, "Not bad thinking. I have to agree. We've

got to keep him interested in talking to you. Next time stall him as long as you can. String him along. Amazingly enough, he was on the phone with you a long time. Longer than someone worried about a trace would be."

Denny answered, "But it was his first call to me. Who would be expecting him to call?"

Wexler pushed on without answering Denny's question. "If you could somehow bait him into a face-to-face meeting . . . massage his ego. You can tell the guy has a big ego. We'll be walking a thin line here. We have to be careful we don't provoke him. I don't want innocent lives on my hands because we goaded him into some action. Better that he gets away altogether than he kills innocents because of us."

Denny ruefully replied, "I'd love to meet him face to face."

"Denny, Felix has fixated on you. You're his foil, his alter ego, maybe his other self. You can lead us to him because I think he'll be drawn to you like a moth to the flame. You're his nemesis. Somehow we'll ferret him out."

Denny tried to keep from smiling at Wexler's use of the word ferret.

Wexler handed Denny a yellow cell phone and a number written on a card. "If Felix calls again, give him this number for this phone. Carry it with you everywhere. Leave it on in case he calls. It'll be a bother carrying your own cell phone and this special Felix phone, but that way we'll know for sure it's him, and he'll be able to reach you anywhere. Please don't use this for anything but Felix calls."

Later when Wexler was alone with Millau he said, "Denny is no boob. We're not dealing with a dumb

Irishman here. He's bright, well read, very savvy about movies, and cultivated in his own way."

Frank said, "His biggest asset is that he has the ability to put himself into the mind of someone like Felix. He may be our best hope in the end."

20

Felix lay on his bed in the attic room of a Brooklyn brownstone. He flipped back and forth between cable news channels on his television set. They were reporting on the raid in Queens. "Three members of a terrorist cell have been killed in a lethal raid on their headquarters. Two FBI agents lost their lives in the deadly assault.

"The apparent leader of the cell, the infamous Grand Central bomber, was not found. The FBI has reported that the cell members called yesterday's bomber Felix the Cat, a name that was written in red ink across a photograph of the bomber found in the terrorists' Queens apartment."

Felix was saddened by the loss of his three compatriots, but he had not been close to them, was not close to anyone, really. In his business, the business of sowing terror, it paid to be a loner.

He watched the footage of agents outside the tenement. In a brief shot he saw Denny talking to other agents on the street. Felix thought, *There he is again. It's like fate. Our paths crossing. Who is he? A big shot or only a cog? I have a feeling that I'm going to run into him again.*

On all the stations the name Felix the Cat had taken hold. The media now had a label, a brand name, to hang on the man. He would become the notorious Felix the Cat. Felix's cinematic senses were pricked, alive to the possibilities of this development; they had a marker, his nickname. Good. This would make the whole thing more interesting. A good career move. Good for his character arc.

One chance at death down, eight to go if he was very, very lucky. He had already come close to giving up some of his lives earlier in Egypt, Lebanon, and Syria. Many close calls that left death always lurking, waiting, ready to take him. What the hell, go for broke now. No one would dare laugh at Felix the Cat anymore.

To Felix the world was an ironic, unjust, tragic, dangerous place. The world had taught him to be a fatalist. He thought about his life, his back story. He used the term *back story* when he thought about his life because his whole being had been focused on screenwriting for as long as he could remember. He saw events through the camera; his life played out on a screen, based upon a story that spun out in his head. His was a world of slug lines, action lines, character tags, dialogue, and cinematic clichés.

As a young man he had written television scripts in Egypt and other Middle Eastern countries. One of his teleplays had been seen in Israel of all places. His telestories were moody pieces about desperate people, but they had had a certain raw power, one critic had said. One of his teachers said that his scripts had misshapen premises, whatever the hell that meant. Another had said to ditch the overwrought dialogue.

As a screenwriter of feature-length releases, Felix was a wannabe. He had never sold a feature film script, had never even come close. He wanted the fame and the money that would come with produced screenplays. He'd had no fame until now. He desperately wanted recognition. Years of toil on scripts had not yielded even the encouragement to continue. His scripts reeked with the stench of mediocrity. It nagged at him. It was frustrating being a nothing, a nobody. Maybe now with this living script he would become famous, infamous.

The child of a Saudi father and a Syrian mother, he had grown up in Damascus and Beirut. Possessed by the screenwriting bug, he had gone to Cairo and Alexandria for university training, become very proficient in American English, and returned to Beirut.

People who knew his lineage called him a mongrel. He knew he would never be accepted into polite society; his only acceptance would be through what he achieved in life. In Lebanon, where he taught screenwriting, he became familiar with many Palestinians. He had brief affairs with several Palestinian women.

It was his contacts with the suffering, poverty, and degradation of the Palestinians, especially the women and children, that had forged his fanaticism and activism. He had grown up hating Israelis, and had acquired by osmosis his antipathy toward Jews of every stripe. And Americans—he hated them for their arrogance, their greed, their smug belief in their place in the world. Along with the Jews, they thought of themselves as the chosen people.

His hatred had seeped into him over the years, becoming more consuming as he matured. He was a decisive person, an activist who didn't believe in sitting on the sidelines. He had worked on his body so that he was strong and well muscled. But his hatred was channeled through a cold and calculating mind. He would light a powder keg, but would try not to let himself be consumed by the explosion.

Felix was not a devoutly religious person and only nominally practiced the Islamic religion. No one in his family had been particularly religious. It was not religious fanaticism that drove him; rather it was a determination to change the world in political terms. Terrorism was the answer. The military might of the United States and Israel could only be counterbalanced by terrorist attacks on their homeland populations. Terror on their home turf paid greater dividends than battlefield assaults. Yes, the homeland. Terrorize the homeland. Make the homeland crumble from within.

Slowly he had become a political zealot and then a militant who embraced the world of terrorism. In the nineties he had been trained by a Palestinian group in the art of bomb making and the skills and craft of terrorism. He never left the Middle East for training in Afghanistan or elsewhere.

In the mid-nineties he had been recruited into a cell that was vaguely related to Bin Laden's Al Qaeda network. He shared some of Bin Laden's goals, but the small cell he eventually headed was not part of Al Qaeda although they did get considerable financing from them in a roundabout manner.

He had been given and continued to receive large sums of money to perform terrorist acts in the United States. In January 1999 he had entered the States, carrying with him all sorts of fake passports and identification documents.

He went to live with a Syrian couple in their late fifties who owned a three-story brownstone in Brooklyn, a building at the dead end of Shelton Terrace, a commercial street of warehouses and garages. The brownstone adjoined a large garage, which the couple also owned. This garage had been used for truck repairs for years and had then gone out of business. It had huge doors that could accommodate large trucks and vans. At present, six vehicles were parked inside.

The Syrian couple with their one son, Asa, now thirty-five years old, had entered the States in 1980 with fake Israeli passports. They became the Levins. Eventually the three became citizens and kept a low profile. They kept to themselves. Their son left the garage almost daily in his battered van. In this commercial area there were no neighbors to spy on them.

Felix and six members of his crew lived in the Levin house with the Levins and Asa. They never walked outside. When they wanted to go out, they would enter the garage through a passageway that had been built between the house and garage. They would then climb in the back of one of the vans, scrunch down, and Asa would drive out of the garage seemingly alone. When he returned, again seemingly alone, Asa would open one of the garage doors by remote control so he didn't have to exit the van. Felix and the other cell members had never been seen anywhere in the neighborhood.

Between January 1999 and September 2001, Felix and his crew had squirreled away all sorts of explosives, detonation devices, and heavy arms that had been shipped into the States in containers originating in the Middle East. From time to time a complete container on a flatbed would be driven into the garage and unloaded. They had unloaded several short-range rocket launchers. If an explosion had occurred in the garage, that whole section of Brooklyn would have been leveled. The munitions were well hidden in the back of the garage in a chamber with a false wall that had been camouflaged to resemble the garage's rear wall.

Felix had all of 1999, all of 2000, and most of 2001 to stockpile materials and make plans. After the Nine-Eleven World Trade Center disaster all stockpiling came to a halt. They did nothing further to call attention to themselves after that attack.

Felix occasionally left the apartment house in Asa's van. When he did, he would go to a multiplex and see two movies and parts of others to keep up with the latest Hollywood efforts. He had continued his screenwriting. Asa brought in the daily newspapers, magazines, videotape and DVD rentals and purchases, and a variety of foods. Everyone in the house lived only for the others, and there was no socializing with outsiders. Asa was known by a few merchants some distance from the house, but he stayed polite and detached.

Ma Levin was a superb cook, who made meals for Felix and his associates. Asa bought plenty of Middle Eastern staples. She found out the foods that each liked and blissfully cooked for them. She was a zealot in the kitchen as well as in her unwavering political beliefs. The dining room table had plates of four types of dark Mediterranean olives. She avoided American efficiency foods. She set her table with all sorts of Middle Eastern treats for her adoring husband and son and their guests. The whole group feasted around her table, except for the day's designated lookout and Felix. He would come to the table, make up a plate for himself, and take it up to his room. She understood; he had a lot on his mind.

Felix stayed in his attic room watching television and videos, reading, working out for hours with his weights and exercise equipment, and writing screenplays on his laptop. He used the latest screenwriting software, *Final Draft,* and wrote in English. Over and over again he watched a videotape of Syd Field's *Screenwriting Workshop.* Felix had received it along with his screenwriting software.

Felix slavishly followed Field's three-act structural dogmas and always placed his plot points at the proper intervals recommended by Field's dictates. Not that he submitted screenplays while in the States. Anyone who wrote screenplays as bad as Felix's would have to learn to live with rejection. Unfortunately and tragically for the world, Felix was a better terrorist than he was a screenwriter.

There were always at least six or seven rented videotapes available for the house. As well as their VHS players, they also had two DVD players. Asa resupplied them with fresh tapes regularly. Sometimes one of the gang would pull Asa aside and order pornographic girlie flicks. Never Felix. Asa would oblige. Many popular videocassettes and DVDs had been purchased and were part of their library. The house was full of books and magazines. Asa did not buy any Middle Eastern newspapers or magazines, only the city's papers and American magazines.

For Felix it was a monastic life, a dedicated life, but now his mission had begun. If he were pitching his script, he would say the waiting period had come to an end, and America would shake, rattle, and mourn.

21

The night of Felix's call Denny was in Joe Allen's, talking to Kevin.

"Kev, I just thought of something. Remember that time you were talking about a screenwriting course? You figured if you wrote your own script, you could write a juicy part for yourself?"

"Yeah, sure."

"Did you go to that school?"

"I did go. I loved the course."

"What was the school?"

"You know those flyers you see in those racks all over town, put out by the Gotham Writers' Workshop? That's the school. Wait a minute, I've got one in my knapsack. Never know when I'll be ready for that big career change."

Kevin fetched the flyer and gave it to Denny.

"Thanks."

Denny studied the booklet. He saw a ten-week summer workshop called *Screenwriting I* with ten different sections being taught, including one taught on the Internet. Denny figured that would be a large number of students. *Screenwriting II* was an advanced course with four divisions, one of them online. As for *Screenwriting III,* this was a master class with one section taught online and one on site.

Ten weeks of classes probably taught four times a year. All those sections, all those classes; just think of the number of students over the years. Plus all the other screenwriting classes taught throughout the city, by correspondence and over the Internet by a myriad of schools.

There were also two sections of *Film Analysis,* which was taught from a screenwriter's point of view. One of these was an online course. Denny thought that it was very possible that Felix had taken one or more of these online courses. It would have probably been paid by credit card, and the school would have had to give Felix a password to get into the system if he were an online student.

It wasn't yet eleven. Denny dialed Wexler's cell phone. He told him about the school. "It's just a chance, but Felix might just be the kind of guy who would do this. They have a number of different courses. The problem is they must have had thousands of students over the years."

Wexler reacted, "He could have used any name. No way of knowing what name he'd be under. But I think this is a more likely bet than a formal college or university course. We'll get Felix's picture to every course instructor they've had."

"I'd take a guess he would have used the name Felix. The name didn't mean anything up until a few days ago. See if by chance there was a Felix."

Wexler answered, "It's a real long shot. And, Denny, let's remember that this guy seems to be very proud of himself and his abilities. He may have felt he was above and beyond any screenwriting courses."

"This would be a class taken before Nine-Eleven, I think. Something maybe in '99, 2000—sometime before September in 2001. Because after that date this guy probably would have gone into deep cover. He's no doubt Middle Eastern and might have been pulled in if he was out in public."

"Thanks, Denny. Now would you try to get yourself some sleep? You can't work this case twenty-four hours a day."

"Look who's talking. Good night."

Denny thought, *I'll have to do some research on ferrets, see if they need much sleep, see if they're nocturnal.*

In Brooklyn Felix had just finished a night of screenwriting. The protagonist in his script had just reached the plot point where he calls the investigator. His script would be the first in which the terrorist was the good guy, the justified avenger fighting for the underdog. He wondered how many more plot points he'd be able to work into his script before his own inevitable end. *Hell, they ain't seen nothing yet.*

22

Everyone in Felix's cell had kept an especially low profile during the millennium scare, when alerts were out for possible terrorist attacks. The year 2000 had been uneventful. Felix took orders from no one overseas; he was an independent contractor. It was up to him when and how he would strike. The group had continued to stockpile explosives in the garage next door. And they waited, patiently. Felix would know when to give the word.

On September 11, 2001, Felix was watching television in disbelief. He was amazed by the precision and the audacity of the attack. Felix was as surprised as anyone when the attack took place. The various terrorist cells and factions were so compartmentalized and so autonomous that one cell had no idea what another one was planning.

He had had no advance word; in fact, he had never heard of any plans for such an attack. It was on a greater scale than he could have managed. He put the plans he had been making on hold. His attacks would be a great follow-up and help to destabilize the public, the government, and the economy. Felix thought each terrorist attack would bring the States closer to a totalitarian state in its effort to control the situation.

When Nine-Eleven happened, Asa stayed in for a week and did no shopping. After the attack Felix watched television and read newspapers to see the effects it was having on the economy and on the psychology of Americans—New Yorkers in particular.

On one of his then rare movie forays in October 2001, he saw the fear in the eyes of the Manhattanites. They had lost a lot of their smugness. He heard them talking. Before, they had existed to be entertained, to be culturally stimulated, to be titillated, to be pampered and massaged. Now many of them had that proverbial deer-in-the-headlights stare. He heard them talking of quitting the city. Some mentioned friends or relatives who had bugged out. The terrorists had done their work; they had terrorized the population.

For months anyone with a Middle Eastern look was suspect. He and the others for the most part lay low. He decided that June of 2002 was his time to act. If he waited too long, law enforcement might get wind of them, arrest them, and confiscate their horde of explosives and equipment. Then his would be a failed and wasted mission.

His scheme might end in death for him, but he would not court suicide. His missions would be dangerous and life threatening, but if he carried them out according to plan, he might get away to do more damage in the future. He had decided on a series of terrorist acts to throw the country off balance. He would rock them off their feet and continue to do so as long as he could. His lieutenants had been trained to continue his work if he should die.

His goal was to terrorize New York and Washington directly. Other cells would probably cause other kinds of turmoil, but his cell would demoralize the East Coast and ultimately the whole country. What a screenplay he would write if ever he was allowed to do it—if he survived to do it.

His current screenplay was on the computer screen; it began with the slug line:

INT. GRAND CENTRAL STATION—MORNING

The screenplay then went on to describe the planting of the explosives in Grand Central, the blast, and the aftermath. The protagonist was the bomber himself.

Felix's days in the movie studios had paid off in other ways. He had learned a lot about makeup and disguise. With his makeup kits he practiced various disguises. Sometimes Mrs. Levin would help him by sewing costumes. He had fat suits, wigs, hats and caps, thick glasses, sunglasses, fake beards and moustaches. He practiced changing the shape of his nose, changing the look of his eyes and ears.

Felix could make himself look older, heavier, handicapped. He practiced slumping over to alter his height, walking with a cane, a limp, a permanent stoop. He learned to change his hair color, change its styling.

Felix had promised his fellow terrorists in the training camp that he would indeed make waves and shake up the world. Felix had no minders; he was an independent operator whose only mandate was to cause fear and suspicion in the hearts of the Americans. His financial backers had faith in him, and they had supplied him with all the equipment and explosives he desired. Money was no object.

One of Felix's goals was to sway American public opinion away from the country's pro-Israeli policy and drive their forces from the Middle East, though not their oil dollars.

Felix knew when his first attack would be. He didn't need a signal, a sign, an order. The decision was his to make, when and how, with the materials and personnel at his disposal. His dictum was to do it when the maximum disruption would take place. Do it when the public had become complacent. Strike fear in their hearts. Make a mockery of their settled, pampered, ordered lifestyles.

One day in May, before the Grand Central attack, he had been scrunched down with his copy of *Variety* in a Manhattan movie theater, waiting for the movie to start. The movie was *Insomnia,* with Al Pacino and Robin Williams. He liked the darker Williams persona better, couldn't stand the star's saccharine do-gooder image.

Two young men and a young woman had ducked out early from work to see the movie. From their seats in the row behind him Felix couldn't help overhearing everything they said. They were oblivious to everyone but themselves. To Felix they were loud, privileged, brittle, precious New Yorkers. They knew every movie, every play, every cable dramatic series, every good restaurant, all the good gyms, the best doctors, best personal trainers, the best brunches on weekend mornings. They sounded like they had ingested *New York* magazine.

They could tell you about the actors, which off-Broadway plays they'd been in, which television program they'd been on, who they dated. Which directors were hot. Who was in, who was out.

Felix could tell that they had good jobs, made big bucks, had nice cars, nice apartments, nice lives. They were serving their apprenticeship as cosmopolitan, sophisticated, cultured entertainment gurus, show business experts. He didn't think the men were gay; these guys weren't show business literate as part of the gay culture or lifestyle, they were just New York–type professional show biz groupies.

And he hated them. Not because they knew more than he did about the biz, because they didn't; he followed show biz as avidly as they did. He hated them in part because he thought they might be Jews, but mainly because they had centered their whole lives on nothing important, nothing of real substance. The little Palestinian child sitting in the dust—hungry, confused, desperate—meant nothing to them. *Fuck them. They'll soon be shivering in their boots, figuring how they can get out of New York. They'll soon wish they'd paid more attention to the world and less heed to their petty lives and show biz concerns. Dissolve to three pampered, privileged scum cowering in a bomb shelter.*

23

Friday morning, the fourth morning after the attack on Grand Central, Denny was sitting in the Vesey Street field office with Frank, going over leads that had come in. They had divided the stack of leads into two equal piles, one for each of them.

Denny said, "You can tell that most of these sightings are bogus. They *think* they've seen someone who looks like Felix. This guy has just faded into the woodwork."

"One thing he can't disguise: his broad shoulders and muscular frame."

"That's true, except he could make himself look fatter with padding."

"Den, do you think this guy is finished? Or will he strike again?"

"I have a feeling he'll do it again and again until we kill him or catch him. With all those pictures around, he'd be dead meat for the rest of his life. He has nothing to lose now. He'll go for broke. Wouldn't you?"

"Hey, I can't even put myself into the mind of a psychopath like that."

"But, Frank, that's exactly what we have to do. Think just like he does so we can anticipate future moves. First concentrate on outdoor public spaces, crowded places. I'd say he'll strike in the streets. Most big indoor spaces have some sort of detection system at entrances. Too much trouble to penetrate."

"Every subway entrance is being checked for anyone with luggage, large bags. A big play is being put on checking vehicles for explosives."

They worked through the afternoon, sifting through evidence reports, agent interviews, files from foreign law enforcement agencies.

At three-thirty Wexler came into Frank's office. He said, "Forensics is still combing through the raided apartment for any evidence. Fingerprint men are dusting everywhere. We desperately need some prints for Felix. A few prints were found and checked with U.S. and foreign databases, but no matches so far. Overseas police and intelligence sources are being queried about the name Felix. We know from the CIA that Syrian and Egyptian security forces are holding back on us. The State Department is trying to put the screws to them, but we may not be lucky."

Denny asked, "Why would Syria and Egypt not cooperate?"

"Because they have nothing to gain by sharing information with us. They figure that it's our problem, not theirs. Factions in their countries wouldn't be happy to see them looking cooperative."

"Bastards."

"Join the real world, Denny. In the movies you send out a request and Interpol comes back with a complete dossier. Uh uh. It's whatta you got to trade for my information? Whatta I get for helping you?"

Wexler was on a roll. He continued, "The computer found at the scene, so far it hasn't offered up much of real value. The computer users sent out e-mails to Middle Eastern destinations, mainly Lebanon, Egypt, Jordan, and Syria. No e-mails within the States. We checked with overseas. The men were sending messages to cybercafes and office service places, Kinko's-type facilities, in the Middle East. Hard to track down. The men surfed the Internet, but mainly for free porn spots. They weren't quite dumb enough to order from Amazon or bid on items at eBay.

"Their telephone and internet services were registered under false names and were paid in 7-Eleven money orders. They had prepaid cell phones and a stack of telephone calling cards. No identification has been made on any of the three dead men. Our main effort has to be on Felix the Cat. Let's hope that he calls you again, Denny."

Wexler told Frank and Denny that he had called Chris's parents, and they had been understanding. Chris had always wanted to be an FBI agent. He and they had known the dangers. The father had said, "I just didn't think anything bad would happen. And if something bad did happen, I didn't think it would be so soon."

Before he left, Wexler added, "I don't have to tell you how much the media and the White House are ratcheting up the pressure."

At nine-thirty Denny left the Vesey Street field office and decided on a long walk to clear his head and get his body doing something. He'd have to watch himself because he was a great walker, capable of walking for hours and for miles around the city. He walked south and surveyed the progress on the World Trade Center site. Not much was new. Denny had known the Twin Towers well. To him the most striking thing was the absence, the physical and psychological holes left from them. You could feel where they had been, soaring skyward, dominating the southern tip of Manhattan, now nothing. Nothingness and an eerie stillness. A lack of something, an absence, a hole in your life. Like a death, but here many deaths. That enormous gaping hole for what had been the foundations of two majestic skyscrapers.

Heading north up Broadway, he passed City Hall and

started counting the blocks. Six blocks and he was at Canal Street. He was going at a good clip.

Still heading up Broadway, another six long blocks and he was at West Houston. Then north through Greenwich Village, past NYU and Washington Square Park. Had he miscounted or was it twelve blocks when he reached East 14th Street and Union Square? This was the point where he'd have to make up his mind. Keep walking all the way home or take a subway or cab? He decided to keep going. What the hell. It was the only exercise he'd gotten in several days. When he was walking, his mind was basically blank, thinking of his footing and observing the street scenes around him. Walking took his mind away from his cares—Monny, those who had died, Felix the Cat, Big Mac.

Broadway headed toward home. Was it just him, or on this night hadn't he been hearing an inordinate number of sirens and rushing fire engines, cop cars, and ambulances? Most of the emergency services were on overtime, twelve hour shifts since the blast. It was called "showing the flag." Even if you could not accomplish much, make your presence known. It made the populace feel safer—maybe. The heightened security and heavy police presence also increased uneasiness and that jittery feeling in the air.

At almost every block he saw blinking lights, knots of uniformed men, emergency workers. All the utility companies seemed to be out in force sealing things off, checking out, anticipating attacks. It was a city under siege. The few pedestrians on the street were scurrying. The homeless looked more dazed, confused, and out-of-it than ever.

Herald Square, the Empire State Building, Macy's—he kept slogging on. Sweating now. When he reached

Times Square, he had a decision to make. Which of his bar–restaurants would he visit? He knew of scores of places where he'd feel at home. No Joe Allen's tonight. Give it a rest.

He decided on the Heartland Brewery & Chop House on West 43rd Street. It was down the street from the Henry Miller Theater, where he and Monny had seen *Urinetown.* They had both roared at the musical's ridiculous and absurd material; it was the last play they had seen together before Monny decided that they needed a trial separation period.

He remembered that she'd said of their marriage, "Den, it isn't working now. Maybe if we both get some space and give it some time we can work it out. Right now I need to be alone: I need to think, and you need to sort out your priorities. We're not singing from the same hymn book, that's for damn sure."

And Denny had answered, "I'll agree we're on different pages in those hymn books, but let's find a page we can agree on and go from there."

Monny had replied, "Den, I wish it were as easy as that."

He liked the Heartland—big drinks and generous portions of good food. The barmaid didn't know Denny, but he quickly made an impression. A young, good-looking Irishman with a winning smile, and wasn't she a lass from the old sod? She put the big rocks glass in front of him, his vodka martini. On the next one he'd have to teach her to go light, much lighter, on the dry vermouth. He studied the huge menu and settled in for a good dinner, either at the bar or at one of the small tables to the side.

24

Maybe Denny would never again know what normal meant, but Saturday was almost a day of routine. He worked at Vesey Street, went out on two leads with Frank—leads that turned out to be dead ends. But you kept working the leads until you struck pay dirt. One was from a woman who reported that she had seen Felix. When they got to her apartment, which smelled strongly of cat urine, she pointed to her cat and said, “He morphed right in front of my eyes and turned into Benjy here.” She had two obsessions in life: sci fi and cats.

At six Denny was cut loose from Vesey Street. He visited Mac in the hospital. Mac was still out of it and wasn’t doing too well. Before he left, Denny placed his hand against Mac’s forehead and said, “Mac, you gotta get well soon. You’re my hero, man.”

He and Barb sat and talked about happier days, barbecues on Long Island, fishing off Montauk.

By eight he was back in his flat taking a nap on the living room sofa. At eighty-thirty the phone rang.

“Hi, it’s me. Terry. How ya doing?”

“I’m doing par for the course. You having any trouble?”

“No, the TV and press have let up, so I’m beginning to get a little peace and quiet.”

“For a while you were all over the media.”

“Hey, Den, a dazzlingly seductive young woman, crippled and confined to a wheelchair? Just think what a poster gal that is for those jackals.”

“I’m really glad that you’re getting out of the limelight.

You never can tell these days. Lots of crazies out there."

"Now I'm beginning to get some peace and quiet. But I see you are taking my place in the papers. Denny, I wondered if you'd like to stop down at my apartment tonight. Are you free about ten?"

He hesitated. He didn't want their one-night stand to have a follow-up. She sensed the hesitation.

"Fran will be here. I want to show you my new gym equipment. I've got everything I need here to work out with when I can't make therapy. You gotta see it."

Childlike eagerness in her voice. Maybe after everything that had happened, a stab at normality.

"Fran and I are going out to run some errands. I need to relax. We'll be back before ten. Is that too late?"

"No, I can swing by your placc at ten. I'd love to see your workout stuff."

"See ya."

"Watch yourself. Be careful."

"Thanks, Daddy."

Denny would be glad to see Terry's roommate, Fran, again. *She's a knockout, great tits. Hey, I can look, can't I? I'm only half married right now.*

At nine-fifty Terry returned to her downtown neighborhood with Fran, her roommate. She pulled her SUV into a parking space off Water Street. Fran unloaded the wheelchair from the back of the vehicle and brought it around to the driver's side front door. Terry lifted herself out of the van and into the chair. She slammed the door shut and propelled herself to the corner using the large rear wheels.

As usual the streets were deserted, no signs of life. A commercial area teeming with people during business hours, at night it was like a graveyard. Fran walked a short distance behind, making sure that she only helped out when it was absolutely necessary. At the corner incline Terry easily rolled herself up the few inches to the sidewalk.

As Terry and Fran reached the sidewalk, they heard the roar of the car. A black sedan bore down on them, screeched to a stop, and double parked near the corner. Terry craned her neck to see the rear of the car. A man dressed in coveralls, his face covered in a ski mask, ran toward them with a drawn handgun. He opened fire on Terry from about forty feet away. Fran dove for the pavement. The masked man fired three shots at Terry and then ran back to the idling car driven by another man. The shooter jumped into the car and it sped off.

Terry had been hit. She lay sprawled out next to her wheelchair, which was lying on its side, its upright wheel still turning. She was gasping for air. She had a wound in her chest. The chest wound was seeping blood, staining Terry's gray sweatshirt. Fran had not been hit; she immediately dialed 911 on her cell phone.

"There's been a shooting outside 1284 Waters Street. Please hurry. A woman has been badly hurt. Hurry, please."

A few seconds went by. The dispatcher told her that medics and police had been dispatched and started to give her instructions for treating the victim.

"For Christ's sake, hurry. It's outside 1284 Water Street." Fran held the cell phone to her ear while she applied pressure to Terry's wound, trying to stem the flow of blood with her own sweater. Terry was conscious, and Fran could hear her pleas.

"Dear God, please . . . "

Minutes that seemed endless passed, and then an

ambulance and a police car arrived simultaneously. Then another police car.

When Denny's cab pulled around the corner near Terry's building, he could see the flashing lights, the headlights of the police cars parked askew in the street, the ambulance. He jumped from the cab and rushed to the scene. He pulled his FBI ID card and lanyard out from beneath his shirt. Terry was on the gurney about to be rolled into the ambulance. He saw the patches of blood on the pavement. He pushed his way to her side. Fran was leaning over her. The IV bottle had been attached, and they were about to place the oxygen mask over her face.

"Terry, jeez, Terry, God . . . "

Terry recognized the voice. Her eyes opened. Denny leaned over her. She could barely be heard when she uttered a word. "Zion," she rasped. Again, two more times. "Zion . . . Zion." The medics placed the mask over her mouth and nose and fastened the strap. One medic was caring for her wound.

Denny reached out to Fran. Her face was flushed, her eyes red from crying. They hugged one another.

The medic said, "Only one friend or family member in the ambulance please. We need space to work with her. Thank you."

"Denny, I'm going with her in the ambulance. They're taking her to St. Vincent's. Take the chair if they'll let you. Here's the key. Put it in our apartment. I'm praying to God she'll need it again."

Denny asked, his voice choking, "What happened?"

"A man in a mask pulled up in a car, got out, and started firing. Den, is it because she knows something about the bombing at Grand Central?"

"Fran, I don't know. What does 'Zion' mean?"

"I don't know. I've never heard her say that before."

Medics carefully placed the gurney in the ambulance. A medic and Fran climbed inside next to her. Already policemen were tying yellow plastic crime scene tape around the corner.

After the ambulance had pulled away, Denny looked at the wheelchair which had been pushed up against a building; he could see a hole that had been torn in its canvas back. A bullet had passed completely through Terry's body. Denny asked one of the cops if he could bring the wheelchair up to Terry's apartment to stow it. The detective told him not to touch anything since it was crime scene evidence.

Denny decided to take a quick look in Terry's apartment. Inside, he looked at the corner of the large, high-ceilinged living room where Terry had set up her treadmill and other workout equipment. Tears came to his eyes. On her cocktail table was a copy of the *Post* with a huge picture of Felix and a blaring headline: WANTED DEAD OR ALIVE: FELIX THE CAT.

Denny walked into Terry's bedroom. He looked at the queen-sized bed. Months back Denny and Terry had had a one-night stand here. It had been an evening of heavy drinking. She was in her wheelchair, and he had rolled her around on a pub crawl to some of his haunts near Grand Central. They had decided that she was in no condition to drive home, so he threw the wheelchair into the trunk of a cab and they had gone down to her apartment.

One thing led to another, and they had had sex. Though it was a boozy pairing, it had been good for both of them. Afterwards she said, "You're very good at charity work. Comforting the crippled and handicapped." He had answered, "Uh uh, Terr, I've been wanting to shag you ever since I first laid eyes on you. You're one of the most beautiful women I've ever met."

He got home very late that night. He hadn't known that Monny was awake when he came in. It became part of the friction between Monny and him even though he had never told Monny about what had happened.

He knew that Monny suspected something. Weeks earlier she had said, "You're always talking about Terry. Terry did this, Terry said that. Boy, you two certainly hit it off well." And one time Terry had called him on his cell phone at home to talk about an assignment.

He left Terry's apartment, making sure it was tightly locked. When he got to St. Vincent's, Fran told him that Terry was in the operating room. Whcn she had arrived at the hospital, Terry had been unconscious. Fran approached one of the nurses who had been with Terry when she was taken to the operating room. The nurse said, "We can't tell you anything now. She's being operated on. It'll be some time before the doctors know one way or another."

Denny was hoping and praying that Terry would pull through. Hours later a doctor—Denny thought either an Indian, Pakistani, or Bangladeshi—came into the waiting room. Hc said that Terry had been hit by one bullet, and that it had not hit any vital organs. Her condition was still very precarious because she had lost a lot of blood. She was getting blood transfusions.

Terry's mother arrived, soon followed by Terry's sister. Denny said the usual appropriate things. The mother was looking for a motivation for the shooting. "Dennis, she admires you so much. Does this have anything to do with that awful bombing in Grand Central Station?"

"I honestly don't know."

Soon after, Denny broke away and headed toward home. But of course he didn't go right home. He stopped at Ryan's on Eighth Avenue and ordered the usual. A New York *Post* was in front of him on the bar. It was open to a big car ad with a large patch of blank white space. Denny kept writing the word ZION in the space. He was thinking as he sipped his drink. *I've got to be Inspector Morse. I've got to do some lateral thinking here, the way he would solve a crossword puzzle.*

Denny had graduated to the Thursday crossword in the New York *Times*. They got more difficult as the week went on. The Sunday puzzle was a different kettle of fish altogether, and he was fairly good with those larger puzzles.

What other meanings does Zion have? Denny had written the word Zion several times with a capital Z and the rest in lower-case letters. Then he started to write ZION in all capitals. The letter Z, the letter I, the letter O, the letter N? *Wait, what if I make a Z then the number 1, then the number 0, then an N. Z—ten—N. The last letters and numbers of a license plate, the first letters, or the whole plate?*

He took a sip of his drink. He thought for a moment, got out his cell phone, and punched in the numbers for Frank Millau.

"Denny, I told you to call me anytime, but I didn't think you'd have the balls to call me this late. Where are you? Some bar?"

"Yeah. Sorry, listen . . . "

He told Frank about the shooting of Terry. "Oh, jeez, Denny, I was so impressed by her when I met her in her tech center."

Denny explained his hunches about ZION. He asked Frank to run a check on license plates with the various combinations starting with the three metropolitan states: New York, New Jersey, and Connecticut. Frank said he'd get on it right away.

After he hung up, Denny decided he'd better cover all the bases and make sure that the NYPD was doing a search as well. Was he being paranoid? He wasn't sure, but Terry would want him to do everything he could. Next he called the 54th Precinct of the NYPD and asked to talk to a Lieutenant Lansky, whom he had known for years. He knew that Lansky worked the graveyard shift. Lansky also knew Terry. When Denny got through to him, he told him about the attack on Terry, and asked for a search of registration plates. Yes, Lansky assured him, they'd search their computers for the tri-state area.

Denny swirled the liquid of his second drink around in the glass. *Jeez, they use small rocks glasses. The shooting . . . it could be the work of the bombing cell. There's a long shot I hate to even think about; it might be the Feds themselves trying to silence her for something she knows and shouldn't know. But what would she know? She knows more about the surveillance tapes than anyone alive. Could there be something on those tapes? Something incriminating to the Bureau?* Wexler had said Denny was paranoid. This whole conspiracy thing with the Bureau was off the wall. He had to stop thinking that way.

Another long shot: Terry's shooting could be related to one of the cases she had worked in the past. It could be a member of that crazy Carrino family or one of their buddies. Maybe seeing Terry on TV, being the FBI's poster child, had triggered them. After all, she had been getting veiled threats from somebody about her shooting of Frankie Carrino.

It had been a long, stressful day. Denny walked

home without stopping anywhere else and dragged himself into his darkened apartment. The apartment was beginning to get that funky smell from too many boozy nights of collapsing on his bed or sofa without undressing. Denny opened all the windows, undressed, lay down, and within minutes was out of it.

25

The next morning, Sunday, June 18, Denny's phone was ringing at eight. It was Monny. "Denny, I heard about Terry. It's terrible. I'm heartbroken. Oh my God, I said awful things about her. And I really like her a lot. You guys are so good working together. But you told me she was under police protection."

"Not on a regular basis, she wasn't."

"Why not?"

"Terry was under what they call a light police watch. It meant a cruiser drove by her apartment building a couple of times a night. Maybe, on a slow night. On a busy night I'm sure she got zilch."

"Why weren't there bodyguards?"

"There were no direct, credible threats against her. Just vague stuff. She was getting calls that brought up Carrino's shooting death, but nothing concrete linking the calls to the Carrinos . . . "

"So she was left out there to fend for herself. A target. What about you? What if they're gunning for you? You've been in the papers, on TV. They might go after you too."

"Why should they go after me? Whoever they are."

"I'm angry about all this. That they would do this to her. And I'm worried about how safe you are."

"I'll be fine. Look, Monny, would you please meet me for dinner Tuesday night after work? Please? I'll meet you outside your building at six. Okay? I want to see you. Just to know you're still there, not just a voice on the telephone."

"Yes, Den, I'll be there."

Denny felt more upbeat after his conversation with his wife. He went out and bought the Sunday editions of the *Times* and the *News.* He stopped in one of his favorite coffee shops on Eighth Avenue for coffee and a bagel while he glanced through the papers. They were full of terrorist coverage and articles about Felix the Cat. The *Times* had a background story on the history of the cartoon character Felix the Cat as a fixture in pop culture. Denny read the story.

The character Felix had first appeared in a short film on November 9, 1919, conceived by a cartoonist named Otto Messmer and titled "Feline Follies." From that point on the character took off, became a craze, and appeared in a whole series of films. In the 1930s he hit the comic books. Over the years he had been reincarnated in television programs, a feature film, in tie-ins like toys and dolls. He had become a worldwide sensation, and the name became a household phrase.

The fictional cat, like a real one, is mischievous and curious. Stories about him have been built around the proverb "Curiosity killed the cat." A book was written about him called *Nine Lives to Live.*

Somewhere in the story of Felix the Cat might be revealed the trigger that had earned the bomber his nickname. Denny decided that later he would surf the Internet to see if he could find Middle Eastern connections. One possibility was that Felix was his real name.

Denny went home and called Frank to see if anything had turned up. The car used in Terry's shooting had been identified. Its license tag was 18Z10N. Eighteen—Z—ten—N. It had been stolen in midtown Manhattan just hours before the shooting. It was a black Honda Civic. Now a hunt was on for the missing car. A "Be On The Lookout Alert," a BOLA, had been issued for the Metro area. Denny thought the car had probably been abandoned soon after the shooting. The conventional pattern for none-too-original mob hit men. Frank was at home getting some needed rest, and he advised Denny to take the day off and rest as well.

Denny decided that on that Sunday above all others he had some serious praying to do. He walked over to his favorite church for the eleven o'clock Solemn Mass. The church was on his street just a few blocks from his home east of Seventh Avenue. The Church of Saint Mary the Virgin was a large, Gothic-style Episcopal church with its entrance on West 46th Street, a church similar in size and gravitas to some cities' cathedrals.

The church extended through the block to West 47th Street. Outside, the exterior of the church was sublimated, crowded in by the buildings around it. There was really no vista from which the church could be viewed and appreciated, but inside it was impressive and beautiful.

In the vestibule he was given a program which declared the day to be the fourth Sunday after Pentecost. He sat in a rear pew. The choir was behind and above him, and the impressive nave's soaring, lofty, newly painted ceiling towered over him. The gleaming, brightly lit altar fronted the wall out to 47th Street.

Those in the know called it Smoky Mary's because of the quantity of incense that was wafted in the air during High Mass; it was a bastion of the traditional service. Denny, though nominally a Catholic, felt at home here. It was never too crowded for masses. Its parishioners were largely locals from the theater district, and a number of gay and lesbian worshippers.

The church's gay membership had been ravaged by the AIDS epidemic.

Denny loved the ritual, the structured rhythms of the service, the stately ceremony, the sense of mystery, the beauty and the incremental progression of the rites. It was a time of release and calm for him. He felt enriched by the soaring organ music which thundered and echoed throughout the church. For Denny it was only a slight stretch of faith to make him a believer. A mass ignited epiphanies within him. He was an ordinary, needy person reaching out for something bigger than himself.

It was during the course of that mass that Denny labeled himself an alcoholic, really for the first time. He felt that it was an admission he had to make, one he had been refusing to acknowledge for quite a while.

In the sermon the rector talked of the bombing that had taken place Tuesday. "We are a city in mourning and in sorrow for those who gave their lives. Terrorism has struck our beloved city yet again. That great rail terminal is only a few short blocks from this place of worship. We are neighbors, so this has struck terror close to this home.

"For me, Grand Central Station has wonderful personal memories. I've walked through that concourse many times, on holidays to and from Yale, on summer vacations to and from Martha's Vineyard, to and from trips to West Point and further north. What the terrorists do is a form of desecration; they know that places once tarnished by their heinous acts can never be the same, can trigger fear in the hearts of those who are in those places in the future. The memories of the loved ones so foully murdered there will dwell on in us.

"The terrorists' mission is to turn the ordinary, the

mundane, and our common places into fearful and dangerous minefields, so that we see danger and death lurking everywhere in our daily lives.

"Why do these horrible things happen? Why are we being tested? These calamities are tests of our fortitude and our faith. We must renew our faith and rely on our faith to help us through these difficult days. God grant us the strength to do what is right and necessary. We . . . "

After mass Denny decided to go on one of his ritualistic walks; he trudged north up Fifth Avenue past Saint Patrick's, his parents' church, past all the expensive stores and prestigious businesses, and entered Central Park across from the Plaza Hotel. At the perimeter of thc park was the line of hansom cabs with the shaggy, heavy-legged horses. They had spilled their oats all over the street, and armies of robotically moving pigeons were feasting on their spillage. *There's been some spillage in my marriage,* Denny thought, and added irreverently: *My marriage runneth over with transgressions and oversights, with neglect and selfishness.*

He walked up the east walkway between the phalanxes of benches. Even though it was a pleasant, warm June day, the park was much quieter than usual. Yes, bike riders, in-line skaters, joggers, people strolling, but far fewer in number. It was more like a weekday than a Sunday. The people he passed seemed jittery, quieter than usual, more apprehensive, checking people out, checking out their surroundings. Why did that old man drop that big plastic bag into that trash barrel? Why . . . ?

Denny walked for hours, deliberately wearing himself out. When he was walking, his mind stopped thinking worrisome things as it concentrated on the walk itself, on his tired body. With his overall tiredness came numbness.

When he finally did get home around five, he got a call from Monny. Was the dinner still on for Tuesday? Definitely yes.

Fifteen minutes later it was a call from his father and mother. Denny's mother was saying, "I finally talked Dad into a colonoscopy. He's going in early in the morning. It's the first one he's had in ten years."

His father interjected, "Yeah, your mother likes the idea of some doctor sticking a light and a camera up my ass and into my bowels. She loves that."

"What'll they do?" Denny asked.

"They'll look for polyps. If they see any, they'll snip them off right then and there and send them out to be biopsied."

"Your Dad's been having blood show up in his stool. He's been having stomach pains and cramps."

"The day before I go in for the procedure I'm to have no solid food, a complete liquid diet, no red stuff. I drink this laxative gook, a whole gallon of it, and all day and night I'll be shitting my brains out."

His mother cracked, "Thank God you don't have much in the way of brains to evacuate."

"Evacuate—that's such a nice word for a damn dirty process; it's taking a dump, dear."

"Dad, I wish you all the best. Let's hope they don't find anything."

His father wanted to change the subject, shift gears away from himself. "Kiddo, the bomber, this Felix nut-case. Be careful. You're playing with dynamite in this one. For God's sake, don't be out front. Play it smart. Stay safe to enjoy your pension."

"I will, Dad."

"The boys you're helping out, the Feds, have a tendency to leave a guy like you out there alone, twisting in the wind—all by his lonesome, if you get my drift."

"I'm playing it safe, Dad, don't you worry. You take care of yourself and that cute little Irish bun of yours. Didn't Jake Sigman tell you once that you had the cutest little bun in all of Hell's Kitchen?"

"Yeah, how's that mink jacket of his?"

"I think he's got a thing for you."

"Yeah, ycah, wise guy. Do me a favor, Braveheart, and take it easy on the sauce. Even down here I hear stories once in a while. People are telling me that you've been going overboard with the drink. Listen to me, from a guy who's been there."

"I will."

"And tell old Mac that I'm pulling for him."

26

On Tuesday afternoon, June 18, at 5:45 P.M. Denny was waiting for Monica on the corner of West 47th and Broadway at the side entrance of Morgan Stanley. Diagonally across 47th Street was the Edison Hotel with its Rum House, one of Denny's regular watering holes. He had considered stopping in there for a quick confidence-building belt, but knew it would be suicidal that night.

Monny came out of the building. She had redone her makeup and made sure her light brown hair was looking its best. Monica was a very attractive woman. She was five foot six and had a trim body. She exercised regularly and watched her diet. Her mouth was wide, sensual. When she smiled as she did at this instant, men perked up and took notice.

"You look gorgeous," he exclaimed.

He hugged her and gave her a more-than-glancing kiss on the cheek. He stood looking at her. The old feelings pulsed through his body. This was the woman he loved, the woman he had married, and the woman he'd fight to hold onto. He knew that somehow he had to win her back. He could smell the usual scent she wore.

"Hell, Mon, this is a start, isn't it?"

"Sure, Den, it's a start. I must say that you've had a terrible week."

"The most traumatic of my life. Talk about stress and tension. But how about you? You're looking great, hon. Where would you like to eat?"

"How about right down the street—one of our favorites, Pierre au Tunnel?"

"Great."

"Tell me how everything is going."

He filled her in on the latest as they walked the short distance to the restaurant that had been in New York forever. In the restaurant the maitre d', Jean Jacques, greeted them like long lost beloved relatives and showed them to what used to be their regular table.

Monny ordered a glass of the house white wine, and Denny followed suit. He didn't dare order his signature martini. Monica smiled as he took a tiny, genteel sip of the wine. *Hey, maybe he would change. Marry the man today and change his ways tomorrow,* she thought. *Fat chance* popped into her mind very quickly.

Denny raised his glass in a toast. "Here's to us, babe." The glasses clinked. He took a tiny taste. *Watch your drinking, stop, on this of all nights.*

They covered all the basics in Monny's current life: her job, her commutes to Mineola, how it was living with her sister in the Long Island apartment, her sister's chances of getting back together with her husband which Monny rated as nil. Monny described her long walks along towns on the North Shore, her favorite walk around Roslyn Lake, her moviegoing, her gym workouts.

She pressed her husband about the investigation's status, whether they had any leads on Felix, Denny's brushes with death in the station and on the Queens raid, Mac's condition, and Terry's condition and the motivation for her shooting.

Denny answered each of her questions as well as he could. "Terry's making pretty good progress. Mac isn't. Barb says he responds a little bit but is basically in a semi-coma."

The dinner and the night went along pleasantly. They shared a Napoleon and each had a decaf espresso. Each had stuck to a single glass of wine. Denny left a little in his glass, a symbol of his newfound sobriety.

When they were again out on the street, Monny said she was going to walk to Penn Station to catch her LIRR train. Denny insisted on going with her. During the walk they were both quiet for long stretches. As they neared the station, Denny said, "Mon, this is from the heart. I need you and want you back. Please, Monny, I'm begging here."

"Den, when you have licked your drinking. When you know you have it beat, and only then, I'll come back."

"There isn't another guy, is there?"

She laughed. "How could there be another guy? I'm not a fast worker. You of all people should know that. Guaranteed, there's no one else. That I swear."

"Mon, on the drinking. I'm getting there. I know I am. I can feel it. I know now that I'm an alcoholic."

"When you've beaten it, you tell me. Den, I know you. You're like your father. When it got to be too much for him, he quit—in time, before he lost Mom. I know you're capable of doing the same, but until then, let's hold off."

"Mon, I'm getting there. I promise."

They hugged, and there was a long, lingering kiss. Monica almost gave in. It would have taken very little for her to turn around and walk back with Denny to their home and their bed. But she didn't. At this point there would only be a replay of the old problems. It was up to Denny; the ball was in his court, not hers. She turned and hurried for the escalator that would take her down to the LIRR trains.

Later Denny sat in a bar on Eighth Avenue he'd never

been in before with a vodka and tonic in front of him. He knew that if he drank a succession of vodka and tonics he could hold out longer, and he wouldn't be hit as hard. The booze would not hit him with the impact that it did halfway through the second vodka martini. That was deadly straight vodka. And Denny's staying power, his capacity with booze, was not that great.

This time he had asked for a glass of ice water as a backup. He was on his third glass of water. He wanted to kill his thirst so that he wouldn't be trying to quench it with the liquor. If he really swilled down the water, he'd drink less booze, and it would have less of an effect on him. He had pulled a big dish of pretzels in front of him. Tonight he would nurse the drink, take little sips, glom down munchies, and put away as much water as he could.

If he were drinking martinis, he knew from vast experience that midway through the second drink it would hit him. He'd start feeling woozy, disoriented. He almost always did. If he stopped at two martinis, he'd be all right, but lately he seldom stopped. It tasted so good. The buzz felt good. It loosened him up. His father, who had been a heavy drinker, really never had gotten out of hand with his drinking, but liked to quote Jackie Gleason: "I drink to get drunk."

In a restaurant, sometimes Denny was able to fill up on bread and put in his dinner order before the full effect of the martinis hit. While eating, he'd switch to a glass of wine.

Over the last year his drinking had taken control of him. Instead of him going for a drink, the drink was going for him. He had at times become an antisocial drinker rather than a social drinker, because often he'd go into a strange bar to drink to avoid people he knew, just as he was doing then and there. Ironically, his father had told him, "You'll never meet anyone worth knowing in a bar. You'll just meet barflies who have nothing better to do with their lives. Bar buddies are trash."

He wondered why his father spent so much time in bars and had so many good and loyal friends from his years spent in bars if he felt that the barflies weren't worth knowing. It was a father's way of discouraging his son from becoming an alcoholic while he, the father, still luxuriated in being a barfly himself.

Denny thought his Irish boozer's genes had kicked in, had taken over. His father had had trouble with booze from time to time, was a jolly drunk, never abusive or mean after having a few too many. He had never come home and abused his family when he was on the sauce. He was a loquacious drunk. Since moving to Florida, he hadn't drunk at all; Denny wondered if it wasn't the stress of the police work that had made him such a drinker. Where they lived in the city, it was very easy to be a bar person and then ease into becoming a seasoned boozer.

For the past year Denny had been drinking partly out of boredom. His job had been boring, his life boring. Had his marriage become boring? Had Monica become boring to him? No, not at all. The only way Monica could seem boring was to view her through a haze of alcohol. His drinking had affected their sex life.

His sexual desire for Monica was as strong as ever. Monica was bigger than life. She had many interests. She read everything, loved and read all kinds of books, read the *Times,* did the paper's crossword puzzles. She had a keen sense of humor. She and Denny were avid movie and theatergoers. Because the Broadway theater district was their neighborhood, they saw almost every show. Often they'd go on free passes that Denny would get through the wide array of theater people he knew.

Maybe it was depression. He'd seen his doctor. The doctor had prescribed some antidepressants, but the drugs had only made the situation worse. The side effects caused more trouble than the malady. Denny had stopped taking them.

Now, when the lives of hundreds of people might depend upon him, he had to straighten out. But nothing in this investigation was going his way. He desperately wanted to make love to Monny. Just hold her in bed. Just . . .

27

For Denny, the week following his dinner with Monny had rushed by: following up leads, reading the reports from overseas intelligence agencies, interviewing people. And then his personal obligations: the funerals and memorials to attend, and hospital visits to see Mac and Terry. Terry was progressing; she could soon be released. When she had been questioned about the shooting, she had little to add. She could hardly remember any details and had no recollection of saying *Zion*.

Mac's heart was giving out. Doctors spoke of the need for a heart transplant but were worried about his overall condition; other serious health problems made an operation too risky at present. He had started talking, but he was weak.

In a letter to Chris's parents Denny had tried to express his admiration for the young man—a man he hardly knew, but who had the courage to perform under fire.

Denny's drinking hadn't abated. It seemed like the only way he could relieve the stress of the job was by his nightly binges. It wasn't getting worse, but he wasn't cutting down much either.

The Grand Central bombing had happened on Tuesday, June 11. It was Friday, June 21, ten days after that devastating blow. Denny was up early, making coffee, watching TV, wandering around his apartment in his briefs. Maybe someday, he thought, things would start getting back to normal.

On West 46th Street going west beyond Restaurant Row toward the Hudson River, between Tenth and Eleventh Avenues amid run-down factory buildings and garages, is a parking lot protected by a high chain-link fence and razor wire. This is one of the staging areas for the thousands of stainless steel hot dog carts seen throughout the city. The vendors set up shop on street corners under umbrellas advertising Sabrett hot dogs or some other company's product.

Most sell hot dogs, but they sell every possible type of fast food, including foods like sausage and peppers, falafel, shish kabob, knishes, giant pretzels. Whatever can be cooked on a gas grill is peddled. After a cart is stationed, soda cans and bottles lined up on top of the steel casing announce all of the liquid refreshments available.

In the morning one can see men rolling or pulling these heavy carts uptown, downtown, and to the East Side. Hareem, one of Felix's men, pulled a cart from the staging lot and headed east on West 46th Street. Near the corner on Ninth Avenue he pushed his cart behind a van.

From the van's rear doors stepped Felix wearing a goatee and lightly tinted sunglasses. He wore a baseball cap and a jacket with the New York Yankees logo. Seleb climbed down from the driver's seat of the van. Felix and Seleb started loading boxes with soda logos into the cart's compartments, while Hareem emptied out the supplies he had just taken on at the cart depot. They worked very quickly. To passers-by a cart was being resupplied.

They finished with their work in very short order. Seleb reentered the van's front seat, and Hareem climbed in the back of the van. The van took off. Felix started to pull the heavy cart crosstown, heading for the East Side.

Felix started lugging his load through Restaurant Row between Ninth and Eighth Avenues. He plodded along, pulling the heavy steel cart that shone in the morning sunshine. He was approaching the canopy advertising La Ferme restaurant.

At a living room window in his second floor apartment above the restaurant, Denny was looking down on the street below. He had a mug of coffee in his hand, taking a moment to relax before he went into work. His hand still shook slightly from last night's drinking, but at least he hadn't gone overboard. He was staring at the street below with its litter from last night and a few puddles from an early morning shower.

He glanced at the man in the cap and baseball jacket as he pulled the cart along the street, just one of a constant stream of those who made their way heading east in the morning and west in the afternoon and early evening. To Denny, looking down from two high stories above the street, the man pulling the cart had been foreshortened by the distance. From Denny's perch he looked dwarfish, with a big upper body—a figure out of a multipeopled Brueghel painting with a slightly grotesque, gnarled body.

Denny could see the top of the man's cap from above. The cart hit a pothole, and the man was jounced by the impact. *Poor bastards,* Denny thought. *Pulling those heavy carts. Have to be strong to do that work. That's a grueling, brutal way to try to make a living.* He turned back to glance at the TV news, which was giving some kind of amber terrorist alert.

Felix continued on his mission, trying to avoid the trucks and cars that didn't slow down, just rushed by.

One passing truck splashed water onto his work pants. He cursed the driver and plodded on. At avenue crossings he waited for traffic lights to change, and then kept pulling the cart, his head down, continuing on, just another hardworking stiff in the cityscape.

He crossed Fifth Avenue. The various cart vendors were very jealous of their established territories, so he had selected a corner where a cart could be left temporarily. At the corner of Lexington and East 53rd, outside a busy subway stop in front of the Citicorp Building, he halted and glanced around him. No one was paying any attention. He opened a metal door and fiddled with some controls, then turned and strolled north, away from the cart. At East 54th he headed west. As he was crossing Park Avenue the whole area was rocked by an enormous explosion. The sounds of the blast reverberated through the canyons of the city.

Already jittery New Yorkers stopped in their tracks and looked around, not knowing what this new blast was. Fear, anxiety, and desperation were etched on the faces of many.

At the bomb site was an all-too-familiar Israeli sight: cars overturned, fires, smoke, blood, carnage, bodies blown apart, an overloaded bus with its side ripped open like a can, wailing, shouting, cries for help, dazed and concussed bystanders, empty shoes, twisted metal, and shredded pieces of a stainless steel hot dog cart. In no time sirens were screaming, response teams were hurrying to the scene, a city was again in chaos, a city was spinning out of control on the edge of an abyss.

28

On the night of the hot dog cart bombing massacre, the media were in a frenzy. Who did it? Was it the work of Felix? When could the authorities stop these horrible attacks? What the hell were they doing anyway? Was there a plan to protect New Yorkers? Were they being left out there on their own, twisting in the wind? What was developing was a feeling that New York was becoming like present-day Israel, or London during the World War II blitz.

That night, after spending a long, fruitless day investigating the explosion, Denny had downed two vodka and tonics with his steak dinner, but wasn't drunk by a long shot. He had just climbed the few steps up to the street from the entrance of Broadway Joe's on his home turf, West 46th. He stepped to the curb, looked to his right down the one-way street, saw no cars coming, and headed across.

When he got about ten feet into the street, the engine of a parked, darkened van facing him was suddenly gunned into action. The van barreled toward him at an alarming speed. The hurtling van roared toward him, aimed like a heedless juggernaut to plow into him. Denny reacted fast: he pivoted, bolted to the curbing he had just left, and dove across to the sidewalk like a baseball player sliding into home. A streetlight beside him prevented the van from coming after him. The van missed him by inches as it veered into the curb, then spun to the right and raced toward Eighth Avenue. At the corner the driver made a sharp left, barely missing a taxi as it raced north on Eighth Avenue.

Denny was sprawled on the sidewalk. Lenny Harrington, an acquaintance of Denny's who wrote for the *Daily News,* had just stepped out of Joe's and had seen the whole thing. He rushed to Denny's side.

"Jesus, Denny, are you hurt? That fucker tried to kill you. That was deliberate."

Denny stood up slowly. He moved his arms and legs, checked himself out. Only a few bruises and scrapes, thank God. His shoulder hurt, but he didn't think he had any broken bones.

"No damage that I can feel or see. That son of a bitch. I couldn't possibly get his plate number. Did you, Lenny?"

"No, I looked. I'm pretty sure he didn't have one. The guy was laying for you. I'm sure that this was a hit. What is it you know that would make people want to silence you? Someone wants you out of the way real bad."

"I can't think of any reasons for this."

In no time Denny was on *his* cell phone to the FBI and NYPD. He saw Harrington on his cell phone, calling in the story to the *News.*

He knew in his heart that it had been an attempt on his life. It was no accident or chance event by a drunken or crazed driver. It had all happened so fast that he couldn't ID the van or its driver. It was like the attempt on Terry's life.

That night Denny had to spend several hours being debriefed by police and FBI. By the time he got back to his flat he was too worn out to drink. He hit the sack and passed out.

The next morning Denny had several calls from the media, which he fended off. Before Denny's brush with death on West 46th, his name had been appearing in some news accounts, but it had not been featured like Terry's name. Because of a big breaking foreign news story, Denny's close call had not gotten much play, even in the *News,* which had broken the story under Harrington's byline.

His photograph had appeared a few times as one of the Grand Central bombing investigators. In one of his run-ins with Tony Tessitore, Tony had called him a headline grabber, a publicity hound.

News accounts lately had mentioned that he had alerted the FBI to Felix on the surveillance cameras, that he had been present when Terry had been shot. A few of the accounts mentioned that he was a native New Yorker who lived not too far from Grand Central. He was mentioned as someone who was involved in the ongoing investigation.

Denny was just as happy that he was not a lead player, because he didn't want to be haunted by the media. He was pleased that he was getting some recognition, but he wondered if the publicity hadn't made him a target, just as the publicity about Terry had probably made her one.

The following day experts confirmed that the explosives used in the hot dog cart blast and the Grand Central eruption were undoubtedly from the same source, confirmation that Felix was responsible for both atrocities.

29

It was nine in the morning on a Sunday, two days after the hot dog cart explosion and the attempt on Denny's life. Denny was sitting by a living room window. The telephone was ringing. On his hangover headache scale Denny had a three or four. Not too bad. It'd be gone way before noon.

He answered the phone.

A voice he knew all too well.

"I took a look at a map and at your address again, and I realized a coincidence. Not too long ago I was pulling a hot dog cart along Restaurant Row past your apartment. I was wondering if you happened to see me go by? Did you know that it was I?"

"No, I missed out. If I'd seen you, I'd of blown you off the face of the earth."

"Mon ami, but no. Our movie would have become a short subject. Can't let that happen."

"What do you want, Felix?"

"I wanted you to know that we did not shoot your wheelchair-bound friend Terry. Nor did we aim a vehicle at you, my friend."

"Why not? What do you care if I think you tried to kill Terry or me? Why would a little thing like that bother someone like you, a mass murderer who has no conscience at all?"

"Because we shouldn't be linked with petty, everyday American crimes that we did not commit. Because we want you to look closer to home for the people who are trying to silence you and Terry."

"But you do things much more horrible than trying to kill two cops. Are you developing a conscience after the mayhem you've caused? What you've done to innocent people?"

"In this war no one is innocent. We are all guilty. All are combatants in this struggle. This is modern twenty-first-century warfare. Your country and Israel kill hundreds of so-called innocent civilians and call it friendly fire or collateral damage. Put a man in uniform in a tank or in a plane, and he has a license to slaughter, to kill hundreds of these innocents. When a man or a woman in ordinary clothes plants a bomb or becomes a bomb, then he is a homicidal devil to you people. Such a stupid distinction. A death is a death no matter how it is inflicted. Men and women—yes, children—in and out of uniform, all are potential targets. Today everyone is a warrior in the struggle."

"Can we meet?"

"Avec moi? What possible use would that be? What purpose would it serve? This is not a personal battle between us two. You and I are small cogs in a huge piece of machinery that is lurching out of control. You are merely a law enforcement officer who is doing what he takes to be his duty, and I am the cog of vengeance and fear.

"No, this call is meant to alert you to the fact that you and your friend Teresa have other enemies. Perhaps your own government that seeks to control the world from its bunkers. Watch your ass, as they say. You're a threat to someone."

"Oh, Felix, before I forget—I've got a cell phone number for you. Call me at this number when you want to get in touch with me from now on. You'll be able to get me anywhere."

Denny gave him the new number.

"Sure, why not? Your minders gave it to you and put in some new gadget that they think will make it easier to trace. Uh uh, it won't work. They'll never learn. Assholes, one and all. Denny, how are you doing? Are you and your wife Monica still separated?"

"That's none of your business."

"And you still have a problem with your drinking?"

"I could ask you where you're getting all this crap, but I know you're picking it up from the scandal sheets."

"Exactly. Where did you think I was getting it? Do you think I'm in the flat across the street, peering in your window with binoculars?"

Denny instinctively looked across the street to the building directly opposite his. The curtains were suddenly pulled together in a third-floor window as he looked over there.

"Do you think I have a stakeout at your domicile, eh? No, that's your friends in the FBI who are keeping you under such close surveillance."

Denny looked over again and saw a blind move in another window. *Jesus, who needs enemies when you have friends like I have? I'd like to take my gun and fire a shot over there, just graze the side of the building. But then they'd get get me on reckless use of firearms.*

Dennis decided to change the subject. "Why are you so intent on these murders of innocents? Are you that dedicated?"

"Almost everything I've done in life, long before my present campaign has been a journey toward such missions of revenge and retaliation. You didn't grow up experiencing what I did, seeing the Palestinian refugee camps, living the way I had to live, seeing others suffer."

"But you know we'll get you."

"Of course, that's the point, isn't it? So far you people have been unable to thwart me. Don't blame me for being a survivor. I'm a survivor in spite of myself, because of your pitiful efforts. Perhaps I'm a survivor to spite you."

"We could talk about . . . "

"Not now. I'm bored. I'm busy. Bye, Den-Den."

Afterwards Denny called Wexler. He started to skate on thin ice when he asked, "What about Felix's accusation that forces closer to home—suggesting the FBI itself, the U.S. government—are trying to silence Terry and me?"

Wexler tried to make his remarks measured. "Dennis, he's just trying to keep the pot stirred. His call was really designed to sow doubts in your mind and get you worked up. He knows that you have a lot of friends in the media that you could talk to."

"I haven't talked to anyone in the media about this investigation. I can guarantee that."

"Denny, try to give your paranoia a rest. These labyrinthine plots, these conspiracies, are great in the movies, but they are pure bullshit in the everyday world you and I live in. I have no agenda other than trying to get this madman before he destroys the morale and the will of this city."

Denny was still steaming at the word *paranoia,* but he took another tack for the sake of his future and was soon off the phone with the Ferret. He turned on his television.

Lily Dish, New York's premiere gossip columnist, who had had a cameo role in a Woody Allen movie and was now on the Fox network, was buzzing about Felix the Cat. "He has nine lives. He's used up two of these, and if he isn't stopped, he'll have seven more acts of barbarism to inflict upon us.

"He'll either be captured, killed, or sacrifice his own life. Be on the lookout for this master of disguise, and we advise the public to be ready to help capture or kill him. Good riddance to bad—nay, putrid—rubbish."

This seemed to be a call for the public to resort to vigilantism. New Yorkers were in a vicious mood. They wanted blood. And Denny not only sympathized with them, he agreed with them.

"Are we going to let one man terrorize a whole city, hold us hostage, immobilize us? All of our security and law enforcement resources are on high alert. The stock market is tumbling. Felix's aim is to instill fear in us. He is transforming the Manhattan landscape, draining from its inhabitants their psychic energy, devastating their morale. Some put up a brave face, but many are hightailing it out. The city has been devastated."

Denny turned off her rantings and got ready to go out for his Sunday *Times* and bagel and coffee.

30

The week following Felix's second call and the attack on him, Denny thought of Wexler as a ferret chasing its own tail. At one meeting Wexler had used the expression "the urgent crowds out the necessary," and this made everyone wonder what was the necessary and what was the urgent. "Everyone has to get out there, get motivated, and try to ferret out information," he declaimed. Denny thought *Oh yeah, the Ferret is back in business.*

Then on Tuesday, June 25, a report came in that got everything spinning off in a new direction. In a Newark garage a black Honda Civic was discovered. The garage was behind an unoccupied house which was up for a bank estate sale. A real estate appraiser had discovered the car there and reported it to the Newark police not knowing that it was a hot car. The car's vehicle registration was that of the stolen car with the 18Z10N plate.

The car was transported to the FBI's big investigation and forensic garage on West 40th Street. Wexler sent in the Bureau's best team of three fingerprint experts. Every surface of the car was examined for prints. The owner's prints, of course, were everywhere. He had reported that he was the only driver, and that he did not transport anyone else in the car. The experts knew at once that whoever had used the car had worn gloves, but there was always the off chance that at some time the perp had taken off a glove to get a better grip on something in the car. The FBI fingerprint experts knew a few spots where prints might be harbored.

The three spent all day and night Tuesday examining every object and surface inside and outside the car. On Tuesday night one of the experts got lucky. Someone—it could have been a garage mechanic, a valet parker, a car wash employee, or the perp—had touched with an ungloved hand a metal rim next to the device for moving the driver's seat forward.

The print was of the first three fingers on the left hand; two impressions were full, one partial. The prints were sent for comparison to the Washington master database.

Denny and Frank were gathered in Wexler's office late Wednesday morning when the report came in. The prints matched those of Lou Carrino. His prints were on file; he had had a number of arrests over the years for minor offenses and had served time for an aggravated assault conviction. His brother Vinnie also had a rap sheet with a record of arrests for minor crimes around the North Shore of Long Island.

Denny roared, "Those sons of bitches. Like dogs gnawing a bone. Terry killing their brother kept bugging them. She did it in the line of duty, out of necessity; they could never see that."

Wexler called in his teams. He explained about the attack on Terry and Terry's justified killing of Frank Carrino. "I've just gotten in touch with the Glen Cove, Long Island, police department where the Carrinos live. Members of the department will be waiting for us. I'm sending three teams out there. Denny, you and Frank will go with Hastings and Morrow. Sadler will head a team of four, as will Jacobsen. Frank will be Agent in Charge for the mission.

"We can be pretty sure this guy was operating with his brother Vinnie. I'd be willing to bet it was the two brothers. They would both want to be in on it. Bear in mind that as far as we know this has nothing to do with the Felix terrorism investigation. It's a tragic coincidence that Terry's attack coincided with the bombings."

As Denny listened to Wexler, he thought that the Carrinos could be ruled out as his attackers. It seemed too far-fetched that they would make any linkage between himself and Terry unless possibly they had been stalking her and had seen him enter her apartment the night of their liaison. That seemed too far out in left field to him. What would be their grievance with him? No, he felt his attack had a different genesis, a more sinister one.

Later the teams met in the Glen Cove Police Department with Detective Lieutenant Bill Gonzalez, a heavy-set, late-thirties cop with a thin line of moustache. Long, errant brow hairs shaded his eyes.

"Your boys, Lou and Vinnie, just left in their boat a half hour ago from a launching ramp in Oyster Bay. They're out on the Sound, fishing.

"The three Carrino boys always wanted to be wise guys. Mob guys. They wanted to be connected. That's all that ever motivated them. They're small-time operators, once in a while providing the muscle for some real mob people. They were just lucky that they could learn to tie their shoes. The two younger brothers worshipped Frank, the one who was killed in Grand Central. He was the boss of a hopeless gang. Talk about the gang that couldn't shoot straight. He developed a bad drug problem and was headed for disaster when he finally bought it there in that train coach in your bailiwick.

"When they were kids, they were bullies. They grew up to be dysfunctional adults who couldn't connect in relationships with women. None of them ever got married. The women they met figured them out fast, and nobody wanted them. You've got to understand that the three of them had a collective IQ of 110. We are not talking about computer scientists here. These are very low-wattage hoods. The Glen Cove Schools Special Ed Department loved the whole Carrino clan; they've been their bread and butter for years.

"Two or three times a week Lou and Vinnie take their powerboat out from Oyster Bay and go fishing in the Sound off Bayville. They're out there for four, five, six hours in all kinds of weather. Too dumb to come in out of the rain, if you ask me.

"When you tell me that you've tied them to the Terry Kerrigan shooting, I know that's exactly what they'd do—try to avenge Frank's death. I'd say the best time to nail them is now when they're coming back on their boat from a day out fishing. They're worn out, they're dizzy from being out on the water, and they won't be ready for you."

Frank said, "I'd like your guys to be backup."

The agents set out in their cars for the boat launching ramp in Oyster Bay on Long Island Sound. Most of the agents were armed with automatic weapons. All wore flak vests. Jacobsen and his four men commandeered a Boston Whaler and headed out in the bay some distance from the ramp, where they could keep an eye on incoming boats and cover any escape route by water.

Frank, Denny, and Gonzalez took up a position behind a pickup truck. The other agents were stationed out of sight in and around the boat docks. One agent with a high-powered rifle and scope climbed the water tower, where he had a perfect view of everything on the ramp. On the perimeter the local police shooed away all members of the public.

It was a quiet day for boating along the Sound; overcast with rain threatening. Few boats were going out. The Glen Cove police were keeping watch on the Carrinos' boat off the Bayville Beach. The two Carrinos had anchored and were tossing down beers. They were listening to a baseball game on their portable radio.

The agents waited. Hours passed. Then the word came from the police: "They're heading in." Denny looked out into the harbor. Time went by slowly for the waiting agents. Then the Carrino boat, a twenty-one footer, was heading in, taking its time. Vinnie was at the wheel and Lou, the fatter one, sat in the stern; he looked as if he were asleep, his head bowed.

The boat came into the launching dock. When the bow was almost up out of the water, Vinnie at the helm yelled to Lou in the stern. Lou climbed over the side and started up the ramp, probably headed for their SUV. Vinnie remained at the wheel.

Frank didn't want to wait until Lou got to the vehicle. He raised his bullhorn. "Freeze, Carrinos, freeze. This is the FBI. We want to talk to you. Both of you. Raise your hands over your heads. Don't make any false moves. Repeat, raise your hands over your heads."

Jacobsen and his men in the Boston Whaler had eased in fifty feet behind the Carrino boat.

Lou stood motionless at the top of the ramp; he hadn't raised his hands. Just stood there, a vague look on his face, his hands slack at his sides. He didn't know what Vinnie was going to do, what the agents were going to do, what he should do.

The bullhorn roared again. "FBI. Raise your hands above your heads. Now. Do it. Hands above your heads."

Again no action from Lou. He didn't raise his hands. He just stood frozen in place. Suddenly Vinnie ducked down behind the boat's gunwales. The FBI sniper on the water tower had a clear shot of him through his scope.

Lieutenant Gonzalez with Frank and Denny whispered, "They're not buying it. They're probably packing."

Frank repeated his message. Instead of reaching his hands in the air, Lou, almost in a trance, very slowly started to make a gradual move with his right hand behind his back to his waistband.

Two cries went out. First to the Carrinos: "Freeze." Then agents to each other: "Duck, get down."

Denny had his gun sighted on Lou, but he did not fire because he couldn't yet see a weapon.

From their position on the motorboat the five agents could see Vinnie. He was crouched down behind the windscreen of the boat. He had a gun. They had a clear shot. One agent was in contact with Frank. Denny edged around to the tailgate of the pickup truck.

Everything was still in slow motion until Lou's hand reached behind his body. Then automatic fire erupted from everywhere. Lou's body was hit by scores of deadly missiles, any one of which would have killed him. Denny had not fired, hadn't needed to—his shots would have been grotesquely, obscenely redundant.

Now it was Vinnie's turn. He rose from his safe position, his gun drawn, firing wildly at the shore. The return fire was more than deadly from the shore positions, the sniper on the water tower, and from

Jacobsen's boat. His body was riven and shattered. Again Denny had felt it unnecessary for him to fire.

Later, on the drive back to Manhattan, Denny sat looking out at the plague of cars on the Long Island Expressway, thinking of the two FBI raids. In this one not a single agent had been scratched, but again the subjects of the raid had been wiped out. No interrogation, no testimony, no trial. A neat package.

A gun had been found in Lou's rear waistband. Probably one of the Carrino guns would match the bullets at Terry's shooting, but no one would be sure that Vinnie had been on Water Street with Lou that night. The odds were very strong that the two had acted together to avenge Frank's death.

In another way Denny was happy for Terry. This might end her constant fear of being targeted. But he thought the old saying used to be "The FBI always gets its man." But hadn't they taken pride in capturing most of their fugitives and bringing them to trial? Couldn't they have shot to wound instead of to kill and overkill? Now they seemed to be an execution squad, and, of course, he was one of them. He would gladly execute Felix, but he wondered if in its zeal the FBI wasn't losing a chance to get at the real truth, whatever that might be.

31

It was a very clear, warm, and humid night—Friday, July 12, a month after the Grand Central bombing. On West 44th Street the theaters had just let out their crowds. The mounted policemen, sitting atop their majestic glistening mahogany-colored horses, were in the street. Rows of taxis and limos were picking up passengers.

Felix the Cat was alone, driving north on Eighth Avenue in the gray stretch limo with the heavily tinted windows. The back of the limo was piled with cases, kegs, and a small detonating device. He made a right onto West 44th Street, where thousands of people were streaming from the theaters, heading for home, hotels, clubs, and restaurants. People were laughing, talking, feeling upbeat. Some were apprehensive, fearful, but after all, life had to go on. Wasn't that what the nation's leaders were advising?

The St. James on the south side of West 44th housed *The Producers,* still the biggest hit on Broadway. Across the street was The Majestic, with *The Phantom of the Opera* and further up the street was the Broadhurst, featuring Sondheim's *Into the Woods*. The Helen Hayes theater was temporarily dark.

A limo had just pulled out of the line of limos beyond the St. James Theater, and Felix edged his limo into the space. Anyone looking at him and comparing the man they saw to the widely circulated photos would have a difficult time matching the two. This man wore a chauffeur's cap, thick tinted glasses, shoulder-length hair, and a goatee. The nose was bigger and the eyebrows were much fuller.

Leaving the engine running, Felix stepped out of the car and walked to the front of the limo. He was holding a large placard over his head with the name *Delaney* on it. He cut across the street holding up his placard as if expecting a client. A policeman in front of the St. James, who was trying to facilitate the movement of traffic, blew his whistle and shouted to the pretend-chauffeur, telling him to stay with his vehicle.

Felix quickly blended with the crowd on the other side of the street, and the police officer lost sight of him. Felix hurried east on the north side of 44th Street, heading toward Broadway. His pace was fast, but he was not running. He was hustling along briskly, weaving in and out of the crowds.

Two mounted police on horseback had been distracted by some sort of commotion at the corner of Eighth Avenue. A man, Hareem, was yelling about some fight further down the avenue.

Felix turned into Shubert Alley and was halfway through when the enormous blast went off. The ground shook from an explosion of enormous force. Utter devastation took place at the impact point. Windows were knocked out in buildings on the street and on Eighth Avenue. The limo was ripped open and spewed shrapnel everywhere. Scores of human beings were obliterated. Carnage everywhere. The two policemen were on the ground, badly injured, bloodied. Their horses were still writhing, one in its last throes, the other in agony. A Jaguar sedan had been lifted off the street and flung into the crowd on the sidewalk. Felix was creating Hell on earth; he was the devil incarnate.

On the margins of the blast chaos and panic reigned.

Deafened, shocked, dazed, traumatized people reeled around. What had been well-dressed theater patrons were thrown to the ground, their clothes ripped and shredded, their faces dripping blood. Bits and pieces of theater programs floated in the air. On one woman's face were tiny shards of glass, blood, and tiny theater program bits. Again, vacant shoes were tossed around everywhere amid the wreckage.

When he heard the huge blast go off, Felix feigned his horrified expression and mimicked the looks and head-shaking of the people around him. Some bystanders started to rush toward 45th Street. He followed them at a fast pace.

At 45th he crossed and hurried through the enclosed driveway of the Marriott Marquis, which cut through the block to the next street, 46th. He was not running; he was endeavoring to fit in with others around him. There was a general rush to get as far from the bombed area as possible. Taxis were picking up and letting off passengers in the covered space in the Marquis drive through.

When he reached 46th Street Felix the Cat ducked around cars and sped across the street to the back entrance of the Edison Hotel, where a long hallway led through to the lobby. He hurried through the passageway to the lobby with its long registration desk, rushed past the Edison Café and into the street. He exited the Edison's main entrance on 47th Street.

When the blast went off, Denny was seated in the Rum House, a bar off the Edison Hotel lobby. The small lounge was one of his regular watering holes. Denny had heard the blast echoing through the canyons of big buildings, though he had no idea where it had gone off. He ran out into 47th Street. The theater crowd across the street at the Ethel Barrymore Theater, where *The Tale of the Allergist's Wife* was playing, were panicky, looking in all directions trying to figure out where the bomb had gone off. Traffic was badly snarled on the street.

As Felix exited on 47th Street, Denny saw him about twenty feet away, looking up and down the street. Their eyes locked for a few seconds. Beside the door on the sidewalk was a yellow Vespa motor scooter, which a cell member had parked earlier. Felix had the key to the scooter in his hand. He hurled himself on it, rolled the scooter to the curb, and started edging his way through traffic.

It took Denny a few seconds to process this information. A bomb had gone off. This broad-shouldered guy rushed out from the hotel and jumped on a motor scooter. Denny thought. *It could be. It was him! It was Felix the Cat.*

He ran after the scooter, which was having a difficult time threading its way through traffic. Denny had pulled out his lanyard with his badge and FBI ID. He shouted, "Police! Stop! Police! Stop!" He had his Walther out as he ran after Felix. He kept yelling and running. He couldn't risk a shot: too many pedestrians in the way, too many cars blocking his view.

At Broadway the motor scooter turned right, threading through traffic, zigzagging its way around vehicles as it attempted to head south in the direction of 42nd Street.

A motorcycle cop was heading south. Denny flagged him down. "The guy on the yellow Vespa is the bomber. Let me on, I'm FBI."

The cop didn't hesitate. Denny climbed behind the officer, and they started to give chase to the scooter.

The police motorcycle started lurching its way through the heavy traffic. The small scooter was a half block ahead, weaving its way through snarled traffic that was frozen in place. Horns were tooting madly. Sirens were coming from every direction. At the corner of 44th Denny saw the crowds and the smoke. Several vehicles were on fire, sending black plumes down the street and into the air.

At 42nd Street Felix made a sharp left turn and headed his scooter east toward Fifth Avenue. The motorcycle gave chase. Traffic on the wide street was moving somewhat faster. Pedestrians and motorists were dumbfounded by the mad chase going on between the Vespa and the motorcycle. At Sixth Avenue the lights were turning red, but the vehicles hurtled on.

Bryant Park, the small two-block-wide park behind the New York Public Library, was on their right. Felix jumped the curb. He tore between two kiosks, one selling Knorr soups and the other Starbucks coffee, bounced up over two sets of three concrete steps, and raced through the park. The motorcycle was in hot pursuit, the police driver gunning his engine, with Denny holding on for dear life behind him. The Vespa plowed ahead; at one point Denny got off a couple of shots, his gun ringing in the ear of the hapless cycle driver.

From the sidewalk Felix raced his Vespa down steps into the series of walkways that sectioned off the park. He threaded his way through benches and the small folding chairs that were distributed around the area. The homeless with their carts, some crack dealers, and a few unwitting tourists were sent hurtling out of the way.

Felix spun onto a graveled area leading across the

park. The motorcycle followed, but it entered the gravelly section at the wrong angle, tipped at a dangerous pitch. Suddenly the motorcycle skidded, swerved, and heaved over sideways. Gravel flew into the air. Little green slatted chairs were sent flying. Denny was thrown from his mount onto the grass some distance from the cycle. The driver was trapped under his bike as it careened and spun sideways into a concrete plinth. Denny's shoulder was bruised. He tried to get up. His legs gave way under him.

Felix glanced back, saw the accident's aftermath, smiled, and sped forward, driving his scooter up a few steps and onto another walkway. Male and female bums and the ravaged homeless scattered; a shopping cart full of plastic bags went in all directions. He drove the Vespa out onto West 40th Street. He reached Fifth Avenue where he headed south, barely missing a slow-moving bus.

Denny got to the motorcycle driver. He switched off the Harley's engine and tried to assess the driver's injuries. He was still breathing but was unconscious. With his cell phone Denny called 911. "Officer down. Critical. Bryant Park. Hurry. Officer down. Bryant Park."

The Vespa raced down Fifth Avenue, then cut west onto West 35th Street. Halfway up the deserted block Asa and Seleb were waiting with the van. The three of them lifted the Vespa into the back of the van and Asa took off. Felix and Seleb scrunched down in the back. Asa drove carefully, at a normal rate of speed. Eventually he crossed the Williamsburg Bridge and headed for the Brooklyn safe house. Felix had struck again, bringing death to many and fear to all.

32

Saturday, July 13, was a hectic day for law enforcement in the city. Denny had spent hours in the Vesey Street headquarters and had shuttled back and forth to the theater district bomb site on West 44th Street. Where had they gotten the limo? became question number one. It was quickly answered. A few hours earlier it had been stolen from a parking lot in the Bronx. The limo was a victim of Nine-Eleven, as it turned out. After that catastrophic event limo rentals had dropped off, and the limo had been mothballed there until business picked up. It was an unguarded lot. The thinking was that the thieves had brought along a spare battery in case it was needed.

No one had seen anything at the lot. As usual. The city was on a heightened state of alert, but at critical times either there were no witnesses or witnesses refused to come forward. Members of the public may have been frightened off; after all, if they had been reading their papers carefully, they knew that two police officers associated with the investigation, Terry and Denny, had been targeted and attempts had been made on their lives. Felix might have been responsible for the attempts, particularly the one on Denny, as a means of intimidating future witnesses.

The media were in an uproar. This had to be stopped. Felix had struck a third time with impunity. The bomb in the theater district had killed forty-one people and one hundred four had been wounded. His hot dog cart explosion had made people leery of even the most casual of street situations.

A moratorium had been placed on hot dog carts in the streets "until such time as a method can be found to insure that they have been properly inspected and supervised before their placement in the streets or before they are allowed to travel in city streets." Thousands of vendors and provisioners had been thrown into the ranks of the unemployed. But what could city officials do? The carts were latent and deadly mobile bombs. The attempt to use bomb-sniffing dogs had not worked; some dogs were too distracted by the food smells emanating from the carts, even though their handlers denied it.

Felix had targeted different segments of Manhattan life; he had disrupted rail transportation, normal street corner life, now theatergoing. He'd done what he'd set out to do: terrorized the population, demoralized the citizens, destabilized society, disrupted the economy. One reporter said, "He sure as hell has got our attention."

The headline writers were blaring that Felix the Cat had struck three times, that he might still have six lives left. A widespread search was going on, it was reported. But where were they supposed to search? The searchers were under fire. It was kill-the-messenger time, and law enforcement was coming under attack.

Saturday was a long, depressing day for Denny. He and Frank were following up a lead about an embedded sleeper cell that had acquired bomb-making skills. It proved to be bogus. He followed up the numbing day with a bout of drinking that ended with him in a stupor on his living room couch.

The next morning, Sunday, July 14, Denny rose at nine-thirty. The restaurant on the ground floor of his apartment building, La Ferme, was decorated for

Bastille Day. Denny walked to Eighth Avenue, bought his Sunday papers, changed his luck with a cinnamon raisin bagel, attended mass at Smoky Mary's, and returned home at one o'clock to plan the rest of his day. Wexler had told him to be ready for a Felix call.

Denny was reading the Sunday papers, which reported about a New York and a nation in an uproar. Felix had demoralized the city, and the rest of the country was trying to distance itself from the target city. Felix had struck three times with devastating results, but now there was talk of isolating the problem, preventing the spread of violence to the rest of the nation. Confining it to the now rotten Big Apple.

The FBI was under heavy fire. They were accused of being ineffective, bungling, irrelevant, useless. New York's governor had activated the state's full National Guard. They were even now being deployed throughout the city. Demands were being made in Congress that the president send in the U.S. Army to take over the city. Terrorist experts from Israel, Russia, and Great Britain were advising American law enforcement agencies. Heads would roll soon, it was said.

Denny was trying to nap in the early afternoon when his phone rang. It was his mother. "Denny, Dad told me not to tell you in advance, but I have to. He's asleep in the bedroom. He took a sleeping pill."

"Mom, at two-thirty in the afternoon? What's up?"

"Friday when Dad's biopsies came back, they weren't good. He told me not to tell you right away. He knows how much you have on your plate, but now . . . It's malignant—cancer in the colon. The surgeon says he is going to have to operate. They're going to be taking out a large section of his colon . . . oh, Denny . . . "

"Mom, they're doing what they have to do."

"It doesn't look good, but if the operation is successful, they may stave off the cancer for a few years. Dad may have to wear a colostomy bag."

"I've known guys who've worn those bags for years. These guys are still ticking. One guy told me that before the operation his diet was very limited. After, he could eat whatever he wanted. Mom, when's the operation?"

"This Tuesday morning."

"I'll be down there tomorrow to see Dad before he goes under, and I'll stay there for a few days after."

"He'll appreciate that, son. And it will be better for me to have you here. I know this is a bad time for you. These bombings are terrible. How is this case with Felix coming? People in the city are really upset about it. We've been getting calls from friends of ours. Aunt Grace said he's making everyone want to pull up stakes, pack up, and get out."

"We'll get him. He'll slip up somewhere, and we'll have him. Sooner rather than later."

"Your Dad's going to need bucking up. He loves you so much."

"I love both of you. I'll be there tomorrow. Don't get yourself all stressed out. We don't need two patients."

Denny called and explained the situation to Wexler, who quickly agreed with Denny's plan to see his father. "Just make sure your Felix cell phone is on at all times in case he calls. I'll plant a story in the press that you are in Florida visiting your ailing father to let him know you're out of town."

33

Monday morning, July 15, Denny was on Delta Flight 263 from LaGuardia to Fort Lauderdale. The plane landed on time at 4:20 P.M. He caught a cab at the Fort Lauderdale–Hollywood International Airport. It drove north on Federal Highway, U.S. 1, to his parents' home in the Coral Ridge section of the city. It was a sprawling Boca pink house that they had bought in 1985. Three bedrooms, three baths with a large pool in the back—a deep pool with a diving board.

Denny rang the bell. No answer. He walked to the side of the house and looked through the garage window. His father's car was there but not his mother's. Years ago they had given him a key so he used it to open the front door. The house was cool—no downright cold—from the air conditioning. His parents had gotten used to the cold clamminess that pervaded so many places in South Florida.

As he was drinking a glass of water in the kitchen, he looked out the window into the backyard with its bright Windex-colored pool, the sun's glare blindingly bright. Greenery and color everywhere: the fanning areca palms, the ixora with its red and pink blossoms, the terra-cotta pots with the blooming desert roses, the high ficus hedge for privacy, the purple and red bougainvillea by the corner fence, and the line of pony tails in pots next to the pool—all of it so familiar to Denny. Outside on an ixora branch a gecko was puffing out his chest into a blood-red fan that attracted mosquitoes and other flying insects. It was a jungle out there.

This had been an ideal spot for his parents to spend their retirement after the shabbiness and hectic pace of West 46th Street. He had spent many weekends and vacations there, many in later years with Monny, who loved the pool.

Two small wild green parrots were perched on a power wire that ran behind the house and between the house on the next street. They were squawking loudly. One raised one of his legs and looked like he was grooming it. More loud squawking. The jarring cackle of the parrots stopped for a few moments while they became airborne, but they soon began another series of shrill screams as they roosted in the broad fronds of a lofty royal palm several backyards away. From there they kept up their piercing chatter.

Denny was soon in another taxi, heading north again on Federal Highway to Holy Cross Hospital. An ancient female volunteer at the reception desk directed him to his father's room on the third floor.

When he came in the door of his father's room, his mother was sitting on the bed and his father was lying on it, still in his walking shorts and a loud Hawaiian shirt.

"Here's the conquering hero now," his father yelled. Denny gave them each hugs.

Denny said to his father, "You're looking chipper."

His father, Eamon, was sixty-one years old, deeply tanned, with a full head of white hair perfectly combed and arranged. Looking at his florid face there was no doubt he was an Irishman to the core. Denny's mother, Carole, was a trim, stylishly dressed sixty-three, not at all the dowdy policeman's spouse.

She had worked for years for the Shuberts and had been in charge of all theater box office sales when she retired. She always talked about the Shuberts like they were members of her family. Her makeup was perfectly applied; she looked far younger than her years. Both his parents cared about their appearance, and they worshipped each other.

Denny knew they were both vain about their looks. They made an attractive couple; both looked and sought to look younger than they were. It was something Denny was careful not to kid them about; it was just a fact of life, and he was proud of them for looking their best. When they walked into a restaurant arm in arm, they looked and acted like somebodies, maybe actors. Hey, that was the way they were, and they certainly were not selfish people. Living on Restaurant Row had made them conscious of their appearances and neighborhood celebrities.

Eamon said, "Well, I'm going under the knife on the morrow. Jeez, I hate that expression 'under the knife.'"

The three talked about the operation, the purging preparations he had gone through.

"For the last day and night I've been sitting on the toilet."

Soon their conversation turned to the situation in the city, the police and FBI efforts. They worried about the number killed, the injured, the family members affected. His mother was incensed by the bomb in the theater district, which threatened to derail the upcoming theatergoing season. She lamented that the marquees and facades of the theaters directly in the blast had been badly damaged.

"The Shuberts are devastated."

Denny and his mother tried to steer the conversation away from the operation, but it drifted back as his father said, "I haven't been in a hospital overnight as a patient since I was a kid." Several times Denny saw his father wince and close his eyes when he changed position on the bed. He could tell that he was in pain.

His mother said, "Monica called. She's coming down day after tomorrow, Wednesday." This was news to Denny. He had told Monny about his father's condition and his trip to Florida, but he hadn't expected her to come down to Florida; yet it was like her. She had always gotten along very well with his parents; there was a close bond there.

Denny and his mother stayed with Eamon for an hour, chatting and reminiscing, and then they left on his orders so that he could be prepped and get some rest.

At eight-thirty Carole and Denny left the hospital after having sandwiches in the hospital cafeteria. After Denny and his mother returned to the house, Denny started to get antsy. He asked his mother if she wanted anything at the stores. She couldn't think of anything.

He walked over to the Walgreen's on Northeast 26th Street a few blocks away and bought a 1.75-liter bottle of Popov's vodka and a two-liter bottle of diet tonic. That night Denny watched television with his mother in the Florida room. Several times he went out and made himself a drink. She noticed the drinking but said nothing. She had a rule: Don't talk to a drinker about his drinking while he's at it. Bad timing, she knew from experience.

At one point she said, "Your Dad has a lot of grit. He'll get through this, I know."

Denny wandered around the house. On one side of the large L-shaped living room and dining room was his parents' master bedroom and bath. On the other end of the house was a hallway leading to a bathroom, a guest bedroom, and a third bedroom, which had been converted into a den with tall bookcases, a computer, desk, and sofa bed and chairs.

On one wall was a large newspaper article framed under glass. It told how a New York City detective named Dennis Delaney had foiled a Manhattan jewelry store robbery by killing the two robbers after they had killed a security guard. He had been cited for his heroism.

Denny wandered out to the dinette near the vodka bottle. The cell phone in the left-hand pocket of his shorts started vibrating. A call from Felix. He went out into the back yard by the pool.

"Hello, is this Dennis the Menace. Felix the Cat here. We're both in the funny papers. Both kind of has-beens in the comics pages, aren't we?"

"Yes, what's happening? What's up?"

"I hear you're in Florida. I'm calling to find out how your dad is getting along."

"How do you know about that?"

"Don't you read the tabloids at all? They report on you every time you fart, dear boy. But even down there the media must be reporting on how fearful everyone in America is becoming. They're all afraid of their own shadows. What's next? Who's next?"

"Yes, so you're getting the results you want. So?"

"I want your superiors to hear this. I deal in fear. I sow fear. Just as your media and your government constantly do. Make the people fearful and afraid, and you can sell them anything. I sow fear, enlist fear, in the service of the greater goal. The goal is to make America butt out of Moslem concerns. Either butt out of the Israeli–Palestinian war or force a settlement. Stop proselytizing your Christianity and sanctimonious attitudes while selling the rest of the world your violent, sex-exploitive movies, videos, music, and games. Get your commercial crap out of our lives."

"Felix, you have no soul, no conscience."

"I have too much soul, too much of a burning conscience. It is your people who have no soul, no conscience, no commitment other than to destroy us."

Denny had memorized a line for one of these calls. He used it now.

"Felix, they say your enemy is someone whose story you haven't heard. Felix, tell me your story."

"Why am I doing this, you mean? All my life there's been a shadow lingering over me. I knew that I would never be anything more than a third rater living in a third-rate country. Look at what the U.S. has done for Israel. You have made it a first-rate prosperous country, militarily powerful with nuclear weapons. It is capable of wiping out the Arab world, the whole Muslim world too. But what is going to happen when Muslim countries get the bomb? Pakistan has it now. Iran may already have it."

"Felix, a priest described you to me as someone with such a shallow soul that you don't comprehend the full extent of the evil you possess and the great damage to human beings you are inflicting."

"Enough of this bullshit. We both need less bullshit and more sleep. Good night."

Denny stood looking at the yellow cell phone in his hand. What had he accomplished? Nothing. Unless they had been able to trace the call, which he doubted. A check with the field headquarters revealed that it was made from somewhere on the New Jersey Turnpike.

Early Tuesday morning Denny was sitting with his father in the hospital room. Irene—his dad's red-haired, pudgy, fortyish prep nurse—came in. She was the cheerful, upbeat type. "Soon you'll be getting your joy juice and flying to the moon, Mr. Delaney."

Eamon introduced his son. Irene joked, "Your dad thinks he's Frank Sinatra. The only trouble is he mixes all the songs' lyrics together. He starts with "Fly Me to the Moon" and you get a medley of ten other Sinatra standards all scrambled together. My dad was a Sinatra fan, too, but he kept the lyrics straight. Your dad has a better voice than Pop, but a rotten memory."

Eamon crooned, "Love and marriage, it's only a paper moon . . . "

When Irene stepped out of the room, Denny kissed his father on the forehead. Eamon said, "All these babes in the hospital keep giving me the eye, hitting on me. Your dad hasn't lost it yet, my boy."

Later Eamon Delaney was operated on. Denny and his mother stood watch in the waiting room for three hours. The doctor, Dr. Welch, a gray-haired pallid man, called them out into the hall. He addressed Denny's mother. "Carole, I've gotten to know you and Eamon quite well in the last few months. I'm going to be very straight and up-front with you.

"After we made the incisions and did some initial investigating, we found that his abdominal cavity . . . had been consumed by . . . the cancer was widespread. We did what we could, but basically we ended up taking out only a small section of colon. We felt that more invasive procedures would do more harm than good. We closed the incisions. There will be a period of healing. The colon will be useable in a short period. He'll be home in a few days unless there are complications.

"The prognosis is not salutary . . . not good. I think his oncologist is going to recommend chemotherapy or radiation or a combination of both. As a surgeon, I would not call for any further surgical procedures."

Denny was ravaged by the news. Later he could hear his mother on the phone with his Aunt Grace. "The doctor said . . . that Eamon's body is riddled with cancer. They took out what they could, but they sewed him back up because it was so widespread." It was strange the way laymen could lay it out in much more graphic terms than the doctors. They cut to the quick faster.

To him his mother said, "Den, it looks very bad. He's going to need us."

"Will they tell him?"

"No, not right away, but I'll tell him in a day or two. That's the deal we made years ago. We don't hold anything back. He was always honest about my health problems, my operations, so he'll expect the same from me. You know your father. He's a very strong guy, gutsy . . . oh-oh, wrong word, hon. Later he's going to be in a lot of pain. Doctor Welch said that eventually he might be on morphine."

"You know how Dad feels about that. He always said he wanted to go out in full control of his faculties. He'd stand the pain rather than be doped up."

"Dad will do what has to be done. I think he'll even do the chemo and radiation. After all, a lot of his friends have undergone it, and it seemed to work for some of them. He's going to be heartbroken when he loses that beautiful head of hair. Your father's very vain, you know."

Denny had to smile inwardly at this. His mother was equally vain, very careful about her appearance, her wardrobe of stylish clothes, her weight, which she constantly monitored.

But now the facade crumbled. She broke down for the first time during all of this. Denny hugged her; her tears brought on his tears as they clung to each other.

His parents were two strong people. He thought it was living in the pressure cooker of Manhattan's Hell's Kitchen that had steeled them. It worked the other way too. Some Manhattanites turned to mush because they were so pampered and spoiled. Not his parents. Tempered steel most of the time.

Tuesday night both Denny and his mother were at home most of the time while the father remained in the hospital, recuperating from the effects of the operation. Carole Delaney watched her son as he walked out to the kitchen several times to refill his glass. She said nothing, but it bothered her. Denny had never been much of a drinker. *We all have a lot on our minds,* she thought. His demons with the terrible bombings would be a huge burden to bear.

34

On Wednesday morning Denny picked up Monica at the Fort Lauderdale airport using his father's car. He told her the latest news about Eamon, filling her in on anything that had happened since they had talked the night before on the phone. When Monny got to Eamon's hospital bed, he brightened up. A good-looking woman always perked up his spirits. His hair was neatly combed, he had shaved, and he looked haler than she had expected.

Monny and Eamon had always gotten on very well. For him that day, she was what the doctor ordered. Denny just had to stand back and watch the two close friends interact. It was a love fest. Monny did not weep and wail; she was supportive, humorous, and upbeat. When Denny's mother appeared, again there was a close bonding between the two women.

The day went on, with trips back home, a restaurant lunch stop, consultations with nurses and doctors, tube insertions, the checking of vital signs, and all of the hospital impedimenta. After their final visit of the day Denny, Monny, and Carole went to the Old Florida Seafood House on Northeast 26th Street for a light supper. Denny ordered his and his father's favorite—crab cakes. Both women had white wine, but they noticed that Denny stuck determinedly to Diet Coke while he compensated by wolfing down the bread basket's three blueberry muffins. He craved a martini, but he knew when to play it cool.

At his parents' home that night Denny talked to

Wexler by phone. Afterwards he told his mother and Monny that he would have to go back the next afternoon, Thursday.

"I can always fly back down here later, but right now they're worried about the next attack. I've been talking to the bomber, Felix the Cat, on the phone. He's made contact with me. I'm going to ask both of you not to talk about this to anyone."

The two women were aghast at this revelation. His mother exclaimed, "For God's sake, how did he get in touch with you?"

Denny explained the situation to them without telling them any of the content of the calls.

When he was in Fort Lauderdale, he always took walks along the beach wave walk. He was jumpy and wanted some exercise. "I'd like to take a walk along the beach. How 'bout it, Mon, join me?"

"No, I'm beat. You go. I'll stay here and find out what Carole's been up to."

After Denny went out for his walk, Carole and Monny sat at the dinette table with cups of decaf. Carole started to talk about Denny.

"When Denny was growing up, he was going to right the world. He was a kind, unselfish kid. He worshipped his father, wanted to be like him. Some nights when he was a teenager, he'd check along 46th Street to see if his dad was drinking with his buddies in one of the restaurants or bars. Even then he was a detective doing his undercover work. It wasn't a case of him going into the bar and pulling at his father's coattails, begging, 'Oh, Father, dear Father, come home with me now and come home to Mother. Stop drinking the demon rum.'

"Eamon was a drinker, but he wasn't a drunk.

Eamon knew how to nurse his drinks. He was mainly a beer drinker. He could pace himself. He knew when to stop, but he loved the fellowship, the camaraderie, of the pubs. He knew everybody who worked on that street and a lot of the customers, the ad men, the theater people, the news and television people, the columnists, the Broadway crowd, actors, stagehands, playwrights. He was one of the crowd. Just as Denny is now, following in his father's footsteps.

"And Denny is his father's son. He'll always be a junior version of Eamon. You guys live in our apartment, he went into the same line of work, you work within walking distance of the flat the way I did."

She paused, took Monny's hand in hers. "Monny, whatever you do, stand by him."

"Oh, I intend to do that. But he's got to get that drinking under control."

Carole answered, "Oh, I can see that. I couldn't help but notice his drinking the last few nights. I've told Eamon about it."

Monica continued, "Lately Denny's become very much a high-maintenance husband, whereas before, he was a snap to live with, strictly low maintenance. I agree with you that in many ways he is selfless, but believe me, this drinking is selfishness at its worst. Drinking is all about self. Carole, you and I are social drinkers, but we never go overboard with it."

"Monny, in about the sixth year of our marriage, Eamon and I started to go through a tough spell. I thought he had a girlfriend on the side at the time, and he seemed to be overdoing his drinking, but he and I worked at it, straightened things out. As I say, it was touch and go for a while, but it worked out because we wanted it to work out. Living with a cop as you well know is tough. The hours, the temptations, the cop culture.

"Denny, like his father, is a keeper. You caught each other and you should stay together. You'll never find a husband who is as basically selfless as he is. If I know him, he'll get the drinking under control, and right himself—for your sake as well as his. He's his father all over again. Don't lose him."

"No, I know. I don't want to lose him. I'm going to fight to keep the marriage going, but right now we're going through some rough spots. We're going to work it out . . . I hope."

"Monny, I don't want to lose you in my life, especially not now when Eamon . . . "

They clung to each other.

Denny came back in at ten-thirty. He looked as if the walk had really been more of a jog; his tee shirt was soaked. At eleven his mother announced that she was going to bed. Denny knew that meant that she'd be in bed reading one of her mysteries until midnight. After she had kissed them goodnight, Denny turned to Monny. "I can sleep on the living room couch or on the one in the Florida room."

"Uh uh, I want us to sleep together in our room. Sleep with me in the same bed. We're husband and wife. We have to behave as such. Your mother has enough on her plate without seeing you on one of the couches."

"If I sleep in there, I can sleep in the chair or on the floor."

"Have you lost your hearing? No, Den, you're going to sleep in bed with me."

"But, hon, I won't be able to control myself, keep my hands off you. I'll want to make love to you."

"That's the general idea. Den, sometimes you can be very dense for a guy who is supposedly a smart cop. Get ready and come to bed. Take a shower. It's been a long time. We deserve each other."

When Denny came into the bedroom after the shower, his towel tied around him primly, his hair neatly combed, smelling of Listerine, Monny smiled. She undressed slowly, languidly. He could smell her scent, the fragrance he had bought her for special occasions. His eyes closed for a few seconds as he inhaled the poignant fragrance that he had known for so long.

Denny sat on the side of the bed while his wife took off her bra. Her breasts were full, the nipples erect. Denny was erect himself in short order. In bed on top of the comforter they held each other very closely, flesh pressed tightly against flesh.

They kissed fervently. Mouths open, tongues exploring and claiming in an act of mutual possession. Denny entered her slowly, tentatively. The motion of their lovemaking was slow and measured. Each wanted it to last as long as possible. Their clinging bodies knew each other, each aware of the other's needs. It was a sexual experience built on loving years. It was an evocative, lyrical coupling.

Soon Monny was above him. Her body was moving, arching in rhythm to his. Penetrations, sensations, joinings. Rhythms were altered to increase the deep pleasure.

For some minutes the sexual joining went on. Climaxes, the coming. These were two people who had not satisfied one another in months. Now they were seeking to make up for lost time, lost lovemaking. After a resting time, they made love again and continued with bouts of lovemaking through the night. No words were spoken, only sounds of pleasure and contentment.

35

The next day in the hospital Carole and Monny left Denny alone with Eamon, who had announced that he wanted to talk to his son alone.

Denny smoothed his father's forehead and carefully pushed back his hair. Eamon reached up and held his son's hand. "Kiddo, I'm going to try to lick this cancer business or at least give it a good run for the money. Bring on the chemo, the radiation, whatever. We'll see."

His father patted the bed beside him and Denny sat down. Oh-oh, here it comes, Denny thought.

"Right now I want to talk about you. Your mother told me how much you're drinking. She says the drinking is at the heart of your troubles with Monny. Den, that's not good. It almost destroyed me and our marriage. It was a very close call.

"Don't I know how the job gets to you. It sure as hell got to me. Burned me out. I used the liquor to ease the memories, to blot out the inhumanity, the ways that human beings can mistreat and destroy each other. Some of what we see we wouldn't dare tell our wives for fear they'd think those awful things have become part of us—which they have.

"We saw this stuff day after day; we blotted it out with the booze, but it's a fool's game. You get lulled into thinking you can handle it. But it handles you; it runs your life. You don't control it. It's the boss.

"For Christ's sake, son, take hold of your life, preserve and save your life. Don't throw it away. It's God's gift to you. It's my and your mother's gift to you, the most precious gift we had to give. Don't squander it on alcohol. Believe me, I went through the whole thing.

"I did it cold turkey. Stopped. Made myself stop. No AA, no nothing. My willpower. Me against it. Eamon Delaney, a man versus a thing, an addiction. A human being versus the booze. You can beat it. You have a real cop's tough mind. I know you, and I know you can beat it."

Denny spoke now, quietly. "Dad, I know you're right. In years past I did stop drinking for months at a time in order to lose weight. I still went to bars and didn't mind drinking mineral water, juice, or soda. Today in bars there are actually a number of people who are completely comfortable sitting there with their designer water. That wouldn't be an impediment to me. Times have changed from the times when it was the macho thing, you had to have an alcoholic drink. Today it's just as manly to sit with a bottle of water."

"Yeah, I know all that, kiddo. You're begging the question. When are you going to get your boozing under control?"

"Dad, very soon. Very soon."

His father insisted, "How do you conquer the booze? By force of will, that's how. Willpower. If I could will this cancer away, by God, you can be damn sure I'd do it."

That afternoon Denny was on his way back to Manhattan alone. He and Monny had made a good start toward reconciliation. The love was still there, the better-than-ever sex.

His dad would face the cancer head-on, and he knew that he'd have to do the same with the boozing—face it head-on before it licked him. And meanwhile there was Felix. Maybe they could terminate him as he risked his fourth life—which was just what Felix was doing as Denny's plane headed north.

36

Thursday, July 18, was a bright, clear, hopeful day. The plan was later described as involving relatively low-level technology, yet it was the most high-tech of all of Felix's missions so far. It was a scheme that demonstrated that no matter how tight security seemed, where there was a will there was a way.

A truck lettered with the name *The Smithsonian Institution* drove down a quiet street about ten blocks from the White House. The driver of the truck, wearing some type of uniform and cap, parked it beside a closed gas station lot and stepped down from the cab. He casually climbed into the passenger seat of a small white car. The car's driver took off at a normal rate of speed.

The sides of the truck were unusually high. People might think it was perhaps transporting some unusually large, bulky exhibits to the museum. The truck's top, which from above looked metallic, was actually made of a thin gray canvas the same color as the sides of the truck.

Inside the truck was a set of modified missile launchers that could fire rockets for several miles. Guidance equipment and remote control devices were set up to work in conjunction with the launchers.

In Maryland, miles from the parked truck, a beat-up van sat in the back of a diner parking lot. No one was in the front seat of the van. In the rear of the van sat Felix, looking intently at a laptop, the glow from the screen reflecting on his face. Another man, Seleb, sat across from him, holding a cell phone to his ear.

In Lafayette Park across from the White House, a woman in a business suit sat on a park bench, talking into a cell phone.

Seleb queried, "Ready?"

The woman replied, "Surely."

Seleb nodded to Felix, who was staring hypnotically at the screen. The screen had three boxes that could be activated. One said *Fire,* another *Abort,* and a third *Pause.* A kindergarten kid could have figured them out.

Felix put the cursor on the *Fire* box on the screen and pressed *Enter.* At the truck site there was a sudden loud crash and a whooshing sound. Smoke hovered over the top of the truck body. The whole truck shook as a rocket shot through its roof, shredding the canvas.

The rocket sailed over the low surrounding buildings and honed in on the roof of the main section of the White House. There was a large explosion and a burst of flame on the roof. The rocket had hit the Secret Service detail manning the anti-aircraft battery on the roof.

The detail members had seen the incoming rocket before it hit but had only seconds to react—unfortunately not enough time. Four men were obliterated in the blast. A huge hole had been torn in the roof of the Executive Mansion and reached down through two stories. The blast had started a fire in the structure; wood, tar, paint, and sheetrock were ablaze.

A dog was barking in the living quarters. A valet in an attic room had been thrown against a wall and was bleeding heavily. In the White House below there was general panic.

On the cell phone the woman in Lafayette Park said simply, "Yes."

Seleb nodded at Felix and gave him a thumbs-up. Felix, now wearing a slight grin of satisfaction, pressed the left mouse button and with the cursor on *Fire* pressed *Enter.*

Again the Smithsonian truck shook violently—a loud burst—and a second rocket sailed over the rooftops toward the Executive Mansion. The second missile exploded on the lawn in front of the East Wing. Two uniformed Secret Service officers were killed by the blast.

The first rocket launch had shaken loose some of the truck's equipment and moved the truck itself a few feet to the side.

At the Smithsonian truck's site passers-by and residents had seen the truck's erratic movements and the sound, the whoosh, and the rockets issuing from the truck bed. Calls were being made to 911 about the truck.

The woman in the park had risen from the bench and was mimicking the behavior of the excited and frightened onlookers around her. She seemed to be talking on the phone about this horrific attack on the nation's first building. On the phone she whispered, "The shoes were discounted by three hundred dollars."

Seleb repeated the message. Felix brought up another screen. He made an adjustment on a calibration dial. When the screen was fixed on three hundred feet north he pressed *Enter* and returned to his activation screen. There his cursor arrow was on *Fire.* Again he pressed *Enter.* The truck's last missile rose up in a fiery trajectory.

The missile hit a parking lot behind the White House. A dozen cars and vans were hit. Some were ripped open, some overturned, some exploded as their gas tanks ruptured. Three television crewmen were seriously wounded.

Seleb had already climbed into the driver's seat of the van, and he was pulling out of the restaurant parking lot. Felix had taken over the cell phone.

On the cell phone the woman said, "Prices are out of sight lately."

Seleb had the van rolling. It was heading north toward the Jersey Turnpike. In the back of the van Felix brought up another screen. This one had a representation of a digital clock. He moved the clock ahead twenty minutes and pressed Enter. Then he brought up a different screen. He brought his cursor to the word Detonate and pressed Enter.

In twenty minutes the Smithsonian truck would blow up from the explosives that had been well hidden under its cab. Felix hoped that law enforcement officers would be scrambling and swarming all over his booby-trapped rocket launching equipment when it detonated.

He yelled up to Seleb, "Hit the road, babe."

The van headed toward the bridge that would bring it eventually onto I–95, headed for New York.

In the park the woman had put away her cell phone. She along with others was staring at the heavy smoke coming from the White House roof. Flames reached up; black smoke spiraled above the Executive Mansion. In the distance scores of sirens could be heard. Hundreds of people were running from the grounds. It was panic.

A woman next to her cried out, "Oh my God! They'll get us all."

The woman in the suit put her hand to her face and cried out, "What's happening to our country?" She saw people hurrying away from the park and joined them.

She was glad she had not worn those spiked heels. She was soon in the subway, headed away from the city center.

In the back of the van Felix had switched to his modem connection and was on AOL. They had already started reporting the breaking news from the White House. "The heart of our nation has been struck. Missiles have rained down on the White House. The president and his family are safe. One of the president's beloved dogs is missing . . . "

37

As Denny emerged from the ramp at his gate into the Delta concourse at La Guardia Airport, he had a bad feeling as he saw groups of people clustered excitedly around the television sets mounted at each gate. Denny knew that this meant breaking news, big trouble. Something was up. He stopped at the closest screen. On CNN he could see flames and smoke coming from the roof of the White House.

He heard the anchor intoning, "The rockets have done damage to the White House. We have reports that the Secret Service and others are fighting the fire inside the president's quarters. The fire has been largely contained. People have been killed. The president and the first lady got out of the building safely, as did key members of the president's staff."

In the crowd he could hear the phrase repeated again and again: "Felix the Cat." One man growled, "That son of a bitch can hit us anywhere, anytime." Another yelled, "He's unstoppable. What a fuckin' excuse for a country this is." Another pleaded, "Bomb the hell out of them, the fucks. Nuke 'em."

Denny wondered who *them* referred to. People wanted to lash out at a known entity, a country. Felix wasn't a country, in all probability did not represent any country or even an international movement; he was an independent contractor intent on his own mission of causing death, destruction, and disruption. Most of all he was in the business of sowing fear in the American psyche while segments of the American media and certain demagogues in the government had made a goal of spreading this twenty-four/seven reign of fear in order to further their own ends.

The picture on the screen had shifted to a scene of desolation on a Washington street. A reporter said, "Here on this street are the remains of the truck from which the rockets were launched. Teams of police, ATF, FBI, and Secret Service agents arrived at this scene minutes after the rockets were fired. They were very careful not to approach the vehicle immediately.

"A D.C. mobile bomb squad robot was sent in to investigate the truck and its contents. The robot was going through the cab of the truck when a tremendous explosion erupted. The truck had either been booby-trapped or fitted with a timed explosive. Luckily all agents and law enforcement were well away from the truck when the bomb went off. You can see in these live pictures the desolation caused by the planted bomb. The mangled truck parts are lying all over this area."

Before getting in his taxi outside the terminal, Denny called Wexler on his cell phone. He told him where he was. "Denny, keep your Felix cell phone turned on at all times. You may get a call from him."

"This doesn't look like his work, does it?"

"Who the hell knows? Denny, get in here as soon as you can."

Denny headed directly for Vesey Street. As usual, the Third World cab driver had to be given directions for any destination other than Times Square.

Later Wexler sat with Denny and Frank. He was on the warpath. "Is it our guy? Has he moved his target area? Branched out? Could our guy have managed this? It's more sophisticated, more high-tech than his previous stuff. Denny, any ideas?"

"I can't say. I just have this feeling it's Felix. His cell has got to be bigger, more complex, than we thought. He's got guys who can mount rockets for him."

Wexler added, "His attacks are coming closer and closer together. He's stepping up his pace."

Denny replied, "Like a good action movie, a good screenplay—as the picture goes on, the pace picks up, actions trip over each other until the final climax. He's scripting this like an action movie. It's called the 'narrative velocity.' The pace gets so fast and furious the moviegoer leaves the theater at the end with his head still spinning."

"If he calls again, I want you to bait him. See if he can give you any piece of information that will definitely link him to the Washington attacks. Any proof at all."

That evening Denny was in Joe Allen's. Kevin had served him the usual before he had gotten a chance to change his order. He could always push it aside. Denny was using his fingers to figure out the number of hours without a drink. His father's words echoed in his mind. He had to get a handle on the booze.

He was distracted by the television set. The drink still stood untouched in front of him. After the White House attack the whole country was in an uproar—much more so than it had been over the New York attacks.

The nation's number one symbolic building had been desecrated. Only an attack on the Capitol building would be as distressing.

What the hell. Denny took a sip. It tasted so good. Why didn't Diet Coke taste this good?

"Kevin, give me a big backup of ice water, will you please, and an order of sweet potato fries." *I'll drink it, but I'll water it down and gobble munchies to deaden any effects.*

The Felix cell phone vibrated. Denny went outside on the street where there was a better signal. He stood under the canopy, shielding himself from a light drizzle.

"Well, good evening, *Denise.* I'm sorry, Dennis. Did you have a nice day? How was the weather when you left Florida? Where are you now? Are you in Joe Allen's, imbibing as usual?"

Denny wanted to keep Felix on the phone as long as possible.

"Felix, when you call me Denise—it's like Anthony Hopkins as Hannibal Lecter saying 'Hello, Clarice' to Jody Foster in *Silence of the Lambs.* Now there was a great flick."

"Overrated, in my humble opinion. Hopkins was good, Dennis, but they missed some great opportunities to make it more cinematic and less like a novel adaptation. I'm looking forward to *Red Dragon,* which is coming out in the fall. That should be really good. Great cast."

What bullshit, thought Denny. *Pretentious, pompous ass.*

"Oh, and in answer to your question, I'm not in Joe Allen's. I'm sitting on a park bench. How do you know about Joe Allen's?"

"Do you still not read the tabloids, me bucko? I am an assiduous reader of the tabs. I love the way you are stringing along this conversation so that they can trace the call. Cut to the chase, dearie."

"Felix, were you involved in the Washington business?"

"Wouldn't it be stupid of me to tell you that?"

"Were you?"

"I take it your superiors have asked you to get me to validate my participation in that Washington campaign? You people are so colossal in your stupidity and incompetence."

"An attack like that would be a feather in your cap, wouldn't it? Wouldn't it be a great scene to tell about when you pitched your movie?"

"Yes, anything that disrupts your country's single-minded destruction of the Islamic world and its culture would be worth doing. I'm going to hang up now, but here's a tidbit of information that wasn't in any of the media. Underneath the truck on its front axle, painted in big white strokes, were the numbers nine-one-one. I'm hoping that in the truck debris you'll find our calling card, that it wasn't destroyed in the blast. Good night, Dennis—enjoy the rest of this balmy night."

"Wait a sec . . . "

He was gone. Denny called Wexler on his other cell phone. "Denny, we got it. We'll be checking on that truck axle. What is the weather like where you are?"

"Drizzling."

"Same here. I'll check weather conditions in and around the Metro area. Wherever he was, it was apparently clear."

After he hung up Denny thought, *Wexler's grasping at straws, grasping at anything he can cling to, no matter how nebulous.*

The next day Wexler told Denny and Frank that he had a report from the Washington forensics team. After searching the debris again and dusting off the axle with light brushes, they found Felix's legend, nine-one-one.

Wexler yelled, "It's him. Grand Central, the hot dog cart, the limo in the theater, and now Washington."

Denny said, "Four lives down, five to go. I'm pretty sure he's back here in New York. This is his base of operations."

Later as a techie agent was reporting, Wexler asked him, "How does he escape tracing while he's talking to Denny on the phone?"

The agent asserted, "He's in a moving vehicle as he talks. We scramble to get fixes on him. He cuts off. The vehicle zigs and zags, ends up in another area. He talks again. Gives us almost enough time to triangulate and find him. He cuts off. And so on. Never long enough in one spot for us to get a fix on him. One time in the Bronx, one time in Queens, et cetera."

Before Denny left the field office that night, the Bureau released the information that they had evidence linking Felix to the White House attack. That night in Crab City, a bar–restaurant at Park Avenue South and East 19th Street, way out of his normal territory, Denny was reading the late edition of the *Post.* The headline read FELIX THE CAT: BRAZEN MASS MURDERER HITS D.C.

The story described Felix as "a man without scruples, an amoral bestial coward who killed civilians wantonly" and "a man with the shallowest of consciences."

Denny felt somehow that the diatribes written about Felix would not even faze him. He had programmed himself to kill as many innocents as possible until he was killed himself. He couldn't be goaded; he was on a mission and timetable of his own.

Denny wondered if it was tenable to talk about civilians in this kind of world. Was any adult in the world really innocent today? Almost everyone was a citizen of one country or another. In America, weren't the adults responsible for the policies of their government?

Felix and others of his ilk were dedicated to terrorizing, to disrupting daily life, to making ordinary people afraid and fearful. When enough people had been shaken up, policies would change. The leaders would start to shake in their boots. If the attacks continued, or even if there was the threat of them, the leaders might start to reexamine their policies.

One columnist had asked if when you hear the sound of a bomb going off, are you hearing the sound of a madman, plain and simple, or you are hearing the voice of a person with a cause? If you won't listen to my grievances, then listen to my bombs until you learn to listen to what I am saying.

Unless and until the supposed grievances and injustices stopped, the columnist went on, this Felix would spawn hundreds of Felixes in the years to come. They would multiply like fruit flies. Already, to fend off this Felix, the country was becoming more of a walled-off, fortress police state.

The claim heard was that the terrorists can never win. In Denny's mind was lodged the thought that they won by default in the first millisecond of their first bomb blast.

38

The week following the Washington assault was a blur. The next week was even more so. It seemed the less Denny had to do or the less significant the work was, the more his drinking picked up at night, despite his best efforts to quit or at least cut down. One day Frank and he were sent to Newark to investigate the possibility of a sleeper cell of Yemenis; another day it was a tip about a terrorist support unit in Yonkers that had financial ties to the Saudis; still another day they were chasing down a large money transfer from a Saudi Arabian fundamentalist offshoot to a splinter cell operating out of the Kuwaiti legation of the United Nations in Manhattan. A narco-terrorist weapons-for-narcotics swap between a group in Singapore and Colombian drug lords seemed to be overwhelming everyone's time and effort.

At the end of the week Denny was frustrated; the investigators were all dispirited, desperate. Denny groaned, "This is all bullshit, Frank. We're down to the dregs, following up on crap leads. This is work for an American domestic spy outfit with international input like MI 5 in Britain, an outfit that we don't have in the States. We're spinning our wheels here, and Felix the Cat is plotting his next move. I'm a cop, and I can intuitively feel what a crook is up to. We're not going about this the right way."

Saturday, August 3, sixteen days after the Washington attack, Denny had a Saturday off. He sat in his apartment, sipping his coffee and nursing a mild hangover. His father seemed to be doing as well as could be expected on the chemo regimen so far, but Mac was not in good shape. Denny had a long talk with Big Barb; she was not optimistic. Terry was back working at Grand Central and also working even harder on her therapy. She now had a detail of bodyguards wherever she went.

Denny decided to go out for one of his Saturday morning walks. At its western edge, Denny's street ended up at the Hudson River. A favorite walk would lead him beside the Hudson River heading south. He and his father had taken these walks many times, and now he liked to reenact the youthful treks of his childhood. Denny thought that if he and Monny were able to get back together, they'd have to start a family. *Before I die, I'd like to have a son or a daughter that I could mentor and take on city walks.*

As he emerged from his building, he noticed how grungy the street looked during the early hours. He headed west on 46th toward the river. A Salvation Army convention was going on in the city. He passed groups of the Army soldiers heading up and down the street. Further on he passed his local barber shop, one of the old-fashioned kind with its lighted barber pole stripes spiraling endlessly toward the top of the cylinder. He waved at Gerry the barber.

He saw a long line of people awaiting distribution from the Saturday morning food and necessities pantry at the community building of St. Clement's. In line were interesting-looking city types, all races and all ages, standing and chatting as they waited with their two-wheel shopping carts. Manhattan street life was always a treat to Denny. Always something going on. All kinds of people interacting, sometimes acting up, but always interesting.

As he crossed over 10th Avenue the area became more commercial, uglier, and duller for walking. He passed one of the marshalling parking lots where the hot dog carts started the day. Now policemen were checking the carts and drivers' IDs when they left the yard.

He was at the river. Ahead was the *Intrepid,* a 1942 U.S. Navy carrier that was now a floating museum, the flight deck loaded with all sorts of historic planes. To his right was Pier 88 where Celebrity Cruises' *Zenith* was docked. It was taking on passengers for its weekly run to Bermuda. It had a black hull and the huge X painted on its superstructure, the logo of the Celebrity line.

Denny started walking south, where a very good walking, jogging, and bike path ran along the river. As he walked along the attractive paved pathway, he passed joggers, bicyclists, rollerbladers, and a few other pedestrians. Not many were taking advantage of this warm August day.

One man on a foot scooter had his little boy aboard while he pushed with one foot and stood on the scooter with the other. Every once in a while they would coast, all four feet on the running board. Denny watched father and son laughing, enjoying themselves, bonding just as he and his father had done in the past. He heard the boy say *Daddy,* and he felt happy for them but sad thinking about his father perhaps facing death soon.

At 42nd Street people were lined up to take the Circle Line tour boats around Manhattan Island. He passed hundreds of disintegrating pilings, reminders of a once thriving port. Ducks and Canada geese were scavenging around the rotting pilings—eerie dark fingers reaching up out of the murky water. A flotilla of brightly colored kayaks went zipping along, propelled by rubber-suited enthusiasts.

Denny, always a creature of habit, took a tiny detour and walked out on Pier 63 opposite West 23rd Street just north of the Chelsea Piers complex. Denny, a frequent visitor to the pier, was greeted warmly by Judy, a sixtyish pier resident in her bathrobe and flip flops, who was watering potted plants scattered around the pier. The old pier had a funky Key West Conch feel to it, and the people who lived on the boats tied up there, or who plied their hobbies there were all characters of one sort or another. They had carved out a little republic for themselves in the middle of Manhattan.

Judy called out, "Hi, Dennis. I see your name in the papers all the time. How's it coming with that Felix scumbag?"

"We're getting there, Jude."

"When you catch him give him a good kick in the you-know-where for me."

On the south side of the pier was the old retired fireboat, the 130 foot *John J. Harvey.* It was owned and kept up by a group of men who loved working on the boat. Some retired firemen volunteered as crew. A group of the old-timers was readying the ship for a sail, loading food supplies and cases of beer. Some women, the wives of the retirees probably, were getting away from the hot sun under a tarp awning that had been strung up across part of the deck. One man was polishing the brass cannons, which would be shooting off water during the cruise. Three of the red-faced men knew Dennis and waved to him.

"Denny, come on out for a sail."

"How's your dad doing? Give him our best."

"You get that Fuckface Felix, for us."

Next Denny walked through the lower level of the Chelsea Piers, a sports complex occupying several piers. Lots of kids were skateboarding, scooting up and down steep ramps, practicing their arcane maneuvers. Other kids in some of the complex's buildings were playing soccer, performing gymnastics, and playing other sports. It was a perfect setting for yuppie parents and their offspring.

Huge high nets had been put up on a pier jutting out into the river, all for the silly desire of people to drive a little golf ball out as far into space as far as they could. A few golfers were at the driving range positions; on the range on the netted pier in front of them were an unbelievable number of golf balls. The profligate, wasteful American spirit: thousands of golf balls dotting the pier's artificial turf, satisfying the whims of golf fanatics.

As Denny headed past 14th Street, he became aware of what wasn't there further south. That huge, blank gaping sky space was the absence of the Twin Towers. He still couldn't believe that those two gleaming towers weren't there anymore. By now they would have dominated his field of vision. Imposing, majestic, huge downtown skyscrapers that proclaimed the power and preeminence of a mighty nation.

They're gone, along with a lot of other things in our lives, Denny thought. Denny's mind was racing with thoughts he dared not say, not as an FBI man at any rate. *Many in the world loathe us, and we neglect and denigrate them. The chickens are coming home to roost. And coming HOME, not just assaults on American assets abroad. Something like three percent of the world's population using up a third of the world's nonrenewable resources. An SUV culture. Wasting fossil fuels, electricity, water, food. Wasting resources for self-indulgent lives.*

As he reached Christopher Street, he wondered how

far south he should go. It was getting toward noon. He was hungry; he needed lunch, and he also wanted to walk back. If he walked too far south, he'd be unable to walk back and would end up taking the subway. There was another reason: he didn't want to venture near Ground Zero just then. It would depress him.

He crossed West Street and headed east on Christopher Street. It looked much better in daylight, and this street—which swarmed at night with all manner of gays, from drag queens to leatherette queens, from the buffed to the less than muscular—was in the daytime almost too mundane, with ordinary people in a workaday place, with folks bringing their clothes into cleaners, walking their dogs, shopping for food, and with other signs of everyday, prosaic life.

At the corner of Waverly and Sixth Avenue he stopped in one of his old standbys, the Waverly, a small diner–luncheonette–coffee shop, a Greek-run place with a tiny kitchen and one of those enormous menus.

He sat at the counter across from the orange juice machine. The counterman stuck small whole oranges, including their skins mottled with black blotches, into the top of the machine, and out of the bottom fresh, delicious, pulpy orange juice streamed into pitchers. Three full pitchers were lined up, but were soon emptied by the demands of the crowd.

The place was full of yuppies and college students having a cheap brunch. Lots of couples. He stole secret glances at some of the couples because they reminded him of Monny and himself. He and Monny had sometimes come in here after a long walk along the Hudson.

One twenty-year-old college girl gave Denny a big smile—a come-on, he thought, a come-hither. He had to look away quickly. Denny was a man to whom women were naturally attracted, a hunk. He had played the field before Monny and had no desire to do it again. Though their interest massaged his ego, he let the advances slide.

Why couldn't he win back Monny? Why couldn't she see what the other women saw? Maybe she did see, but she also saw the dark side. Few people wanted to live with an alcoholic and watch him sink lower and lower as time went on.

He ordered a large OJ, a hamburger, and a cup of decaf. Sitting next to him, an old Irish woman with very thin silvery hair, dressed in a housedress and bunny slippers, ordered soft-boiled eggs. Denny could tell that she was living on a limited budget in a rent-controlled apartment. "Did they get that Felix bastard yet?" she asked the counterman and, by extension, Denny. The counterman was too inundated to answer.

"No," Denny answered softly, "he's still on the loose, unfortunately."

"They'll get him, dearie. I've got two cats, and believe me I know, cats ain't as smart as they think they are. Not by a long shot."

39

Denny left the coffee shop and retraced his steps, west on Christopher and up the walkway beside the Hudson, heading north. He tramped along, making good time. When he was back to his starting point at the *Intrepid,* he looked at his watch; it was three o'clock. He walked beyond the carrier and decided to look in the passenger terminal where Celebrity Cruises' *Zenith* was berthed. In the summertime it left on Saturdays for its seven-day cruises to Bermuda. He went to the upper level of the terminal, where he could see the gleaming black-hulled ship to his left and the river spread out before him. Denny stepped onto a small outside balcony that faced the pier and the river.

Most passengers were already on board. The decks were full of expectant cruisers. On the top pool deck some were in bathing suits. Passengers were hitting the pool before the ship sailed at five. Across the water Denny could hear the calypso music of the steel drum band playing on the pool deck, serenading passengers for the bon voyage party. Waiters circulated among the crowd, pushing tropical drinks topped with tiny paper parasols. A few years back he and Monny had taken this same cruise and loved it.

Fairly recently, as a security measure, the U.S. Coast Guard had decreed the mounting of heavy machine gun emplacements on the bow and stern of major cruise ships hitting American ports. They were manned by a combination of crewmen and Coast Guardsmen. It was like World War II, when merchant ships had to be armed to protect themselves from the enemy U-boats.

Denny looked out into the river. Three small boats were pulling patrol around the cruise ship. One patrol boat was one of the ship's orange-topped tenders, labeled with a huge *Security* sign. The other two were U.S Coast Guard Boston Whalers, each with two powerful outboards. A heavy machine gun had been mounted on the front of each boat. The Coast Guard boats had a crew of four outfitted with orange lifejackets, with the helmsman seated on a high seat amidships. The boats moved around the large liner like small water bugs circling a huge floating log. Blue lights flashed from the sterns of the whalers. The men were all well-armed. *Boring work* thought Denny, *but at least they were out on the water getting sun and fresh air.*

Oh-oh, activity out there in the river. A sleek cigarette boat with its long bow was speeding south, heading downstream toward the passenger piers. Denny thought, *He's really tearing along.* He saw the two small Coast Guard patrol boats suddenly perk up and start to get up speed, forming a blocking action, one coming from the *Zenith's* stern, one moving out from around her bow. Between the two passenger piers the room for maneuvering was limited. The cigarette boat now seemed headed right for the *Zenith.* It started to zigzag as it came closer to the two Coast Guard boats.

Suddenly, from one of the Coast Guard boats, a Guardsman got off several warning rounds of machine gun fire in the direction of the cigarette boat. *Hey, this is serious stuff.* The *Zenith's* decks were now alive with passengers gaping as they began to realize what might be happening. Denny himself was mesmerized by the scene being played out on the river setting in front of him. *What if this is just some hot-dogging wild boater, a waterway reckless driver, out for a Saturday blast? Supposing he's a drunken nut. It doesn't matter. The Guardsmen are doing the right thing—this nut is threatening the safety of the ship and its thousands of crew and passengers.*

Now the gun on the bow of the *Zenith* started to open fire, zeroing in on the advancing speedboat. At first they were just trying to warn it off, but then as it steadily advanced, it became a desperate attempt to shoot it out of the water. The guns in both Coast Guard boats were chattering away. By now it was an all-out effort to stop this boat bearing down on them. Machine gun fire erupted from everywhere. Two New York City police boats were racing upstream toward the scene now.

As the cigarette boat came closer, one of the Coast Guard boats headed directly toward it, trying to head it off. The other one was in a blocking position in case the charging boat tried to sweep around the advance, offensive Coast Guard boat. Would the cigarette boat veer away? By this time any ordinary, sane boater would have turned away. This was either a madman or a suicidal terrorist. In an instant a vision of Felix at the helm of that wild boat flashed across Denny's mind.

All at once the cigarette boat veered to the right. Denny could see a single figure huddled at the wheel. All Denny could think of was that this was Felix the Cat on his last fateful suicide mission. The Coast Guard vessels continued firing. *That helmsman in the lead boat is good.* Suddenly the cigarette boat did a U-turn and headed for the middle of the river. One Coast Guard speedboat and a police boat were closing in. It looked like they were all on a collision course; the three boats seemed to be converging on one another. From where he stood Denny saw a tiny figure leap free of the cigarette boat, hurling himself into the choppy river with its wild convergence of stirred up wakes.

Suddenly the three boats collided head-on with an enormous, all-consuming explosion. That part of the river was covered with an ominous fireball, and thick black smoke rose from the river's surface. Obviously the cigarette boat had been packed with explosives. Denny tried to make out what was going on at surface level, but couldn't see through the black wall of hundreds of feet of smoke that clung to the river's surface. It was impossible to see what remained. The surviving Coast Guard boat and the other police boat were circling the site, trying to edge in closer, but the smoke was too dense.

Helicopters were hovering overhead. A fire boat had come upriver toward the blast site. Huge waves created by the explosion were kicking up a fierce wake at the piers and around the cruise ship. The passengers lining the decks of the *Zenith* now had some terrible sights to share from their camcorders and still cameras. "The day we sailed to Bermuda and all hell broke loose." "How a cruise to paradise almost turned into the cruise to hell." He could imagine some passengers leaving the ship, and he doubted it would sail that day.

The smoke was being blown away. Denny could see that the surviving Coast Guard and police boats had maneuvered into the center of the wreckage. He could see men pulling a torso from the water, but even at this distance he could tell that it was not a living form. Bits and pieces of debris and wreckage were bobbing all about.

Denny's eyes searched everywhere on the adjacent river, looking for signs of a living form swimming or floating away. There was so much stuff floating around that it was hard to tell. A few of the larger pieces near the blast were still smoking. An overturned and sinking hull was the largest piece left afloat. For a long time Denny stood there watching the operation. He could see that it was not a rescue, but a body recovery operation. At least Felix or whoever it was in the cigarette boat had been thwarted. That boat had been loaded to gunwales with explosives.

Now there were more police boats, fire boats, helicopters circling overhead. He recognized one of the copters as an FBI chopper. Some of the copters had fanned out and were searching the river and shore for any signs of the cigarette boat driver. Denny could see no signs of life in the stream. The current was swift moving and could carry a body downstream fairly quickly.

Denny said a prayer: *God, let me be where this guy finally cashes in his chips, and let me be there to speed this bastard on his way.* In the initial blast in Grand Central he had come close to actually being a victim; Felix had passed his apartment on his way to plant the hot dog cart bomb; the theater bombing had been only a few blocks away, and he had chased Felix through the streets; now this attempt on the river, a few blocks west of his home. The only one that had been out of Denny's frame of reference had been the Washington White House attack. He realized that some force had ordained that he was destined to be a witness to this man's mad attacks. He vowed that he would be there at this madman's final scene.

40

Denny was in the FBI field office until ten o'clock on the night of the Zenith attack. The office was a madhouse; everyone was taking for granted that Felix was the perpetrator. Thousands of law enforcement officers were out scouring the Jersey and Manhattan banks of the Hudson for signs of him. No luck. Felix or whoever was piloting the boat may have been killed in the explosion's aftermath or drowned. All sorts of reports were coming in, but they seemed not to bear fruit. The river might quickly take a body out to sea. Divers were at the scene of the collision, but the current prevented much of a search of the riverbed.

Denny said to Frank and Wexler, "I think the *Zenith* attack was a stunt, not really meant to succeed, but meant to prove how vulnerable we are. I think Felix thought it would succeed only if he got incredibly lucky. He meant to stick it to us. Meanwhile he accomplished what he wanted. Thousands of bookings cancelled on cruise ships. The industry headed for a nose dive. The *Zenith* and other cruise ships tied up at their docks."

At eleven that night Denny was ensconced in Joe Allen's with a martini and a big glass of ice water to dilute it. *Mustn't overdo it tonight,* he kept urging himself. He was captivated by the TV. The *Zenith* attack had been caught on videotape by scores of camcorder enthusiasts from the decks of the ship. A wide selection of these videos was being shown, with the moment of impact of the boats repeated over and over again.

The explosion and fireball would become another part of recent history. Another piece of scar tissue, another vision embedded in the cerebral cortex, imagery branded into the brains of billions, to be replayed over and over again in dreams and nightmares.

Jake Sigman, the character actor, sauntered in with a busty brunette showgirl on his arm. He greeted Denny, and they sat down next to him at the bar, waiting for their table to be ready. Jake was drinking Campari and soda. Denny thought that it would be a safe drink for him, might wean him away from the high-test hooch, except for the fact that he couldn't stand the taste of it.

When Denny saw that Jake's date was in conversation with Kevin about theater minutiae, he asked Jake, "No blonde tonight? How come?"

"Den, I don't know why, but blondes are getting to be in short supply."

"Jakey, do you still have that mink jacket? My dad is always asking about it."

"Tell Eamon that I had to donate it to Broadway Cares. The animal activists were getting on my case. I couldn't afford to have someone spray me with dog and cat piss. I bought a synthetic one, but it ain't the same. No cachet to wearing manufactured shit."

Denny smiled.

"Dennis, what about that thing with the *Zenith* today? Was that the Cat again?"

Denny sighed. He really didn't want to talk about the job. It was like asking a vacationing doctor about your ailments when he was on a cruise. "Nothing for sure yet."

"Denny, don't you find that this whole thing is ironic?"

"What's ironic about it?" He noticed that Sigman was slurring; he had raised a few that night.

"I'm quoting someone or other when I say that the price we pay for not understanding paradox is irony."

"I don't get it. I'm just a big dumb flatfoot."

"That's the last thing you are, my boy."

"How do you define a paradox?"

"When people profess to a belief in a monotheistic religion yet they adhere to the doctrine of the Trinity, that's a paradox. A paradox seems to defy common sense."

"What's ironic about the Felix mess?"

"Millions of eyes are looking for a weight lifter, and this guy walks around with no one seeing him. That's because any actor knows that people only see what they think they see. Alec Guinness, the man, could disappear into the character he created. When I met him offstage, he seemed like a nobody; that was his acting genius."

"But Jake, it's a tragic situation—a world in which a madman with a bomb can disrupt and destroy our ordered life."

"For a cause."

"What cause?"

"To prove that this country of ours is not an invincible fortress, nor should it be. There should be consequences for our actions. That's what other countries had to learn long ago. Felix's cause, his message—their message—is to prove to us that we cannot go all over the world meddling, trying to reorder other people's priorities, trying to destabilize and topple governments we don't like, disrupting other people's lives, while thinking that non-Americans are inherently inferior people, that their lives don't count. Who appointed us judge, jury, and executioner?

"Because we crave oil we favor one group of people at the expense of another. These attacks of terrorism are partly about the U.S.'s insane, unquenchable thirst for oil. Just like our insatiable need, demand, for drugs in this country. Narcotics fuel the instability and lawlessness in many countries around the world. The terrible crisis Colombia is in is because of our demand for narcotics.

"Our addictions have a price. Maybe we're starting to pay that price. Maybe these horrible acts of terrorism here in the homeland are partly the result of our insatiable appetites and our wealth, our greed, and our enormous selfishness and need for self-gratification, our need to consume like blind pigs."

Denny said, "That's a lot to swallow."

Jake was on a roll. "The attacks, I think, are mainly in response to and the result of American advocacy and support of a tiny, rich Middle Eastern state's right to exist and survive while at the same time depriving their neighbors of the same right to survive. Think Israel as the oppressor of the Palestinians.

"I am a Jew, Denny, and it pains me to see those horrible suicide bombings in Israel committed by the Palestinians. But I am an American first, last, and always. Israel has every right to survive and prosper in peace, but it has to allow another people the same rights. Israel cannot keep building settlements on Palestinian lands and not pay a price for it.

"I want to see Israel survive as an independent, viable state. But people have to realize that the American support of Israel by both political parties comes at a price. Are Americans willing to pay that price when terrorism has now struck the homeland? The American public has acquiesced to the pro-Israel policies largely by their apathy.

"The Israelis and Palestinians can live and exist in peace. One nation in the world, the United States, has the economic and military power to bring about a peace, to force and impose a peace on both parties, but so far they refuse to use their enormous economic powers of persuasion. So as we keep tilting toward Israel, we will pay a price. We are paying a price now."

"All this doesn't seem like irony to me."

"What is ironic, Dennis, me buddy, is that the greatest power the world has ever known doesn't use its economic power to insist that these two tiny populations, the Israelis and Palestinians, at least pretend to settle their differences and live side by side, not necessarily in harmony, but with a truce of enemies."

"But the Palestinians will continue their suicide bombing, won't they?"

"I don't think so. If the U.S. forces both sides to do what they have to, they will probably stop. The irony is that the U.S. refuses to do that. Why? You tell me."

"But will the bombing here in the States stop?"

"Denny, we should work on those grievances that we know in our hearts are just. Bombings don't stop because of retaliatory killing attacks by an army. And I dare anyone to accuse me, a Jew among Jews, one who has played the archetypal Jew on many stages, of being anti-Semitic."

"Jake, I never thought you were so hip. That you took an interest in anything other than the theater, reading *Variety,* and your blonde protégés."

"Ah, there's the paradox. The fool who's not a fool. As a character actor, I spend most of my time on stage listening to what other actors, usually the leads, are saying. Some of them say some wise things. Of course the schmucks are mouthing lines written by much brighter people. Also, because I often don't have a hell of a lot of lines, I have a lot of time for reading and thinking during rehearsals and during the run of a play. I watch TV news programs and read when I'm between parts or off stage. Besides, my parents always wanted me to be a college professor. They already had a doctor son."

"But things like the mink jacket?"

"Hey, if you're a character actor, make everyone believe you're a real character. It ain't easy being me."

Kevin told Jake his table was ready. Jake patted Denny on the shoulder as he was led to his table. "Denny, give my love to your dad and mom. And protect that cute Mick butt of yours."

Kevin winked at his new theater buddy, the knockout brunette.

41

Denny's Felix cell phone was ringing. It was early Sunday morning, August 4. He looked at the bright green numbers on his clock radio—seven-fifteen.

"Hello, Dennisis, my nemesis. Boy, that's awfully hard to say. It is I, Felix the felonious feline. I couldn't sleep."

"Why not?"

"I'm afraid that I may have ingested some of that foul stuff in your river. I may get cholera or something."

"We should be so lucky. Are you saying you're the one who went after the *Zenith?*"

"I should refuse to give attribution to you blockheads, but it was none other, my boy, than your faithful servant."

"How can you prove it?"

"I knew that your minders would insist you ask me for proof, as usual. One way I can prove it is to tell you that we purloined the boat from that marina in Newark."

"That was on the news; anyone could know that."

"Would the media know that the boat's owner had a skull and crossbones pasted on his dashboard above the fuel gauge?"

Denny knew that when the FBI checked that with the boat's owner, it would prove to be true. "We'll check."

"Of course you will. What else can you do? You people can only go through the motions. You are only reactive. Your government talks about pre-emption, but is incapable of it in terrorist activities."

"You failed this time."

"Not really. I'd be willing to wager that a hell of a lot of people are not going to be booking cruises in the coming months. One of my goals is to hit you economically. And certainly the cruise lines will be hurting. Look at the number of plays that put up their closing notices after I rocked Broadway."

"But isn't one of your primary goals to kill as many human beings as possible?"

"Not necessarily to kill, but to force as many people as possible to rethink their government's policies."

"Such as?"

"String me along as much as you want. They won't trace me."

"Which policies?"

"Many people in your country want to make two things synonymous. Anti-Semitism and being against Israeli governmental policy."

"Aren't you against both, Jews and Israeli policy?"

"Yes, I am, but an American should have the right to be against Israeli policies toward the Palestinians without facing the charge of being an anti-Semite. Especially if he happens not to be anti-Semitic. It's a Catch-22 used by many of your sophists."

"Where are you going to attack next?"

"Wouldn't you like to know, Denise—Clarice?"

"You only have four lives left. I figure that we'll catch you before your ninth. I'd like to be around at the ninth one to finish you off personally."

"Perhaps that can be arranged."

"How?"

"We'll both think about it, okay?"

"You must be running short of cash and explosives."

"Not really. We have an endless supply of financial replenishment, an endless cache of cash, and as for explosives, we have enough left and on delivery to blow up your whole city."

"We'll go after the state, the country, that supplies you with money and weapons."

"You are naïve. Our suppliers are no more countries and states than we are. Our backers and we—their clients, the terrorists—are not states nor do we have any ties to states. You cannot sign an accord, a peace treaty, with a gang because you don't know who we are. The only thing you can do is annihilate us cell by cell. We are insidious. If you wanted to, you could not surrender to us because we are not an entity that would be able to handle a surrender. We are all-powerful and powerless. Enough bullshit for today. I think I'm going to have my stomach pumped out."

Felix hung up.

Late in the day Wexler called with the confirmation. The skull and crossbones had been confirmed by the boat's owner. It had been Felix. Denny thought, *So what else is new?*

42

It was August 13, a Tuesday, when Felix got in a cab near Penn Station. He was headed north. This was to be his sixth life. He was determined to be cautious on this one. Mustn't squander his nine lives now, when he was so close to his goal.

Later the yellow cab pulled up in front of the Graymint Hotel on Central Park West. An old man, heavyset, hunched over, had difficulty exiting the cab. He tried to get his footing with his cane. The doorman tried to assist him. The old man imperiously motioned him aside. An irritable, cranky, crabby old bastard.

The cabbie put the old man's two heavy bags on the sidewalk next to him. The doorman and a bellman wrestled the bags into the lobby. After the doorman assisted the old man up to the reception desk, the old man ransacked his pocket and came out with a dollar bill, which he handed to the doorman as if it were a hundred. *Typical,* the doorman thought; *the more you helped them and the more dough they had, the nastier they were, and the less they tipped.*

In a quavering voice barely audible to the desk clerk, the old man mumbled, "I have a reservation. The name is Genovese. That's G-e-n-o-v . . . "

"I know how to spell it. Yes, sir, I've got it here in the computer. That's for three nights. A corner room with a queen-sized bed."

The old man completed his signing in and slowly, with his left foot dragging, followed the bellman and his luggage truck to the elevator. Once in his corner room with its windows facing out on West 62nd Street and Central Park West, Felix arranged the bags.

A half hour later he was shuffling through the lobby and heading slowly for the entrance. He refused the doorman's offer to secure him a taxi. On the sidewalk he made his way, snail-like, to the corner of West 62nd Street. Once he was around the corner he picked up speed. Seleb was waiting in a panel truck. Felix the Cat climbed into the vehicle and ducked in back where he couldn't be seen. As the truck pulled away, Felix dialed a number on his cell phone. A powerful blast shook the whole neighborhood and the truck. Behind him, through a shower of debris, Felix could see smoke coming from the building. A huge segment of windows and wall had been blown out by the blast.

When news of the outrage reached police headquarters, roadblocks were set up at all bridges and tunnels, but they were too late to catch Felix. Again he had evaded capture.

A television security camera in the lobby of the hotel had caught the old man's entrance into and exit from the hotel. When Denny, Frank, Wexler, and other agents viewed the tape, there was no doubt in their minds that this was Felix.

Frank fumed, "If we could ID him, why couldn't the people in the hotel?"

Denny said, "Because this guy is a real actor and a master of disguise. He creates a persona. People accept and believe in the persona. They are so busy dealing with this personality, that of a crotchety bastard, a curmudgeon, that they forget everything else. He looked shorter, older, bent over, with a limp. He even created a nasty disposition, a different personality. He was playing a part in his own movie. He was Lon

Chaney or Alec Guinness, a man of many faces. A trickster—loving every minute of it."

Wexler added, "They were only seeing what they wanted to see—the ordinary, the commonplace, their day-to-day happenings. A dislikeable old man checks into a hotel. They are so busy disliking this guy that they have no time to ask themselves if he is anyone but who he seems to be."

That night while awaiting a call from Felix, Denny got a call from his mother. His dad was bearing up fairly well with the chemo. He seemed to be holding his own. He had bought a toupee of silver-gray hair. Monny had just left them after a short visit. Yes, he'd be down soon, he promised. Later, thinking of his father's words, Denny had Diet Cokes instead of liquor. A start, anyway.

Watching on TV that night the havoc caused by the hotel explosion, Felix celebrated with a small brandy. His days, his lives, were numbered he knew, but so were theirs.

43

It was a steamy Sunday, August 25, the last Sunday before Labor Day weekend, with the temperature hitting ninety-five. Twelve days after the hotel blast. Hundreds of thousands were going to hit the beach to try to cool off near the ocean, get in the last Sunday of beach before the Labor Day hordes. After Labor Day it would be the fall season, back to school, and people would have other things on their minds. The beach at Rockaway was jammed. People had set up their beach sites like Bedouins, bringing enormous quantities of stuff. Families seemed to be trying to outdo one another, seeing which clan could schlep the biggest monster coolers and the most gear over the sand to their sites, their beach enclaves. Umbrellas, blankets, toys, coolers, beach bags, stuff piled on top of stuff.

The two men walked across the sand, each one holding the handle of a big cooler. On top of the cooler were two bulging beach bags. They wore shorts, no shirts, and were barefoot. Both men were muscular, well buffed. One man was buffed more than the other; he seemed to have shaved off his body hair but not his bushy eyebrow hair. He had a shiny, lotioned, shaved bald head with knots of veins bulging in the back—all in all, an ugly head.

It was Felix, and he was smoking a cigar. He had dark wraparound sunglasses and a nose guard to prevent sunburn, which also helped him become less recognizable. No one had seen him unclothed. His build drew attention away from his face. The other man had a big patch of black hair on his chest. Both men were gleaming with sun oil. They put down their load in a small vacant space in the middle of a crowded area. Few paid them any attention.

The two men stood over their cache of stuff for a moment or two, until two more men and a woman arrived with another big cooler and more beach bags. The first two men hiked back across the beach as if they were going to get more supplies. The two other men soon followed them, strolling leisurely back toward the parking lot. The woman stood sentry over all the stuff. She sat on a cooler for a few moments and then casually, lackadaisically, strolled down toward the ocean.

When she got close to the lapping waves, she walked parallel to the shore for a time; then she turned and walked hurriedly away from the water toward the parking lot, skirting their beach enclave by several hundred yards.

Some people were born nosy, suspicious, wary. Such a man was Xavier Gonzalez, a city bus driver who sat in his two-position back rest with his extended family clustered around him. He was a rotund man with thick unruly eyebrows and a big broad nose. His huge white thighs were spread out in the sand before him. He had watched the men carrying their heavy burdens over the sand. These guys, he thought, were trying to blend in and look like they were having a relaxing day at the beach, but they looked like gangsters to him. They looked Middle Eastern too.

They had deposited their stuff. Why had the woman wandered off? Wasn't she supposed to be watching the stuff the way his own wife did? He craned his neck to spot her down by the ocean. She was strolling along the shore way down there. Then he saw her turn away from the sea and walk toward the boardwalk at a good clip. His brain was working overtime. He shifted into third. Big, monster coolers. Only one woman. No kids. Leaving the stuff there untended. NO KIDS. That did it.

Suddenly he stood up, yelling at the top of his lungs. "A bomb. A bomb. Felix the Cat. Felix!" He pushed his family members toward the water. They didn't wait. Women in the vicinity gathered children and ran toward the water. He kept screaming, "A bomb. Run. Scatter." He waved his hands in a shooing gesture to everyone around him.

It didn't take much. Everyone had been prepped to expect something like this for the past months. People scattered in all directions. He ran around in a wider circle. Pointing toward the abandoned stuff, yelling. "Run for your lives. Scatter. Go. A bomb. Run." His voice was powerful, persuasive. This was a man who knew how to command.

Other people had taken up the cries. A huge wall of people around the site scattered, ran. "Bombs. Run for your life. Run. Get away from here." Kids howled and screamed. The people had cleared a huge ring around the coolers. Several people had called 911 from their cell phones. Some people ran for blocks.

The woman had made it to the parking lot. She hadn't looked back and was unaware of anything happening on the beach. In the lot she got in the back of the van with Felix and the others. Hareem was driving. They were so far from the beach that they had neither heard nor seen any commotion. Hareem headed the van out to the street and toward the causeway. He drove up local streets at a normal rate of speed. They were at the beginning of the causeway when Felix dialed the number. Even at their distance the blast was very loud. Felix winked at Seleb and gave him a thumbs-up.

On the beach it happened. A huge explosion. Deadly shrapnel flying in all directions. A mushroom cloud of sand had been thrown up. The sand bit into people for hundreds of yards around. Only a few people were slightly injured by shrapnel. Xavier took a piece of flying debris in his shoulder, but no one was badly injured. Xavier smiled and raised his arms in victory with clenched fists. "The bastards. We beat the fucks." Strangers came up to him and hugged him, patted him on the back, shook his hand. He was the hero of the day.

The van was on the other side of the causeway, heading toward Brooklyn. A row of police cars and fire engines tearing oceanward toward the beach passed the van. Sirens blaring, lights flashing. The quick response of men skilled in the aftermath but impotent in the area of prevention. Police cars swerved off the road at the causeway entrance and started to form a roadblock. Only a few moments earlier and the authorities might have caught the van in a dragnet. The bombers drove at normal speed back to their lair.

The headline on the extra that night was FELIX HAS STRUCK OUT. Xavier was a hero, lionized by the media. Felix was squandering his lives now, Lily Dish, the gossip columnist, crowed: "Felix is getting sloppier. He's losing it."

44

It was September 11, three months to the day since the Grand Central massacre had taken place. It was also the anniversary of the World Trade Center attack. Commemorative events, memorial services, were scheduled for 8:48 A.M. at the site of the Twin Towers and for 2:00 P.M. in the Main Concourse of the station. The vice-president, the mayor, the governor, and New York's two senators were scheduled for both events, so they would have to shuttle between the two ceremonies.

At Grand Central the invited guests were the families, friends, and neighbors of the deceased, the survivors and their families, and a group of dignitaries. The event was being covered by all of the television networks and local stations as well as the other media. Many of the victims' family members and friends were carrying photographs and icons of those who had perished, their lost loved ones. The audience was kept behind velvet ropes to the north and south sides of the hall. Servicemen lined the perimeter.

Denny stood with Monny on the East Balcony overlooking the great hall. He had invited her over to see the ceremonies and to touch base with her once again. He was there partly to aid in security and partly to witness the rites. Tony Tessitore saw him and said, "Oh, the publicity hound is here again to get some more press coverage."

Denny turned his back on him. Richie, who was standing nearby, said, "Fuck off, Tessitore, you're pushing your luck." Tessitore made one of his derisive faces and stalked away.

Below each balcony's set of three massive arched windows, fifty kilted bagpipers in full regalia had been massed. A bell tolled. This was the signal for the bagpipers to begin their mournful cries, the ritualistic wailing. The pipers in slow step marched down each side of the East and West Staircases. The bagpipers' keening echoed throughout the huge space as they continued their stately pace to the ground floor.

Once they had descended the stairs the two squads of fifty joined forces and then formed a circle around the rebuilt information booth, the epicenter of the explosion. Their mournful tones brought tears to many gathered in the rotunda.

From the North Balcony a chorus of two hundred sang "America the Beautiful" and "The Navy Hymn." On the South Balcony the New York Philharmonic Orchestra played a segment of the funeral music from Wagner's *"Gotterdammerung."* The horns and bass trumpet were amplified throughout the hall. The brasses thundered.

Denny and Monny were holding hands. Both were moved by the ceremony. Denny leaned over and kissed Monny on the cheek. His thoughts were on the Ellises and on the dead FBI agents Chris Simpson and Charlie Snelling.

The mayor stood at the podium that had been set up on the middle landing of the West Grand Staircase. He adjusted his glasses and looked out across the huge space. He introduced the vice-president, who spoke briefly.

The vice-president talked about the obscenity of the attack: "It was the grotesque act of demented, evil men." His praise was expansive for the rescue workers and first responders. Pointing to the huge American flag that hung down from one end of the concourse he called for two minutes of silence. Then the mayor reclaimed the podium and began his own remarks.

"I know that today in this now hallowed space there are many relatives, friends, and neighbors of those who were killed or injured in this horrible tragedy. I know that there are people here today who were witnesses to that infamous act. Many people have called upon me and others to erect a substantial memorial here in this hall to those who gave their lives and those whose lives were forever scarred by what happened that day. I know how you feel and I feel with you, but there is something more lasting we have to do.

"This great rail terminal was an essential part of the vitality and the spirit of a vibrant, living, functioning city. That information booth in the center, those ticket windows to my right, those train gates to my left are real, practical, and part of what was and is normal, purposeful, and functional.

"We must not turn all of America, all of New York, into a series of memorial sites. I refuse to turn this entire city into a mausoleum. We are a city that must live and thrive. If we turn this space or even a substantial part of this space into a memorial, then they, the terrorists, will have won. We must do more than grieve; we must overcome, we must endure, we must live and fulfill our lives, our destinies, because that is how you defeat these murderers.

"Above us on that ceiling are thousands of twinkling stars. On the hour, every hour during the day and night, a certain number of those stars will be the only ones lit; they will burn very brightly and distinctly.

These will be in remembrance of the fallen. A plaque has been placed on the northern wall of this concourse with the names of the victims. But this concourse must serve its original purpose for millions of travelers, commuters, and visitors. This city will go on. This great railroad station will go on.

"I will not allow this city to die in stages. This city shall live and prosper. This city remembers its dead, but a city is a living, breathing organism for the living to function and enjoy.

"This hallowed space will serve as a symbol of the persistence and endurance of our lives. Life has to go on. It is for the living to go about their daily lives and earn a living. We shall catch those responsible for these bombings, and we shall punish them.

"Now we shall hear from our city's poet laureate, Dr. Jacob Brewer."

In 1999 Jacob Brewer had been named poet laureate of the City of New York by the city council. The white-maned, stooped old man in his eighty-ninth year spoke into the microphone in a clear, firm voice.

"In sorrow I must bear witness that our city has been torn asunder by these horrible blasts. Rent is its spirit, yet the heart and sinew of our beloved city is still intact and vibrant. In desperation a people is crying out for deliverance from this evil beast who brings surprise assaults upon its ordered and ordinary life, creating havoc and wanton death for what reason, what cause, only the beast knows. To disrupt, to destroy, to kill and maim in a cowardly way, to strip away the people's faith in their everyday way of living—these are the beast's missions.

"If you, a beast, were fighting a superpower, how would you do it? You have only one weapon other than propaganda; you use subversion, subterfuge, sabotage; you try to weaken the spirit of your enemy, their will to fight; you bring the enemy to their knees by hitting them where it hurts—in their homeland.

"This beast shall be brought to bay, hunted down, and slain unmercifully, as he has slaughtered the innocent so mercilessly.

"When I looked at the devastated World Trade Center site, the cairn that remained, I saw a slaughtering ground, and I vowed that that horrible act would be avenged.

"The Twin Towers were a symbol of success, of economic dominance. They were brought down with enormous loss of life, but those towers were not the only towers in New York. They were not the only towers in America. The people who died there were tragic casualties of war, but those buildings were things, objects, structures. Those beasts destroyed many lives, wonderful lives, but they didn't destroy a nation, a people.

"In this place the beast destroyed many beautiful, caring people, but we must go on. The living honor the dead by remembering them, and they also honor the dead by a new commitment to make their lives meaningful, moral, and productive. May we never forget those whom the terrorists so cruelly murdered, and may we endure and go on with our lives rededicated. This is our resurrection."

After the ceremony had concluded Monny and Denny stood, still holding hands. This was Denny's opportunity. He turned to her and spoke earnestly, almost pleadingly. "Monny, what I'm doing, I may be risking my life. I'd like us to get back together before it's too late for me."

Monny responded, "Denny, you aren't trying to play

the *pity-me* card, are you? Not much time left for us? Den, are you saying that I should move back in with a live drunk because there's a danger that he may become a dead drunk? That would be an existence, not a life, as far as I'm concerned. I know what you are like sober and in control. You're a great guy. When you're drinking most of the time, you're not there. I refuse to play the role of the typical Irish barroom widow. That's a role this gal ain't going to play, Den.

"It's your decision to make, and don't try to frighten me into a wrong decision. Of course I worry for you, I love you deeply, but for more reasons than you know. Felix and all the other Felixes could kill you, but you could also kill yourself with the drinking."

When Monny left him at the Vanderbilt exit, Denny felt that they hadn't solved anything. He'd been given his warning, maybe his last.

45

Denny was in a cab. He had instructed the driver, an unsmiling Pakistani, to follow a pickup truck. In the bed of the truck were three mattresses. His cab stayed a full block behind the truck, and Denny kept urging the unresponsive driver to make up the distance, but they always remained a block behind.

"They'll get away, damn it. Speed up. Catch up with them. They'll slip away."

Ahead the truck was in the middle of a mass of pedestrians scurrying across an avenue intersection. Cabs, trucks, and private cars were all around the pickup.

Suddenly there was a tremendously loud blast as the pick up truck with its load of mattresses exploded. Smoke, huge pieces of debris, the horrible sight of death and maiming.

A blast of air from an open window wafted into the room. Lace curtains billowed. An instant burst of recognition. Denny sat bolt upright, sweating, shaking. *Cripes, what a dream. So real—so believable.*

He was on his couch at home, still wearing his suit pants, shirt, and loosened tie. His smell was wicked, a combination of booze, sweat, and fear. His body was oozing alcoholic fumes. His clothes reeked as if he himself had smoked scores of cigarettes—grimy memories of the smoke-filled bars.

The yellow cell phone rang.

"Hello, Denny? Is this my Denny Delaney, intrepid investigator?"

It was Felix. “Give a message to your friends in the press and to your superiors in the Federal Bureau of Incompetency. Tell your minders that America will pay for Israel’s latest attack on Palestinian civilians in the Gaza. The Israelis killed eight, four little children. Tell them, please.”

“Felix, your last attack at the beach was a real bummer. I think your days are numbered. You’re running out of lives. The public is so aware of you now that you can’t take a piss without them reporting it.”

“Denise, you’d be surprised how much freedom I have to move around this town. It’s remarkable how unobservant you people really are.”

Denny ignored Felix’s words and said some lines he had been rehearsing with Wexler.

“Oh, Felix, I read one of your old screenplays. Kinda amateurish stuff, I’d say.”

“Where would you get one of my scripts?”

“From your school.”

“Pretty basic stuff, wasn’t it? Yes, embryonic stuff. One has to learn one’s craft incrementally, I’m afraid.”

Felix had bitten on the bait they had dreamed up. He hadn’t denied anything. Maybe now they could put the squeeze on the Middle Eastern states. Denny continued in his effort to deflate Felix.

“Well-worn turf. Kind of hackneyed, trite, pedestrian stuff, wouldn’t you say?”

“Not quite that bad.”

“But certainly of unsaleable, unproducible quality.”

“Have you ever tried to write a screenplay, Mr. Delaney? It’s an art that your besotted brain could never master.”

“No, I’m not a writer, but I can tell inferior and shoddy stuff when I read it.”

What Denny was doing was very dangerous. This might really ignite Felix and cause him to do something horrendous. But Wexler's thinking was that Felix was going to do his thing anyway; maybe they could make him become careless, reckless.

"Dennis, I know you have instructions to keep me on the line so they can trace me, but I'm on the move with a cell phone. Impossible to trace me. You give the media and your bosses my message. All of you will pay for that latest Palestinian indecency."

Click. He had hung up. Another prepaid phone would be hurled in the trash.

Late that morning while driving up Broadway, Denny and Frank saw a pickup truck piled with mattresses. Denny, thinking of his dream, made Frank pull the truck over. They searched it and found only used mattresses. The driver thought they were nuts.

Frank was fuming. "Denny, let's not lose our cool now. A dream is a dream, guy."

46

September *13—a* Friday the thirteenth. If ever there was a day of deep apprehension, this was it. Near Sheepshead Bay in Brooklyn a small strip mall was undergoing renovation. Near the rear wall of the mall's main building a large construction dumpster had been placed. Asa had been casing the location for months. Every Friday morning around ten a flatbed truck arrived. It would back up to the dumpster, tilt its flatbed, and the dumpster would be hauled onto it. The dumpster would be affixed to the truck so the truck could dump its load in a landfill site.

The driver would drive to the Verrazano Bridge, which connected Brooklyn to Staten Island. Once on Staten Island the truck would proceed to a landfill site.

At four o'clock on the morning of the thirteenth Felix, Seleb, and Fahd were in one of their disreputable-looking panel trucks. They drove behind the shopping mall building. They had discussed the possibility of one or more police cars cooping there. As Seleb drove in, they saw that the parking area was deserted. Seleb quickly doused the van's lights and parked next to the dumpster. They unloaded several heavy boxes and two black plastic garbage bags. Seleb climbed into the dumpster. Felix and Fahd handed up the heavy boxes and bags one at a time. Seleb carefully camouflaged the bundles, hiding them beneath construction debris. When all of the explosives and a detonating device had been hidden from sight as much as possible, Seleb climbed out. The van pulled away from the strip mall, and they returned to their hideout.

At nine-fifteen the three men were back at the site. Seleb was driving. Felix and Fahd were in the rear of the van out of sight. Seleb parked the van at the end of a line of construction worker's cars. He had a clear view of the rear of the building and the dumpster.

The waste removal flatbed truck always pulled up around ten o'clock. It was hot in the van. Once in a while Seleb would run the engine to air condition the hot van. It got to be ten-thirty.

Felix was getting impatient. "Where the hell is he?"

Seleb answered, "The truck may have broken down. The driver might be sick."

Time passed. Eleven o'clock. Felix and the other two were getting anxious. At one point a worker came over to his car to get something but soon went back to the site. Felix said, "When it gets to be lunchtime some of the workers are going to be going to their cars. We'll have to move."

Eleven-thirty. No sign of the truck. At quarter to twelve Felix was ready to get away from the site. Seleb roared, "Here he comes!"

The truck pulled into the site and backed up to the dumpster. Before the driver tipped the flatbed, he got out of the cab. He climbed up the side of the dumpster and peered in. After all sometimes bodies were abandoned in dumpsters. Then he returned to his truck cab and started the procedures to load the dumpster onto the truck.

With the dumpster loaded on its back, the truck headed through a network of streets and highways, heading for the Verrazano Bridge. The van followed at a short distance. Just before the truck entered the roadway leading up to the bridge approach, the van turned to another road. This road led to a place where they could look across to the bridge from a long distance away. When they had parked at an overlook spot, Felix sat in front, looking up at the bridge. He had his cell phone in front of him. Seleb used his binoculars to follow the progress of the flatbed truck as it crossed the span.

When the truck had almost reached the center of the span, Felix dialed a number. They waited. Nothing happened. Felix listened to the cell phone. There was no sound of connection. He aborted the call and dialed again. No ringing signal. He was angry. "Fuck!"

The truck had passed the soaring towers and was reaching the end of the descending suspension cables. Again he dialed. Still nothing. The truck was out of sight now, off the bridge. Felix was furious, sweating. He dialed again. This time he could hear the ringing. At the fourth impulse they could hear from afar a loud explosion. They watched the bridge traffic. The traffic heading into Brooklyn still continued, and the bridge was still standing.

Felix was philosophical. "Seleb, get out of here. We'll strike again. I swear to you that we shall have another dawning." In his heart Felix knew his string of luck was running out.

The explosion took place beyond the bridge's toll plaza. Cars were turned over. The dumpster and truck were mere shells. A gasoline truck had been ignited. People in private cars were killed. The damage was extensive and devastating, but the Verrazano Bridge still stood.

47

Big Barb was on the phone. "Denny, Mac was very bad yesterday. This morning he's worse. The doctors say he's failing. It's strange, but he's more with it and lucid than he's been since the attack. Could you come and see him before . . . ? He wants to see you, to talk to you. He loves you."

Denny was there in less than a half hour. Down the hall he could make out Big Barb, the two tall boys, and daughter Julie. His chest tightened, his step stiffened. *How am I going to get through this? But more important, how are* they *going to get through it?*

He hugged Barb, and Julie and each son in turn. No one was dry-eyed. Denny and the family knew it was time. How do you say goodbye to a friend, a father, a husband, and how are you going to live with the torn-out hole in your life afterwards?

He went into the room red-eyed. Mac was propped up in bed. He smiled weakly when he saw Denny enter.

"Here he is now. The big FBI guru. How ya doing, Den? How's it going with that bastard Felix? Any closer to nailing the prick? Thank God he didn't get the Verrazano."

"The guy has struck eight times. He has the city tied up in knots. We're not getting any input at all from countries in the Middle East. We're all alone on this."

"It'll only be good old-fashioned shoe leather, door-to-door police work, that will nail this guy. But Den, I wanted to talk to you. Can a dying guy have a last wish?"

"Sure, Mac, but you're going to pull through. You're going to beat this."

"Den, I don't want to pull through like this. I'm a wreck. My body is shot to hell. A bum ticker. Diabetes. You name it. But that's me. You know, lying in this bed I have had a lot of time to think about a lot of things. Barb—solid, strong, there all the time for me and the kids, knowing who she was, what she wanted. The kids all out of high school, all in college. My God, eighteen to twenty-three already. All successful students.

"Academics and scholarship have always been more important to me than athletics. Shit, any black kid can excel at handling a ball. It's getting a good job, being someone, that counts. Tom is a competent lacrosse player at Johns Hopkins, Dave is a fairly good soccer player at Dartmouth, but they're students, not athletes, at top schools. And my Julie at the University of Massachusetts in Amherst is going to be a whiz in political science.

"Remember how over the years you and Monny would rent a car and drive out to our place in Smithtown for barbecues, clambakes, softball games? Big Barb loves you guys, and so do the kids. And all the times Barb and me would be your guests for dinners at different restaurants along Restaurant Row and drinks at your apartment?"

Denny said, "And Monny would say, 'Why should I cook when I've got twenty restaurants downstairs serving every major cuisine in the world?'"

"Yeah, man. But hell, Denny, buddy, I wanted you to see me so I could talk about you and to you. Guy to guy, my good friend, my favorite white guy. You know, even here in bed I hear things from the guys who visit. Your mom and dad have called me. People are worried about you. The sauce. The booze. A lot of good guys have fallen off the edge going the way you're going."

"I know, Mac. I've got to stop."

"Are you just saying it, or are you going to do it? What would it take to make you put your life back together, to save your marriage? Denny, I had a serious drinking problem after I'd been on the force for a few years. I knew that if I didn't beat it, it would beat me. I thought, 'Goddamn it, you're a human being with free will; no one but yourself is making you do this.' I said to myself 'Goddamn it, stop it.'"

Mac took a deep breath. The talking was wearing him out. Denny put a hand on his shoulder, tried to shush him.

"I said, 'Don't let something outside of yourself, something that's not human, control your life. I'm either in charge of my life, or life is not worth living. It's you or the booze. Hell, end it all now. Why die a slow death from the drinking?'"

Mac leaned forward in the bed. "Hell, Denny, this is from a guy who loves you. This is a dying man's wish, request—hell, order. Stop the fucking drinking. Get a fucking life! Now, get the hell out of here and tell Monny to come in and see me. It's time that I looked at another beautiful woman, other than Big Barb."

That night in Joe Allen's, before Denny had a chance to think or to order, Kevin placed a rocks martini in front of him. Before he took a sip, he kept revolving the glass on the bar, staring at it. He didn't drink it.

"Kevin, give me a big glass of orange juice, the biggest you got. And here, throw this out."

He pushed the martini to the edge of the bar. "I don't feel in the mood tonight."

Denny left the bar after he had finished the orange

juice and two bottles of mineral water. In his apartment he turned on the television set, but didn't follow his routine of going to the drinks cupboard for his vodka. That night he took an Ambien and was soon asleep. He awoke the next morning early, feeling good. He went out and took a long jog beside the Hudson River. For the first time in years he really felt good about himself. *Now the tough part. Turn this into something. Keep it going.*

Monny went to see Mac and reported that he seemed to be holding up as well as could be expected. Barb and the kids were strong, a lesson they'd learned from Mac.

The call came two days later from Barb. Big Mac had passed.

48

"Denny, you're probably wondering why I wanted to see you alone like this," Wexler said.

It was Tuesday, September 17. As he sat across from Wexler in the SAC's office, Denny thought, *This is the first time I've ever been alone with this guy. There has always been someone else present, usually Frank. The Ferret looks like a fox today.*

"In a few days I'm going to be replaced, moved back to Washington. Supposedly a reassignment, but it is really their way of saying that I've dropped the ball. The only reason they've waited so long to give me the shove is that I've made a good scapegoat for them. And I have. Believe me, they have been breathing down my neck throughout this whole fiasco. A lot of people in the country are saying the FBI has fucked up on this one.

"Looking at our lack of results, who can blame them? Initially we got those three sleepers in Queens, but after that, zilch. Felix keeps hitting the city, and we're powerless to stop him."

Denny answered, "Look at his latest attacks though. The beach bombing was completely ineffective because an ordinary joe was on the ball. The bridge explosion could have been a catastrophe, but somehow he fucked up. The mechanism was off. The hotel blast was bad, granted, but didn't result in many deaths, and his *Zenith* try fizzled."

"Denny, we can't just measure these things by the number of casualties. Look at the stock markets, the drying up of tourism, the whole economy, the demoralized state of the country. He's done what he set out to do. All with a very small cell. Imagine if we had to contend with multiple cells like this throughout the country. We'd be on our knees, a basket case. A great world power can be reduced to paralysis when a small number of fanatics strike its homeland.

"Felix really does have unlimited lives and can move around the city with impunity. His disguises are working. The director and attorney general keep shouting at me, 'Why haven't you nailed him yet?' 'What are we doing to stop him?' they say. They forget that in World War II Hitler couldn't shut down a growing resistance movement. Sabotage, we called it then. The attorney general has given me orders to kill him on sight. No questions, no protestations. Just kill him. I said great, but where is he? Every FBI agent, every cop, the National Guard, now the armed forces, every law enforcement officer in the country is working this case.

"Denny, I need your thinking on this. Where do you think he is going to spend his ninth life? You must have given it some thought."

"I've been doing a lot of thinking about it. I believe he wants me to be there when he cashes in. I think number nine will be a real suicide mission, one where he hopes to take me out with him. It may seem absurd, unbelievable to you, but I think he'll try striking at Grand Central again."

"Why do you think that?"

"Just intuition, instinct, a wild guess. This is a feature movie we're living here, one hundred twenty minutes, one hundred twenty pages. It's got these nine plot points or high points. It can't go on indefinitely. He wants it to end on a high note, but it has to end with number nine. For a lot of reasons, he wants it to end.

He's beginning to run on empty. He's probably running out of explosives. His attempts are becoming more anticlimactic; he's beginning to lose his mojo.

"But the key point is that this guy gets off on being in touch with me because he's writing and living a movie at the same time—creating it, directing it, as he goes along. In a movie I'd be the protagonist; he'd be the bad guy, the antagonist. Except in his film, with his warped sense of the world according to Felix, he's the hero, the protagonist, and I'm his bad guy, the nemesis representing the satanic American empirical power. In the last act it has to be just the two of us, dueling it out.

"Think about it. In this whole city, where is the one place that he might expect me to be waiting for him? The only place where he could be sure to expect me to be at some future point? Grand Central. I think he expects me to go back there and wait for him. He's been leading me back there. For the ninth strike, one last mission, one last dramatic going-out gesture. A repeat performance at Grand Central. A nice cyclical structure to his screenplay. End where you began. Bring the audience back to the starting point. Send them out of the movies satisfied. Things end where they begin. It's also the place I know best, my only hope of nailing him."

"So what do you want to do about it?"

"I want to go back to the Grand Central Security office and get ready for him. I want enough personnel to monitor every single surveillance camera seven days a week, twenty-four hours a day. I want to be there ready to roll if he turns up. I'll sleep right there on the premises until he shows up.

"Also, I want it widely publicized that I'm being placed back on station security, a reassignment, the end of my TDY, whatever."

"Hell, Dennis, it's better than nothing. Do it. You can have as many agents and other people as you need. I'll get on it with the police commissioner. You'll have everything you need. Just do it. I'll back you all the way.

"If I tell the director and the attorney general we have a plan, he'll put off my transfer. And you'll have my complete support. Denny, let's get this fuck dead or deader, never mind alive. Preferably with a hand grenade up his ass. I don't want a trial. Do you get it?"

"I'm with you all the way."

Wexler stood and shook his hand.

That afternoon it was in all the papers and on television, not as a major story but as a sidebar: Denny had been moved back into the terminal's Security office. It wasn't mentioned that a large staff of transit police and FBI agents were being reassigned there with him.

Tessitore was more pissed than ever, but he got lost in the flood of new people. A large room next door to Security was cleared and cots were moved in so that Denny and others could rest or sleep in shifts. Restrooms down the hall were shut off from the public and designated for the surveillance detachment's use. A workers' shower room was made available.

Every monitor was being watched. When one officer or agent left, another took his or her place. Terry was busy in her Tech Support unit, coordinating the increased surveillance. She had four FBI techies assisting her.

It became a daily routine for Denny. He slept and ate at the station. He had moved in extra clothes, underwear, and toiletries. For Denny it was an alcohol-free period. It was going to be a siege.

49

Wexler was standing in front of a roomful of agents in the Vesey Street field office at 8:00 A.M. on Friday, October 25. A number of other law enforcement agencies were represented by their brass. Frank Millau was there, but Denny was with his crew in Grand Central.

Wexler began, "Listen up, folks. If anything of what I say to you here gets leaked to the media we're all dead meat. This has to be top secret.

"Over the last few days the NSA and the CIA have picked up on something that we think is going to help us break this case. We know that Felix needs financial resources and ordnance in order to keep operating. When he started, he probably had a cache of money and explosives, but about now he probably needs an infusion of both.

"He has sponsors, sugar daddies in the Middle East who can help him with money, weapons, and explosives. How do they communicate with him without implicating themselves? How does he receive their messages without getting caught? The Internet would be one source. We have people monitoring that constantly, but we could never possibly filter out more than a fraction of the traffic.

"The money and arms people overseas, we think, came up with another method of communicating with Felix. They have probably used it before. We have learned that an Egyptian film is going to be released on videotape in a few days. Felix's sponsors have digitally encrypted a detailed message onto the tape.

"Using a specially equipped VCR it is possible to pick up the verbal message embedded in the tape. It's akin to subtitling. We have no idea what the message says, but we do know that the tapes will be released in the Metro area in four days. We know that the video contains a message for Felix and probably other sleeper cells with what we believe to be detailed information on money transfers and container shipments of explosives to be delivered to or already stored in the States. The message is probably in code. Right now we're not interested in the message; it's the tape and the means of delivery that we have to monitor.

"Now there are thirteen outlets in the Metropolitan area that handle this type of Middle Eastern film. It isn't going to be a general release sort of thing. It's a secular—what we would label as an R-rated-movie, so we are sure that mosques, Muslim charities, and religious groups are not going to receive it or want it.

"We are going to stake out those thirteen outlets around the clock. Of course there is a danger that one of these outlets may be staffed or owned by someone in Felix's cell or someone sympathetic to him. We've got to keep our eye on all of them. We have to be on the lookout for someone who comes in around the release date and purchases or rents the tape."

A New York City police inspector asked, "Why couldn't they just air express one videocassette to Felix?"

"We don't know that they don't do that, but we have been told these tapes have messages for more than one cell. There would be too many variables. Too many dangers inherent in express shipping such a tape.

"Somehow Felix, a film buff, will know the release date. We believe he'll send in a flunky, a gofer, to one of these outlets to get the film. The name of the film is *Her Last Flight from Cairo.* It's in Arabic. It's not going to be a video that is in much demand by non-Arabic speaking Americans.

"Working previous cases we've all sweat out the large number of personnel needed for multiple-point surveillance. This videotape rental surveillance is going to be one of the largest surveillance operations we've ever undertaken. This is going to be a full-court press. It's our last best hope."

For the next hours the activity on Vesey Street and in all the involved law enforcement agencies and departments was frantic. Over a thousand FBI agents were involved. Frank had been warned not to inform Denny so he knew nothing of the massive surveillance operation. Wexler told Frank that Denny's own plan was still key to catching Felix. Frank knew that Denny would be royally pissed if he knew he'd been kept in the dark.

50

Jocko Nepeni was a loyal American of Lebanese descent in his early forties. A harried, overworked man with deep circles under his eyes and a will to persist and endure, he ran a video rental store called The Film Harvest in Brooklyn. After Nine-Eleven he had placed a large American flag in his store window.

He carried all the latest hit videos and DVD releases but also had a section of his store devoted to imports from Asia, the Middle East, Europe, and South America. It was strong on Middle Eastern stuff because he read and understood Arabic. He had a large number of Arabic speakers in the neighborhood of the store. The foreign imports provided the little edge that allowed him to compete with the chains like Blockbuster. He worked in the store fifteen hours a day, seven days a week. His wife spelled him for four or five hours a day so that he could run errands.

One October morning when he opened he was greeted by two FBI agents. They told him that they were going to be staking out his store. They asked a lot of questions and seemed to know a lot about him, his past, his associations, all about his family in Lebanon. He assured them that he loved America and hated what Felix was doing to the city and country. Yes, he would cooperate fully with them. Yes, he was expecting a batch of recent releases from the Middle East to be delivered that week. He wasn't sure of all the titles. The distributor sent what was current.

Two agents took up residence in his back room. In

the store itself they had set up a signaling device on the floor below the cash register. It was a foot button that Jocko was to step on if anyone rented or bought *Her Last Flight from Cairo.* Two hidden television cameras had also been placed in the store to record all customers. The men in the back would be alerted if the signal light in back came on.

Jocko hadn't been told what would happen next. The plan, however, was for the agents in back to alert agents in cars outside. A series of vehicles would tail the suspect. An elaborate network of alternating tailing cars would come into play. The agents in the cars would, with any luck, follow the suspect to the cell's headquarters. All of these elaborate procedures had been set up at each of the thirteen video outlets in the Metropolitan area where the tape might be distributed. It involved close to a thousand agents and hundreds of police officers.

It was a Wednesday, October 30. Three o'clock in the afternoon. Late Tuesday, Jocko had put out *Her Last Flight from Cairo* among his Middle Eastern new arrivals. The store's door opened. The bell signaling the door opening or closing tinkled and Asa entered. He smiled at Jocko, nodded hello. Jocko gave him a hello because Asa was a fairly regular customer. This time he had no rentals to return. He hadn't been in for a while. Jocko didn't know that Asa dealt with five different video rental stores.

Once in a while Asa came in and rented five or six films. He sometimes bought one or two videocassettes as well. Lately he had been renting and buying DVDs too, so Jocko knew he had a DVD player. He always paid cash. When he first came in a few years ago, he had presented a credit card to establish his rental security, but he never used it for rentals or purchases.

Jocko didn't recall his name, couldn't possibly remember the name on the credit card presented years before. He was a pleasant enough guy. Jocko thought he was either Lebanese or Syrian. Asa just smiled and was agreeable. He did not enter into conversations, and Jocko was not the garrulous type anyway. Many customers found Jocko to be cold and abrupt, as if he were constantly constipated or henpecked.

Asa walked around the store, looking at tapes, reading the synopses. Gradually he had a stack of five in his hand, all from the new Hollywood release area. It almost looked as if he were about to leave when he made a detour into the foreign release aisle. Asa was now at the Middle East recent arrivals table. He looked over the tapes and selected two.

He continued looking around the rest of the store and picked out *Insomnia.* The last time he had forgotten to get it for Felix. He walked over to the counter. He placed two stacks of tapes on the counter, one with six tapes and one with two. He pointed to the stack of six. "These I want to rent, and these two I'm going to buy."

Jocko checked out the six rentals, all current Hollywood releases, and then turned to the two purchases. The top one was in Arabic with the title *Alexandria: Dawns and Dreams.* The second one was *Her Last Flight from Cairo.* Jocko fought the desire to look up at Asa. He trembled ever so slightly. His foot found the foot button. He hoped the agents would get his signal.

Jocko glanced at the shelf under the cash register. His thirty-eight sat there ready and loaded. He toyed with the idea of pulling out the gun and capturing this guy, maybe shooting him, but the agents had told him to act in a normal manner and just step on the button. He stepped on the button again to be sure they were alerted.

Only after he had totaled up the transaction did he look casually at Asa. When Jocko told him the total, Asa handed him enough twenties and received his change. Asa smiled. The two nodded. And Asa left the store.

The two agents in the back alerted the cars outside. Asa walked a half block down to his dirty, banged-up van. A series of alternating cars followed as Asa went about his business, driving to various food stores, buying magazines and newspapers, doing his errands for the house.

He seemed to make a lot of turns. Wherever he was going, he was taking a circuitous route to get there. The agents were careful. Sometimes it was a utility truck, a pickup truck, or various passenger cars that tailed him. By six-thirty Asa finally felt safe and drove into the Brooklyn cul-de-sac. From a distance an agent in a Federal Express truck saw the garage door go up and the van enter the big garage on Shelton Terrace.

At the FBI field office a hectic time began; teams were being dispatched for a major assault. A perimeter was set up around the Brooklyn neighborhood, but no one in the area would get wise because it was being done with a ragtag group of vehicles. Every person, every vehicle, everything going in or out would be photographed and noted. From the moment Asa entered that garage a dragnet was in place.

At the Brooklyn Borough Building Department maps were studied. The tax assessor's rolls were checked for the garage and adjoining house on Shelton Terrace. The house and garage were owned by the Levins. The name sounded Jewish. An unpromising sign when you were hunting down Middle Eastern terrorists.

This was the biggest SWAT and assault operation that the FBI had ever mounted in New York City. For blocks around the area in the early hours of the morning a massive buildup of forces had begun. No sirens, no flashing lights.

A square had been drawn around the cul-de-sac on a map. At a prearranged time nine city blocks had been cordoned off by hundreds of city police. It was almost exclusively a commercial area, so few residents were involved. Those hapless people who tried to enter or leave the area were held in a quarantine situation.

A light drizzle had begun coming down at four-thirty in the morning, and the wind had started slicing the rain sheets diagonally against heavily armed and armor-vested officers.

Wexler had set up a command center a block and a half from the cul-de-sac. At first light the assault would begin. He figured that the cell members would have too much of an advantage on their home turf if the assault went down in darkness. His orders were clear. Heavy, massive fire power, gas, shoulder-held rockets to get the job done with as little loss of life to FBI and police as possible. Get them dead or deader, he had ordered.

51

The house was quiet and dark. Each night one member of the group was responsible for an all-night patrol, walking around the inside of the house, checking the garage, making sure that the house wasn't compromised. At five-thirty in the morning Seleb, that night's watchman, saw a shadow across the street. He also heard a sound up the street. Better safe than sorry. He awakened everyone. No lights were turned on. They moved around with small pen lights that they shielded from the outside. Each cell member had a post, a pre-set station.

Most of the house's windows had heavy curtaining so that little could be seen from outside. Inside it was a precision operation. Hareem and Fahd rushed into the garage through the tunnel and took up positions near the doors. They had heavy automatic weapons and plenty of ammo. Hareem had positioned one of the vans so that it could make a quick exit.

Krista went into Felix's attic room and took up a position near his gabled window. She had a rifle and removed a machine gun from under Felix's bed. Seleb was near the front door with his weapon. Asa was in the dining room, looking off toward the cul-de-sac's entrance.

Ma and Papa Levin with their Uzis were in the kitchen, across from the back porch and the kitchen door. Tamil and Samin were on the second floor, where they could rake the street below with deadly fire.

In the garage Fahd was readying a huge charge of

explosives to blow up everybody if necessary. He had it rigged so that he could use his cell phone to activate it.

The first rays of light came up on the street. Wexler's voice could be heard from a loudspeaker.

"FBI. Your house and garage are completely surrounded. We are ordering you to leave the buildings with your hands in the air. FBI. Now. Leave the buildings."

Wexler repeated the messages over and over. No targets appeared on the streets for the cell members to fire upon. An eerie silence blanketed the whole area.

Fifteen minutes went by. No movement from inside. Behind the house an FBI SWAT team had taken up position behind a brick wall. One of the team, heavily armored, was about to climb over the wall when heavy gunfire erupted from the back pantry window and the kitchen window. This was the first evidence the FBI had that the terrorists were within. Ma and Papa Levin's Uzis were chattering, firing out the back. This set off a barrage of heavy, deadly fire from the federal agents in the rear, an overwhelming barrage.

Gunfire raked the rear of the brownstone, tearing into the kitchen, the pantry, and the dinette. The return fire from the SWAT teams was devastating. Ma Levin was cut down before she had a chance to seek cover. Papa Levin leaned over her, knew from her riddled body that she was gone. He rose and ran toward the back door and flung it open; his Uzi was spitting fire, but he was firing wildly, his eyes blinded with tears. Again a massive blast of firing from the FBI. A heavy-caliber bullet smashed into his skull. Papa Levin was ripped apart by the barrage.

A warehouse across the street from the front of the house suddenly became a lethal firing base as gunfire erupted from at least ten spots in the warehouse, raking each floor of the brownstone with gunfire. Now from another warehouse across the street the garage was being peppered with fire.

After an enormous fusillade the firing stopped. The SWAT teams waited. Wexler repeated his messages over the loudspeaker.

"FBI. This is your last chance to come out with your hands raised above your heads."

A few minutes went by. One door of the garage slowly rose. A van tore out into the street, its tires squealing. Hareem was at the wheel. He drove with his foot clamped on the accelerator. He had barely gotten the van out the door when heavy fire erupted. A torrent of shots. Every agent was firing at the van.

The windshield shattered. Hareem was hit by scores of shots. His head was thrown back, and the van careened diagonally across the street. It bounced across the curb, grazed a lamppost, and then hit a hydrant, sending a geyser into the air. It plowed into the warehouse wall. Seconds later the gas tank ruptured; and with a roar, flames and black smoke burst from the van.

With the shattered van pouring thick acrid smoke into the air the street was turned into what looked like another war zone. The garage door had closed after Hareem's wild escape attempt. No movement from the house. Everything quiet.

Then suddenly a series of whooshes, bursts of air, as small missiles were shot off by the federal agents. Into every window of the house, into the shattered garage windows, canisters of gas were shot. The canisters burst open, and the gas filled every corner of the house and the garage.

The streets were deathly still. Everyone was ordered

to remain at his post. For over thirty minutes, silence. Then an armored car drove down the street. Six men in chemical safety suits and gas masks, heavily armed, moved to the side of the house. They were on the lookout for booby traps, and there was the very real danger that a massive bomb was set to go off. They made their way very warily to the back door.

They pushed open the back door. In the kitchen they found the bodies of Ma and Papa Levin. The agents were in contact with Wexler at the command post.

"Team Red. Kitchen. Two bodies, older man and woman, dead, gunfire."

A long pause. In the dining room was Asa Levin's body.

"Team Red. Dining room. Male, thirties. The gas has killed him."

Seleb was in the front room, badly cut up by gunfire, dead either from the gas or the barrage.

"Team Red. Living room. Male, late twenties, early thirties. Dead. Extensive gunfire wounds."

Five minutes went by. "Team Red. First floor cleared."

Then another voice. "Team Blue. Cellar cleared. We've found a tunnel leading to the garage. Will investigate."

Minutes passed as Wexler, his lieutenants, and Frank Millau listened.

The second floor revealed the bodies of Tamil and Samin.

"Team Red. Second floor. Two males, late twenties, thirties. Both dead."

Then: "Team Red, second floor cleared."

"Team Blue, very large garage. One male, mid-twenties, dead. Four vans, one sedan. Back wall is phony. Will investigate."

"Team Red. Third floor. Two rooms and bathroom. Female, mid-thirties, dead."

Minutes went by. "Team Red. Entire house cleared. None of subjects is Felix. This third floor area was his headquarters, though. Exercise equipment, computer, TV, tape players, scripts."

"Team Blue. Back of garage is like a munitions dump. Lots of weapons, ammunition, explosives. Garage has only one deceased male. No sign of Felix."

A team on the street reported in. "Street report. Subject killed in van breakout was not Felix."

Wexler looked at Frank. "Shit. All this and we didn't get him. If this guy got away, I'm going to be tossed to the wolves, even though we may have destroyed his cell."

Frank said, "It's all up to Denny now. He's gotta pull this off."

"Let him know what went on here."

"He's going to be one pissed-off puppy about being left out."

52

Denny was in the Grand Central Security headquarters in the squad room, sitting in front of a bank of small television screens that monitored nearly the whole station. He stared at the screens. Constantly he had to pull his mind back and focus on the screens. It was so easy to let your mind wander.

Here he was, back at square one in his life. He could be out of it now, out of the loop. He wasn't in the field office anymore; he hadn't gotten his man, he hadn't even come close. Felix hadn't been in touch for quite a while.

No, but thank God, maybe he had been doing something right. Something in his personal life. For a month and a half now he had stayed away from the booze. He had proved to himself that he could do it. He had been to the gym every day. His workouts had been long and serious. He had been jogging along the path next to the Hudson River. It was a start.

Something had clicked in his brain. Right after Mac's last talk, his doctor had also scared the shit out of him. The blood tests, his blood sugar, his cholesterol—everything was lousy. It was either be a person or be a cipher.

He had started to eat salads, fish, chicken, real food. "Get a life," some force within him had shouted.

He decided to call Monica. He called her at work.

"Hi, Monny, how ya doing?"

"As per usual. How is everything coming along on your end?"

"I'm making progress."

"Getting your perp?"

"No, I think that may be over for me. I'm still at Grand Central watching monitors. As long as I'm back to work here, I may never see that guy again. Lightning doesn't strike twice when it comes to targets like Grand Central. They have tightened up on everything around here. The people using the station are so pissed off at the holdups and delays that we're getting a lot of abuse. But as far as terrorist attacks, I think I'm out of it, out of the loop."

"So what's the progress you talked about?"

"Personal progress, Monny. It's been forty-five days now that I haven't had a drink. I've gone cold turkey, and I'm happy with myself. Now I don't even have the urge. Before, I think I did the drinking partly out of boredom. But no backsliding so far."

"Was I that boring?"

"Of course not. It was me, all me."

"Well, that's a relief."

"I can't promise anything, but hey, Mon, it's a start, isn't it?"

"Yeah, Den, it's great. I'm happy for you. You've done wonders. I'm proud of you."

"No, Monny, be happy for us. Are you dating anyone?"

"Denny, are you nuts? Not only am I not dating anyone, I don't want to date anyone else—ever. I've been waiting for you to hear the music."

"How about us getting together for a dinner? I could take the train out, and we could eat at that Portuguese-Spanish place in Mineola. You know the one near your apartment. Paella, garlicky gambas, iced tea."

"Yeah, I'd like that."

"How about Friday night? I'll meet you there at eight.

I'll make a reservation. I promise I'll just have iced tea, Diet Coke, or fruit juice."

"Great."

"So this Friday at eight?"

"Yes. See ya."

"Thanks, Mon. I'll bring you a surprise."

"No, just bring me a sober Denny."

"Love you."

"Love you too. Oh, and happy Halloween. Goodbye."

That's right. It's Halloween morning.

After he got off the phone with Monica, he began flipping through the channels on his central monitor, the one that was capable of looking at all the camera sites. He looked at a screen showing the Main Concourse, which had been almost completely restored. The vast space seemed much quieter than in early days. People avoided it if they could. In general people tried to avoid crowds as much as they could. No one dawdled. Everyone rushed to his or her destination.

His cell phone was vibrating in his pocket. Not the yellow Felix one. He pulled it out and answered. It was Frank Millau from Brooklyn who told him what had happened: the video from overseas, the video store stakeouts, finding the hideout, the raid and gunfire at the cell's roost. He hadn't gotten around to telling him about the missing Felix when Denny angrily interrupted Frank's flow.

"Frank, I'm really pissed about this. Shit, here I am sitting here out of the action just when you guys confront Felix. Why didn't Wexler let me in on it? I deserved to be there. They probably caught him napping, Felix the Cat in his hideout, planning his next operation, caught with his pants down. Did you at least waste the mother fucker?"

"No, Denny, that's why Wexler wanted you to stay there. We got a lot of them, found Felix's room, but he slipped through our fingers. One theory is that he got some kind of warning."

"He's still on the loose?"

"Yeah. Quite a setup here. This was the headquarters, their cache of explosives, their vehicles. We found his room with all of the weight lifting equipment. Tapes of all the classic movies. Maps of the city. His computer with his scripts. No sign of Felix. He's gotten away, but we finished off the husband and wife who owned the place and a guy who was probably their son. And all the other bit players, the extras. Enough explosives here to blow up Times Square. But one great thing: only two of our guys slightly wounded. No deaths on our side. That's a real plus. Sort of makes up for Chris Simpson and Charlie Snelling."

"I'm glad to hear that."

"We were going to turn this place into a stakeout, figuring Felix might turn up, but the media are all over here. It'll soon hit the airwaves. This place will be useless as a stakeout. The government has asked the media to sit on the story for a while."

"Frank, why wasn't I at least told about the video store stakeouts?"

"Wexler wanted you to stay put. Don't forget you're the one who chose that spot. Felix may still show up there yet. You're our only hope right now. Our guys are going through his computer, hoping that there's a script about Felix the Cat's nine lives, and that the ninth life will be spelled out."

53

Felix the Cat had survived the Brooklyn raid because he knew when not to be a creature of habit. He could act unpredictably when times called for change. The day that Asa was to pick up the message videotape was Felix's trigger. He didn't want to hear it or see it. His own movie was reaching one hundred five minutes out of one hundred twenty. People did not want to sit through more than two hours of this movie genre. It was time to wind things up. Go out with a big bang. A very big bang.

He made a conscious decision about his life. He had had a good run for it, his life so far. No need to drag it out. He would end it on a high note, a spectacular finish if he could. If he was lucky, Denny Delaney would go down with him. That touch would make for a better movie.

Years ago Felix had set up a safe house in New Rochelle with a Palestinian sympathizer. Early on the morning of Wednesday, October 30, Asa drove him to the New Rochelle house, which was a block from the railroad station. They drove into the backyard. Felix got out and unloaded a heavy suitcase and a duffel bag. He shook hands with Asa; both realized that there might be a finality to this. They took a lingering look at each other, a few seconds longer than might be expected. They both smiled; then Asa turned away and drove off to run his errands, one of which was to pick up the encrypted video.

That night Felix slept fitfully in the empty house. The

next morning he got up early to ready his costume. He was busy with his preparations and did not listen to the radio or watch television. Even if he had, he would have heard nothing of the Brooklyn raid. A news blackout had been ordered by the government. It took him quite a while to disguise himself, to get into his fat suit.

His plan depended upon people seeing a grossly fat man and not seeing Felix. It had been a month and a half since his last attack so he was hoping that the public was getting somewhat complacent. On that morning from the back door of a house in a Westchester suburb a fat man emerged carrying a large black suitcase. He trudged the block to the station clumsily, ducklike, seemingly with great effort.

On the platform he bought the *Times*. He was just in time for the train. He boarded the last car, lifted his heavy bag onto the overhead rack, and took a seat by the window, the last window seat on the crowded coach.

Opening up his *Times* he buried himself in the large paper which covered his face for most of the trip. There was nothing in the paper about the raid. He chose the Arts and Leisure section, so he spent most of his time reading the articles and studying the movie ads.

The people around him were intent on their own affairs, reading newspapers, futzing around with laptops, listening to Walkmen, doing crosswords, talking incessantly and brainlessly on cell phones, reading books. A woman across the aisle was reading the latest potboiler, *Nine Lives Too Many.* No one was paying attention to the sloppy-looking, grossly fat man who smelled of sour sweat. One small wisp of a woman, who worked on costumes at the Metropolitan Opera, recognized the unnaturalness of his outfit, but formed a tiny smile; it was Halloween, after all, and this guy had probably dressed for some office shenanigans.

The train was soon in the Bronx. Then Manhattan. They were nearing Grand Central Station. At the station he waited until most of the people around him had exited before he got up. He was carrying the large black suitcase the old-fashioned way, by its handle. He thought that if he were seen pulling a black rolling suitcase, it would spark too many memories of his last visit to the station. In his fat suit he waddled down the aisle of the car and headed out the railroad coach's door to the station platform and the long walk up toward the waiting gate exit. The movie had only fifteen minutes more to run; then it would all be over. All of it.

54

Shortly after his phone conversation with Frank, Denny was flipping through the camera views as if he were shuffling a deck of cards. He saw a figure that interested him. *Something about that guy.* He zoomed in for a larger image. On the furthest end of the Track Three platform was a very fat man trudging toward the gate many cars ahead of him.

A man, a heavy beard, walking stooped over, Quasimodoish, black coat, a fedora. Fat, huge. Something about the man's gait rang a bell. A distant memory. A guy pulling a hot dog cart. A man on video pulling luggage through the Main Concourse of the station. But this man was carrying what looked to be a heavy suitcase.

Yes, he was sure. It was him. He must be wearing a fat suit. He had just gotten off a commuter train from Westchester County. He was at the end of the long platform, shuffling slowly, trying to look old, trying to act as inconspicuous as possible. And yet maybe trying to attract Denny's notice. The gecko puffing out his red fan to attract flying insects. The spider to the fly. Come to me.

Denny pressed the silent alarm button. Every officer in the station would be alerted to a Code Ten emergency situation. It also notified New York City fire and police departments that the station was under a general alert. They would dispatch all available vehicles and personnel.

He spoke into the radio system that was hooked up

to every security officer, but which did not go out on public p.a.'s.

"Code Ten, Code Ten Alert for all of Grand Central. To Able and Baker response teams. Felix is on Track Three platform headed for Track Three gate leading into station. Bearded, fat, very heavy, black coat, hat, carrying a suitcase. Assemble at gate entrance and await further orders.

"To all other officers: evacuate station, evacuate station. Do not sound general alarm system at this time. Evacuate everyone from Main Concourse, all passageways, and all other public spaces."

Denny called the subway and rail headquarters and ordered all arriving trains to be halted. None were to enter the station. All trains in the station were to leave at once.

He turned to Richie, who had followed everything he had been doing. Everyone in the Security squad room was now alerted, tense and ratcheted up.

"Richie, take over here. Call Lieutenant Pressman and Captain Grayson. No general p.a. announcement yet, but have all officers evacuate the station. All entrances to be secured. No one allowed to enter. I'm going after this son of a bitch."

He grabbed his shoulder holster, an extra thirty-eight, which he rammed in his pocket, and his orange vest marked *Security* in big letters, and ran out of the squad room.

Denny raced down the East Grand Staircase. He could see that officers were quickly emptying the terminal. People were rushing for the exits. They didn't have to be told twice. There was no panic, but no one was wasting time either. "Felix the Cat is loose," one man yelled at another as they hurried for the gate.

When he got to the gate of Track Three, Denny saw the group of uniformed patrol officers and plain-clothesmen gathered there. He told four of the uniformed officers to follow him. He started threading his way through the mass of commuters coming toward him. About half the platform had been emptied. Commuters didn't dawdle. Even under normal circumstances, commuters acted as if they were running for their lives.

Denny leaned way over the opposite side of the platform, which had no train parked on its tracks. Then he saw him. At the rear of the army of people was Felix, carrying the large bag, trudging along as if he were plodding through a heavy headwind, slogging through wet sand. A heavy-footed, sad march. This time Denny was convinced that it was a suicide mission, Felix's swan song. Denny hurried down the platform, the four uniforms with him. People got out of their way fast.

Sweat was pouring from Felix. The heavy coat, the fat suit, the hot fetid air of the tunnel. As he neared the middle coaches of the parked train, he peered ahead at the gate on the ascending ramp above him. He saw a commotion; he could see uniformed men swarming. Then closer, ahead, he spotted Denny hurrying toward him, his gun drawn, uniformed men right behind him.

Felix dropped the bag, turned around, and made a run for it. He ran back along the platform toward the last car and toward the tunnel. Felix had his cell phone in his hand, ready to dial the number that would detonate his bag. Denny tried to get a clear shot, but commuters and train conductors were in the way. Denny yelled as he ran, "Get down. Drop to the ground." Some dropped; others hugged the sides of the railroad cars.

Two officers had closed in on the abandoned bag and

prevented anyone from touching it. A panicky man on the platform was yelling, "Get out! Get out now! A bomb is going to go off." A woman screamed. Denny and two officers were closing in on Felix. One officer fired a round at the Cat, but it went wide of the mark.

As he neared the end of the platform, Felix crossed over to the Track Four side. No train there. The track bed and tunnel were clear. He crouched down, shoved the phone in his shallow pocket, and then leapt down to the track bed. He made a hard landing. He quickly got up and started running, but he had twisted his ankle on alighting and was now limping. Denny got off a couple of shots at the fleeing figure.

Denny got to the track side and was able to make a soft landing on the track bed. He immediately resumed his chase. The two officers took his lead, jumped down to the tracks, and followed close behind him.

Felix had entered the tunnel beyond the platform. It was darker there and harder to make him out. At the signal light station, Denny could see the dim figure ahead. He took another shot at him. Denny and the officers edged through the tunnel in pursuit.

As the second officer started down the tunnel, shots rang out from up ahead. This would slow them down. Denny thought, *Felix is armed.* He shouted, "Be careful. He's got a gun."

One of the officers had a flashlight; Denny took it but didn't turn it on yet.

Now their chase was slower, more cautious.

Denny was further into the dark tunnel when he stumbled over a thick mass between the two tracks. He thought, *Good. We've got the bastard.* Denny examined the pile carefully, gun pointed at the mass. It was soft stuff, not a body. Felix had abandoned his coat and his fat suit. The man was getting ready for his run. In the pocket of the coat Denny found Felix's cell phone. This could be a big break. This might mean that he had no way of detonating the bag. Judging from the size of the bag, he certainly wasn't carrying as much explosive as he had on the first Grand Central attack.

In the dim light of the tunnel Denny saw a headlight in the far distance. A train was either just entering, starting to pull into the station, or was stopped there. Denny hugged the walls. He could just barely make out the outline of Felix up ahead. A burst of flame from ahead, a shot thundering, echoing throughout the tunnel. One of the officers was down. The other officer had stopped and was helping his fellow, leaning over the limp body. Denny heard him on his radio, "Officer down. Tunnel Four. Suspect armed. Send response team."

As Denny was readying a shot, Felix slithered into an alcove. Denny began edging ahead slowly, shaving the wall. Was the train ahead coming into the station? It looked closer. He frantically searched for a recessed area. He just barely made it into one when the train drove by. Denny thought, *If that bomb is timed to go off on a delay, this could be a disaster for those passengers.* Denny crept slowly forward. Some passengers in the train saw him and gaped at this man with a gun. What had happened now?

He started ahead again. A shot rang out. He pulled himself back against the wall. When he dared look ahead again, he saw that Felix was on the move, threading his way along the side of the train. It was a long train, and it would take Felix a long time to get beyond it.

Abruptly the train started to back out, its passengers still aboard. Security people on the platform had apparently signaled to or communicated with the engineer to back out of the tunnel before the bomb exploded.

Denny's two-way radio strapped to his shoulder crackled on. "Denny, Richie here. Bad news from FBI. Frank Millau reports that Felix's computer says the bag is nuclear. Repeat. Bag contains a dirty bomb, nuclear explosive."

Denny acknowledged the call. *Oh, shit. Just what we need now. A radioactive explosion. So this is Felix's way to go out with a big finish, a really big deadly bang.*

Denny caught quick glimpses of Felix making slow progress ahead of him. In such a narrow space and poor light it was difficult to get off a shot. Denny tried one shot fairly low, hoping that he might get lucky and hit him in the leg.

It was a long, agonizing time as the train backed out of the tunnel. Then Denny was level with the engine. It cleared him and continued its reversal. It was a dangerous time for Denny—in a clear tunnel with the train's headlight on him. He crouched down to make himself a smaller target.

When the train was well back in the tunnel, it turned darker. Denny made his way very slowly along the track. He mustn't miss anything. In these tunnels on patrol, he had often experienced claustrophobia, a feeling of being trapped in these tight, dark spaces. His breathing was getting more difficult. His chest was heaving, tightening. If only he had taken a Valium to ease his inability to pull in a full breath of air. The more he gasped for air, the less able he was to draw in that full blast he needed.

He could hear shouts behind him, see flashlights. Officers were approaching. He heard a metallic sound ahead. He advanced slowly, sweat pouring from his forehead. He was nearing an alcove. A grating next to the track bed was open. This could be a false lead, a ruse by Felix.

Denny thought, *Where would I go? I'd try to get out of this tunnel.* He spotted a metal ladder affixed to the wall, a metal ladder that descended to the next level. He knew it led to a subway tunnel. He climbed a few steps down the ladder. His hand felt something. He looked and smelled. It was fresh blood.

At the bottom, another alcove. A rat scurried away. Water was dripping nearby. Denny looked in both directions. Which way now? This tunnel was narrower and not as high. He looked north, away from the station. Yes, Felix would have headed away from the terminal. The station would be full of security people.

Denny looked over at the third rail. He must keep well clear of that. He heard a sound coming from a spot about a hundred yards down the tracks. He hugged the wall and edged his way down the tunnel. Ahead of him there was a faint light, but deep shadows, eerie light. The heat in the tunnel was stifling.

Then a sound again, ahead. Dead ahead. Someone moving. Denny continued on, cautiously. Again he stopped, listened. A sound only a few yards away. All of a sudden Denny was being pummeled. His gun went flying. Felix had him from behind, one hand holding him, the other hand jabbing his kidneys. He could smell Felix's hot, garlicky breath. Felix's grip was like a steel hoop.

Denny violently threw the weight of his body and his elbows into his attacker. Felix held him all the tighter. Then Denny unleashed a swift kick, giving it all he had. Felix fell back, stunned, but then he came at him again, striking him with the sides of his hand. Denny pushed him off, but Felix reacted with a jump and a vicious kick that sent Denny flying. Felix was upon him, beating his head against the gravel between the rails. Denny's head was swimming. He had to react. He struck out with a lucky blow to Felix's throat, his windpipe, which sent the Cat flying. Then they were both up, facing each other. Denny had his back to the third rail, perilously close.

Felix lunged at him. Denny spun out of the way and Felix tripped. His body fell over the third rail in a heap. Denny could see the body's last spasms as it was electrocuted. Denny—winded, sore, muscles aching, chest heaving—stared at the body. *Good riddance to a piece of shit.*

In his mind he had imagined a more fitting end, a more eye-for-an-eye ending for this freak of nature. Felix in the middle of the Main Concourse. Ordinary people recognizing him, moving in on him. The crowd becoming a mob as he is kicked, gouged, literally ripped apart by an avenging mass of New Yorkers wreaking their vengeance.

Flashlights were coming toward him. He yelled, "Sergeant Delaney here. Police. Don't shoot. Felix is down and dead."

Minutes later on Denny's two-way radio he heard Richie's voice. "Bad news, Denny. The suitcase Felix was carrying contains radioactive material. The bomb experts confirm it is a dirty bomb, some kind of nuclear device. We're evacuating everyone, even Security, from the station while the experts work on it. A general evacuation of a twenty-block area around the station is being ordered by the Feds. There's confirmation from Felix's computer files in their Brooklyn base that this is nuclear."

55

Denny was feeling decidedly upbeat. Things were going right for him. He was off the booze. He and Monny, now reunited, had just had breakfast together in their Restaurant Row apartment. He had kissed her and sent her off to work while he readied himself for the new job.

As he watched her from the living room window, walking east the few blocks to her office, he felt sanguine about his new life and proud of his good-looking, smartly dressed wife. He glanced at the television set that was still on. A government spokesman was droning on about the Israeli-Palestinian crisis. Denny snapped off the TV and returned to his post by the window to finish his mug of coffee.

He looked across the street at the windows opposite him. A curtain moved. Probably some lonely pensioner surveying the morning's restaurant deliveries. Again, as they had many times in the past months, his doubts and skepticism about what had happened reemerged. All of Felix's associates had been killed. Not a single witness had been left. Wouldn't normal procedure be to try to nab at least one cell member to interrogate, even use torture if need be to get information about the operation? But he could also understand the Bureau's zealousness after two of their own had been killed. But was that deadly gas absolutely necessary?

Who funded the cell? Where did they get their armaments? What was Felix's background? Why hadn't any Middle Eastern country supplied the U.S. government with background information? And why had the CIA, the FBI, Interpol, the highest level of government never been successful in getting any ID or biographical information on Felix from the Middle East? As if he had never existed. No one, no police or security force, had ever presented a single fact about his life, his career, his family, his associates. He remained an enigma.

The three from the Queens raid and the bodies in the Brooklyn raid had never been identified as far as he knew. What were their connections with other terrorist groups? What evidence had been found in the hideout? Had Felix's computer provided any additional leads?

Was it FBI vengeance to just wipe out the whole cell, or could it have been a plot to silence them? He himself had killed Felix and in effect silenced him. He had learned that Felix's body had been cremated a few days after the Halloween battle in the tunnel. Wasn't that done in extreme haste? Had they photographed the face and body, taken fingerprints, kept DNA, examined the teeth, taken body measurements, conducted an autopsy? He hadn't been able to find out.

Then there had been that terrible explosion and fire at the Brooklyn cell headquarters the day after the raid. The brownstone and large garage had been completely destroyed. The official version was that the buildings had been booby-trapped, and luckily no one had been hurt in the explosions and fire. All evidence completely destroyed. What had set off the booby traps? A rat?

The FBI and the government had refused to divulge the nature of the gas used in the Brooklyn raid. A few weeks after the raid in America the Russians used a similar gas to break a Chechnyian rebel hostage crisis at a Moscow theater with deadly results.

And hadn't he seen Felix in FBI headquarters months ago? Doing what? That had never been explained to his satisfaction. Felix had acknowledged seeing him.

He had been there in the Queens raid and killed one man himself when the first three cell members had been taken down, but that was out of necessity. He had also been in on the execution of the Carrinos, so that the attack on Terry was only partially explained. Why had the Carrino brothers been killed so precipitously? It seemed as if no attempt had been made to wound them, only to kill them, get them out of the way. How did he know that they had really tried to gun down Terry? He had gone completely on the FBI's say-so.

He had to stop all this paranoia. The Ferret was right. His paranoia got out of hand at times. But what about the attempt to run him down? Who had done that? Forces unknown. Denny thought, *I don't think I'll ever know the answer to that, or should I say, I don't think I'll ever be given the answer to that.*

Richie had done some quiet checking for him, and it had not been Tony Tessitore, although he might have put someone else up to it. But that was not Tony's style anyway. He dealt in petty slights, not that level of violence. Denny knew Tony well enough to know that he wouldn't go that far.

And in the beginning hadn't there been a rush to judgment by the FBI to say that the Grand Central attack was the work of a suicide bomber? Had this whole thing been some kind of horrible plot, some horrible conspiracy, some mad scheme gone wrong?

Denny had wanted to put his concerns directly in front of the Ferret. "I'll answer one of your questions as best I can," Wexler had said. "After the death of two of our agents in that Queens raid, it was a decision at the very highest levels of the Bureau that after the deaths of so many civilians in the bombings, we were not to put a single man in danger. In the Brooklyn raid I was ordered to shoot to kill, to finish them off. No trials, no period of hand wringing by bleeding hearts. And don't forget you were the one who killed our best witness, Felix."

Could it be that the calls from Felix to Denny were part of a plot to hook him, to get him personally involved? Perhaps Felix hadn't called for the reasons he stated.

God, it was awful being paranoid about all this stuff. Denny knew that his constant questioning and skepticism made him a good detective, albeit a paranoid one.

Enough of this bullshit. Denny had finished his coffee. Now it was time to get to work and pack away his paranoia for another day.

People had said that New York would never be the same. True, but it wouldn't be moribund either. Cities bounced back because the residents in them bounced back. New York was a competitive place where the assets of living and working there outweighed the liabilities for many people. The losers and the faint of heart might move out, but the strivers and those who loved the city, who found it convenient and stimulating, would stay no matter what. Just as London had come back after the blitz. It wasn't the same city, but cities never stay the same. They are always organic, changing, in the process of becoming.

It wouldn't be the same city, but it would be a vital, vibrant place. It would bounce back from Felix just as it had after Nine-Eleven. A terrible hole in life would linger where the Twin Towers had stood. The majestic buildings had gone, part of a city had disappeared, part of one's life had been eaten away. The family, friends, lovers, neighbors of the dead would grieve and never forget their lost ones; the injured, some of them badly maimed, would try to piece together their shattered lives.

The same was true of Felix's ravages. He had caused the death and maiming of many innocents. But it was necessary to look at the city itself—to see how badly the fabric of the city had been rent, become undone, been destroyed. The city had survived. The people had endured. New York would resume its fast-paced lunge ahead in the arts, commerce, sports, media.

New Yorkers were no longer demoralized and dispirited by Felix, but its inhabitants were more aware of their vulnerabilities, and more apprehensive about a gleaming future. Felix had come so close with his dirty bomb nuclear device, which had been disarmed and destroyed in the Nevada desert. Its effects would have been devastating, but it had been a failed attempt.

Monny and Denny had reconciled, and Monny had moved back into the apartment on Restaurant Row shortly after Denny's run-in with Felix in the tunnel. Denny was still off the sauce and was happier for it, exercising, living a fuller life, a life more under his control. His father's cancer was in remission, at least for now. Terry was walking on her own. Big Barb had moved back to the city and was working for a publisher.

Almost as soon as Wexler had finished up on the Felix investigation, he had become involved in a serial killer inquiry because of his previous experience as a profiler. One or more killers in New York City was murdering teenage boys and young men, the victims apparently hustlers. Wexler had begun consulting with Denny on the case.

In a neatly pressed new suit, with an immaculate white shirt and bright striped tie, Denny walked through the perfectly restored Main Concourse of Grand Central, refurbished exactly as before, with everything bright and gleaming. People dispensed train details from the bright new information booth. Everywhere brass and marble gleamed. Everything shone again. Not a sign of the bombing. He bounded upstairs to the Security headquarters. It was a room full of people; all of the monitoring stations were staffed. He said good morning to Richie and exchanged greetings with everyone. At Tessitore's station was a large woman. Tessitore had been transferred to Penn Station.

Denny stopped in to see Terry. She was walking around the room on her own. From her tech support room he crossed over to the left-hand office where he removed his coat, placed it on a hanger, and hung it on the stand. He sat behind the desk with a picture of Monica facing him. At the edge of the desk was the new brass nameplate that proclaimed "Lieutenant (Acting) Dennis Delaney." He and his beloved city had a lot to be thankful for.